HIGH PRAISE FOR BARTON AND WILLIAMS' PREVIOUS NOVEL MANHUNT

"Equal parts classic Western and classic who-dunit. . . . A page-turner spurred to full gallop. Maybe best of all, in Jefferson Davis King, these writers have a Western protagonist durable enough to carry a whole series. I'm already waiting for the next one."

—Bruce H. Thorstad, author of *Sharpshooters*

JEFF KING: He was too late to save his half-brother. But he'll be there for Rachel, Travis, and C. D. Junior—even if it means his life. . . .

TOM TRUEBLOOD: He knows Spivey like the back of his hand. He also knows no lawman in this whole Wild West can bring that mean hombre in without his help. . . .

EDWIN SPIVEY: King and Trueblood want to hang him high. But they'll just have to get in line with the others—and pray that he'll be seeing hell before they do. . . .

RACHEL HOLLIS: She'd like nothing more than to settle down with Jeff. But she knows what the badge does to a man—and she isn't about to bury another husband. . . .

"MANHUNT is a good-time suspenseful read. Get after it!"

REVEREND JAMES WALLACE MELTON: He caught the Dallas night train with a bag full of Christmas collections, and sat down next to the wrong man. . . .

WARNER WILSON: He's witnessed a lot of bad things riding the rails. But he'll never forget that bloody body being hurled from the train—and the dark shadow of the man who did it. . . .

CAPTAIN JOHN SLATER: His many years as a Texas Ranger have made Jeff King's boss an uncanny judge of men. He thinks Trueblood is a queer duck, but he knows Spivey is as deadly as the typhoid. . . .

MYLES BREWSTER: Waxahachie's cantankerous chief of police, he swears no harm will come to the Hollis family in his town—unless it comes after he's in the grave. . . .

Books by Wayne Barton and Stan Williams

Shadow of Doubt
High Country
Manhunt
Live by the Gun
Warhorse

Books by Wayne Barton

Return to Phantom Hill
Ride Down the Wind

Published by POCKET BOOKS

Portions of the article "Successful Writing Team Puts Up with Hassles for End Result" by Georgia Todd Temple, copyright © 1993 by *The Midland Reporter-Telegram*, are reprinted by permission.

An *Original* Publication of POCKET BOOKS

POCKET BOOKS, a division of Simon & Schuster Inc.
1230 Avenue of the Americas, New York, NY 10020

Copyright © 1994 by Wayne Barton and Stan Williams

ISBN: 0-671-74578-6

First Pocket Books printing November 1994

10 9 8 7 6 5 4 3 2 1

POCKET and colophon are registered trademarks of Simon & Schuster Inc.

Cover art by Norman Adams

Printed in the U.S.A.

*To Charles
and
To Stan*

Life itself is but the shadow of death and souls departed but the shadows of the living. . . .

The sun itself is but the dark simulacrum, and light but the shadow of God.

—*Sir Thomas Browne (1658)*

SHADOW OF DOUBT

From the Journals of Edwin Spivey

I WAS COLD AND HUNGRY AND SIX DOLLARS SHY OF PENNILESS when I boarded the night train south of Dallas. The train didn't string to more than three cars and a blind baggage, with hardly anybody riding that night. The only other person in the car was a stringy old man. He sat alone up front, staring out the window at the scattered night lights as the train flowed along south for Waco.

As soon as I saw him, I decided. Even before I knew who he was or what he was carrying or who he worked for. I came up the aisle toward him not even caring whether he might be one of them that was after me, and I decided.

His white hair looked soft as new cotton. That hair made me think he was old. As I came closer, though, I could see his skin was like smooth tanned leather the way I'd expect of a man in his prime fifties.

He saw my reflection in the window and looked up at me with eyes that couldn't have faded much from their young man's bright cornflower blue. He invited me to sit.

I sat. We visited a little until I learned what he was. The Reverend J. Wallace Melton.

"Ed Spivey," I told him. That's proof—giving him my true name. That shows I meant to from the start. "Where's your church from here?"

"I'm the Presiding Elder for the Dallas district." He explained he was some kind of leader for a bunch of churches without being preacher at any of them. I didn't pay much attention, because that wasn't what I wanted to know.

"I'm looking for an old friend from these parts," I told him, watching close. "C. D. Hollis. Used to live close to Dallas. I wonder if you'd know where I might find him or his family. Maybe you've met him in one of all those churches."

"C. D. Hollis? No, sir, the name is not familiar to me. Of course, he might belong to some other flock."

"Very likely. Seems to me Hollis said once his pa had died in the war. Might be he was reared by somebody else."

He frowned, stroking the leather of his chin while he thought. I could see he wanted to help.

"Ye-es," he said finally. "I remember now. Hollis was the name. Became a lawman, I believe. Left here some years ago, and I've not heard of him since. Dr. King."

"Dr. King?"

"Yes, Daniel King. Married Cynthia Hollis in '66—or was it '67? My memory." He chuckled and wagged his head. "I was a young man then, just back from the war myself. He's been dead for some years—Dr. King, I mean. His name was well known in my denomination."

"Where'd he live?"

"In Waxahachie. He and his wife died during the typhoid —'76 or thereabouts."

But I didn't care what had killed Dr. Daniel King. It was C. D. Hollis who interested me—him and his family. After that, I was just making talk with the reverend while I got ready.

"Are you bound somewhere special for Christmas?" I asked him.

He meant to be back home for Christmas—I almost laughed—but yes, he was going somewhere special. He was taking a Christmas gift to a group of orphans.

"Are you?" said I. It pricked up my ears.

"Yes, at the new Methodist Home in Waco."

Before I could stop myself, I said, "I wish you Methodists had built such a home up in the Wyoming Territory forty, fifty years ago."

"Oh?" said he. That was all the words. The rest of his question was in those blue eyes that he'd fixed on me. He sat there in his black suit and boiled shirt and necktie and high-topped black shoes. Watching me with a kindness that invited me into his warm world. He was inside. It let me see that I was outside, like a stray dog looking in at a winter window.

He shouldn't ever have done that, though it didn't matter. I'd decided already. I belonged in the cold. I couldn't stand his kind of warmth. But I couldn't turn away from it either, it was such a temptation.

"A place like that might have meant a lot to me back then."

Would it? those eyes asked. And what would it mean now?

"I was all on my own when I was a boy."

His eyes were a warm blue question. He didn't need any words to ask whether I wasn't still all on my own.

"Things might have been different for me."

The warm blue eyes said things might still be different for me, that I might yet even yet walk into that warm world of his. I couldn't stand the thought.

"No matter," I told him. "Important thing is to do something for those who need it now."

He didn't understand. "Would you like to help?" he asked me.

"Help?"

"With a gift. Money is the gift I'm taking. It's a Christmas offering from all the churches in my district to the Methodist Home."

"Oh?" My eyes fell on a black valise between his feet.

"Yes."

I'd meant to do it anyway. Else I'd never have given him my right name. Never have given him that power over me. Him and his warm world and his church and orphans and warmth and singing and all what I'd never had but once.

3

And God looking out for all of them when He hadn't moved a finger for me.

I put my hand in my coat pocket. The car was empty. The brakeman probably off having himself a nap. My arm shook a little, vibrating to the sway of the train. My heart beat with the same pulse as the great steam engine in the locomotive that drew us. The same power.

Melton stared at my face. "Is something wrong?" he asked.

"I sincerely would like to have a part in that," I said. "What amount would be appropriate?"

His eyes told me that any amount I chose would be appropriate. That a thousand dollars or a dime would be exactly right for a ticket into his warm world full of kept orphans and motherly women and blue-eyed preachers. God, how I wanted to go in! But I couldn't pay God the price it would cost me.

Instead I brought out my six dollars in silver to weight my fist when I hit the Reverend Melton. First I broke his jaw to keep him quiet. And sure enough, he never made a sound but just stared at me, dazed, those blue eyes hurt and questioning. I meant to finish it quick, but instead I hit him again and again, hating him for his warmth and his God who wasn't doing anything for him, no more than for me. Finally, I shoved him up against the window and killed him with one quick short hard blow to his heart.

4

Chapter 1

JEFFERSON DAVIS KING SAT AT THE WINDOW OF THE PASSENGER coach and watched the shades of evening rise out of the east. The sun was setting, closing a short December day. The night train, rolling smoothly north from Austin City, was nearly enough on schedule to bring him to Waxahachie by eight o'clock.

King didn't care. He thought he'd be looking forward to coming home, but things weren't working out that way. He was tired as much in mind as in body, and his arm throbbed like a dull toothache.

He looked down at his right forearm. Bandaged from above the elbow out to the thumb and fingers, it rested stiffly on the arm of his seat.

"You came within an ace of leaving that arm with me, young feller," the doctor in Willow Springs had said. "And you might lose it yet if you don't look sharp. You change those dressings the way I told you. And don't go mixing around in any more gunfights!"

"Good advice," King muttered half aloud. He fumbled

5

for his watch with his left hand, checked the time, then slipped his right wrist back into its clean white sling. He had more than an hour, plenty of time.

Bracing himself against the gentle rocking of the train, he rose and stepped into the aisle. He was a lean, solid man, still in his late twenties although his dark blond hair already showed its first strands of gray. He wore dark trousers and a white shirt with a thin tie. Instead of a suit coat, a short leather jacket, worn and scuffed, lay across his shoulders. The skirt of the jacket almost hid the Colt revolver thrust through his belt for a left-handed draw.

King made his way toward the front of the car slowly, favoring his right leg. Two rows ahead of him, a young couple talked softly, heads close together. Farther along, an older man dozed with his mouth open. Just by the door of the car, a man of fifty glanced up casually, then froze as he saw King's face. His eyes widened in surprise and he half rose, seeming about to speak. Then he let it go and sank back as King passed.

From the car's end platform, King looked back. No one was paying him any mind, least of all the man who seemed to know him. He went on into the next passenger car. It was more crowded, with twelve or fifteen people scattered among the seats. In the aisle, a boy of ten or eleven was wearily hawking Christmas apples from a wooden tray. He looked up at King, mustering a tired grin.

"Evening, mister. Would you want an apple for a nickel?"

King smiled. He rested his sling on the back of a vacant seat, felt in his pocket with his left hand, and brought out a coin.

"No," he said. "But I'll take that biggest one for a dime."

"Thanks, mister. That's right nice of you." He stared openly at King's bandaged arm while King slipped the apple into a coat pocket. "Was you in a war?"

"Sort of."

"Gee rod! Which one?"

King thought about it. "Blackstone County," he said at last. He bent closer to the boy. "Listen, in about a minute, a man's going to come through that door behind me."

6

"Yeah?"

"Maybe you could sort of block off the aisle with your tray while you try to interest him in an apple."

"How'll I know him?"

"Brown Stetson. Short brown beard with lots of gray. Dark eyes. Big shiny badge on his coat."

"Yeah. I seen him up there. The lawman." The boy's eyes widened. "Is he after you? Are you meaning to rob the train?"

"Not tonight. Can you handle it?"

"You bet. I'll see he gets a good look at these apples, never fear."

King grinned and put a quarter into the youngster's hand. "You do that. He looks to me like an apple would improve his digestion."

He slipped past the boy and strode toward the front of the car. As he reached the door, the beginnings of a commotion started behind him.

"Well, hey, wait up! You—hey, boy look out with that tray."

King pulled the door closed behind him, crossed the platform, and rapped on the door of the mail car. A wooden panel slid open and suspicious eyes peered through at him.

"Mail coach, mister. Nobody comes in here."

King stepped close, showing his bandaged arm. "I have horses up front," he explained. "Need to see to them. I'd climb over but for this."

"Oh, yeah. Conductor said you were aboard. Whyn't you say so? Just a second."

The express guard closed the slide and swung back the door enough to let King through. Then he bolted it again while his partner kept a wary eye and a revolver trained on King.

"Sorry. We got to be careful. Railroad policy, mister."

"Just be careful where you point that thing," King said amiably. He passed between bins of freight and baggage to the front door and waited while the guard let him out. Only one baggage car was between him and the engine now, and the acrid coal smoke blew thickly back on the cold wind.

Crossing the platform quickly, he entered a warm, dim, animal-scented rolling barn.

Half a dozen calves lay in a bed of straw at the rear of the car. Two of them lurched to their feet when King came in, then lost their balance and stumbled backward, falling over their fellows. King's chunky roan dozed in a stall a little farther up, barely raising its head as he passed. Near the front, another stall held a pair of matched sorrel ponies. Seeing King, they crowded toward him, making hoarse throaty cries and trying to thrust their noses through the slatted door.

King spoke to them. Then he fished in his left coat pocket for the apple he'd bought. It needed dividing. Tucking the apple into his sling, he drew out his clasp knife and flipped it open one-handed. He was trying to hold the apple against a board and cut it when the main door opened behind him to admit a breath of cold smoky air.

The knife was still quivering in the wood of the stall when King turned, the long six-shooter now cocked in his left hand. The passenger with the big shiny badge looked at the gun, at King, at the anxious ponies, at the clasp knife. Bending down, he picked up the apple, which had rolled to his feet.

"Why, hey," he said. "No need to cut this one up. I've got another you can have." His voice was thin and nasal, his eyes quick, watchful, and without expression. "I'm Trueblood, Thomas T.—Tom Trueblood. Figured you'd know me."

"Jeff King."

Trueblood's reaction surprised King. The lawman drew up, staring at him through the dimness. "What?" he demanded. "The devil, you say!"

"Not the devil. Jeff King."

Forgetting the pistol pointing his way, Trueblood took a step forward, twisting his head to see King from another angle. "I'd have bet money on it," he muttered. "But no, I see now—you're too young. You're the same age he was then, back when we rode together—like he'd never aged. But you surely favor him and no mistake."

"Who?"

"Hollis. C. D. Hollis, his name was."

For a moment, King was silent. Then he said, "C.D. was my brother. He's dead."

"What? When?"

"About a month ago. He was killed—shot."

"Oh." Something seemed to go out of Trueblood. His shoulders sagged and he shook his head. Then he looked up at King. "Then I'm too late. Did you get the one that did it?"

Again, King hesitated. "It's over with," he said finally.

"You're lucky then. Ain't many could've brought Spivey down. He was a mean one."

"I don't know what you mean. There was a—a sort of feud at Willow Springs. Political stuff. It's—over."

"Well." Trueblood shook his head again. "Well, hey, that's good. A man's not worth much who won't stand up for his family." He seemed to remember the apple in his hand. Reaching carefully into his pocket, he withdrew a second one. "That boy you put onto me sold me this. You won't mind if I give it to one of your ponies?"

"No." King returned the pistol to his belt, lowering the hammer to half cock. He took one of the apples and offered it to the nearest colt while Trueblood made a friend of the other. "I don't recognize your badge."

"Back when I knew your brother, I was marshal in Rock Springs. Special investigator for the governor now."

"What governor?"

"Well, hey, of course you wouldn't know. The governor of Wyoming." He looked more closely at King. The short jacket had slipped back and a circled star shone on King's shirt pocket. "That's a Texas Ranger's badge you're wearing, I'd take it."

"That's right."

"You get that bad arm seeing to C.D.'s killer?"

"That's right. Shotgun."

Trueblood clucked his tongue. "Well, hey, you're a lucky man. Where I come from, we say buckshot means burying." He put a hand through the slats of the stall to stroke the colt's ears. "Sure funny how things work out. Here I've come a thousand miles from Wyoming to find C.D., and I miss him by a month. But it's Providence I've found you, sure enough."

King cocked an eye at him. "Oh?" he asked.

"Sure enough. That lady Hollis was married to—what was her name? Rebecca?"

"Rachel." King's throat tightened. He pictured Rachel Hollis—Rachel Porter, she'd been then—standing in a field of half-grown cotton, her dark hair blowing in the summer wind. "They have two boys."

"Well, hey, you don't say! Well, it's my bounden duty to meet them, then, same as you."

The sorrel colt had finished the apple King had offered. It nosed across, trying to get a taste of the one Trueblood was holding out to its twin. King moved away.

"What's your business with Rachel, Mr. Trueblood? And with me?"

Trueblood looked up at him. "Tom," he said. "Not mister. I'm after a fugitive. Edwin Spivey, and he's a bad one."

"From Wyoming? He must be pretty important if they sent you plumb down here after him."

"Important?" Trueblood rolled the word around his mouth as if he hadn't thought of it before. "Spivey wasn't so important. Your brother helped me bring him in, eight, nine years ago. Should have hanged, but he got prison instead. Then he escaped and started killing off the members of the posse that arrested him."

"Killing?"

Trueblood nodded. "Said he'd get us all, back during his trial." He shrugged. "Well, hey, I didn't pay much attention. Lots of them say something like that."

"I know."

"But Spivey meant it. He killed Matt Swanson and Bill McKeever. Thought he'd got me, or he'd be in Wyoming still. I caught the train for Texas, figuring he'd get after Hollis next."

"Shouldn't be much of a problem for Holley now," King said grimly. "How does that tie in with Rachel and me?"

"Old Saul Graham—he was the oldest of the posse—he died before Spivey got to him. So Spivey shot down Graham's widow and their grown daughter. He finds Hollis is dead, which he will, finally, he'll go after his family sure. You, too, if he knows you're a brother."

King stared at him. "That's crazy," he said.

"Some have said so."

"Wouldn't you think so? I mean, to kill a young woman and a couple of boys that weren't even born."

"Spivey can act crazy, all right. When it suits him. Maybe that's all being crazy amounts to. But I know him better than anybody living, and that's not what I'd call him."

"No? Then what *would* you call him?"

Trueblood stepped back and rubbed his hands together, his face serious. "Mean," he said. "Just plain goddamned mean."

From the Journals of Edwin Spivey

MELTON'S EYES ROLLED BACK, TAKING THEIR WARMTH WITH them. That was better. No warmth now. Working fast, I cleaned out his pockets and put the plunder in his valise without looking at it. No warmth.

He was heavier than he looked. But I took him up by the coat and dragged him to the door and out onto the platform. Cold wind whipped cinders past us in showers. There wasn't a light to be seen. Well and good.

I propped the reverend up against the back wall of the car and leaned out over the safety chain to look in each direction. Some places are better than others to throw a man off a train. I needed one where nobody would see that white hair right along the tracks.

I was looking when, close to my ear, I heard a gurgle. It was Melton's mouthful of blood from that broken jaw. He'd let it dribble onto the shoulder of my coat. The whites of his eyes turned over until the blue showed again. His lips came together to spit out the bloody word *Why?* without making any sound.

It scared me half to death!

I reached inside my coat and took hold of the handle to the knife I'd found in the railyards at Dallas. It was a queer thing, hollow, like it was meant to core an apple, only near a foot long. Melton tried to twist away. I helped him until he was facing the outside rail with his back to me. With my one arm clamped at his neck, I reached round him and jerked the odd knife right toward my own heart just as hard as I could.

But the knife punched into his chest instead. When I yanked it out, blood sprayed all over, spilling past the rail and blowing back in the cold wind to paint the side of the last car.

My heart was still pumping with the engine, its power, the engine helping me. Just then, it brought us to a river span with side rails no more than four feet high. I slung the matter out of the knife and dropped the plug cutter on the platform behind me. Then I lifted Melton up high with that pulsing power in me and flung him out over the railing into the cold water below. I guess it must have been pretty far, because I didn't hear a splash.

The money was in his valise. I didn't take time to count it. It was in two, three dozen envelopes. In his wallet he had forty dollars. That and a rail pass that I figured to make good use of. I cleaned up the knife as best I could and put it in the valise with the Reverend J. Wallace Melton's things.

Then I waited for the train to slow down so I could jump off in the dark and cold. I figured to get on another one going the opposite direction before anybody got to missing the reverend. A hard, cold rain had started; if I'd thought God cared, I'd have figured He meant it to wash away the blood.

Chapter 2

THE TRAIN SLOWED MORE SHARPLY, CURVED NORTH ROUND A LOW hill, and snaked back west to stop at the stone depot in Waxahachie. Two men of much the same height and size got off the train as soon as the porter put the steps down. A light, cold rain was falling. Water droplets haloed the oil lamps in the station window, throwing a misty golden light across the platform.

Jeff King and Thomas Trueblood spoke with the porter before they walked back to the stock car to unload two sorrel colts and a chunky roan road horse. King took charge of his roan and left Trueblood to lead the ponies down the ramp.

"Nice horse you got there," Trueblood said. "Good bloodlines. I used to ride one a lot like that in the old days in Wyoming. Called him Blue Steel. What you call this one?"

"Mostly call him horse. Name's Pistol."

While King held the horses, Trueblood lifted King's stockman's saddle out of the storage bin. Two brand-new little saddles followed. Trueblood stroked them and sniffed at the fresh leather.

"How in the world did you ever get money to buy these

fine kids' saddles? They must pay their law better in Texas than in Wyoming!"

"Not likely. No. Those saddles were a gift thrown in on the trade. Where's your horse?"

"Way it worked out, I didn't bring one. Seemed like it'd be less trouble to rent me one after I got here."

"Expect so." King watched Trueblood putting the tack on a green depot cart. "We'll let them store that here tonight. Seems strange you were on the northbound train. Were you headed home without Spivey?"

"Spivey? Why, hey, I hate to admit it to you, but I guess I was. I'd pretty much give up hope of finding him before I had the luck to meet up with you! And then it was getting to be Christmas."

"You got family waiting?"

"No. Sure don't. But it's good to be back in your own country come Christmas, even so." He shrugged. "But, hey, now I've got something to get my teeth into."

"You don't know Spivey will come here."

"Bet you."

"You don't know he's even in Texas. Could be he's dead or in jail someplace else."

Trueblood let it lie. They led the animals into a holding pen, gave the attendant a quarter, and went along to the depot. There the porter stood guard beside their luggage. "Waiting for his dadblamed quarter, too," Trueblood muttered.

The porter grinned at them. "Merry Christmas," he said. King gave him a coin, thanked him, and lifted his leather valise.

"Here," Trueblood said. "Let me lug that for you."

"I'll manage," King said. "I'll get the strength back sooner if I work at it. Thanks the same. Do wish you'd help me get hold of that leg-of-mutton case."

"Why sure," Trueblood said. He picked up the shotgun case and looped the strap over King's right shoulder. "How far you got to carry this, old son? Guess you're headed for the Hollises'."

"To—" King started to explain the house was his, then

changed his mind. He was tired, tired of traveling and tired of Trueblood. Explanations could wait. "Just up the way. We'll get a horsecar at the corner and I'll show you as far as the hotel. It's called the Rogers. Good as you'd want."

King picked his way across the muddy street, Trueblood following. At the corner, they stepped up on the brick curbing. Shiny wooden tracks gleamed in the diffused light, running up the hill toward town in one direction, curving back to parallel the railroad in the other. King drew his hat down over his nose and huddled deeper into his jacket. After a few minutes, a bobbing yellow light appeared along the tracks and moved toward the men.

"Consarned worthless flea-bait animals," a voice said out of the darkness, growing nearer as it spoke. A yellow-painted street car lurched along the line, drawn by two tall mules. "Made us late for the train, and customers waiting. Ahab, Jezebel, ought to be ashamed. What will these gentlemen think?"

The car drew to a stop on the last word. Unconcerned, the mules twitched their long ears and bowed their heads against the rain. The driver was a black man, lean and wiry, with strong thin hands on the reins.

"Streetcar uptown, gentlemen? Only a nickel—why, it's Ranger King, home for Christmas. But you've been hurt."

"Just business, Sam. Good to see you again. My friend is stopping at the hotel, and I need to go up to the house."

"Why, this is just like Denver," Trueblood murmured admiringly as the driver helped swing their bags aboard. "All the comforts."

King didn't answer. He'd been away from Waxahachie for only a few months, but he could see changes in the town already. Two new buildings were going up in the three blocks between the depot and town square. In the center of the square lay a mass of timbers and stone.

"Looks like there's been a battle," Trueblood said.

"They're rebuilding the courthouse," King said. "So I heard, anyway. The Rogers is on the next corner." They passed along the east side of the square until they came to the two-story stone hotel. "Sorry I can't invite you on up to the house to stay the night. Truth is, they're not even expecting me."

"Why, hey, I understand. I'll put up in the hotel for tonight and let you explain all about it to Mrs. Hollis before we spring me on her."

"All right."

"I'm a kind of private person anyway. Always liked a room of my own. Merry Christmas."

Sam held up the mules until Trueblood went inside the hotel. Then he clucked to his team and the streetcar clacked north. King looked out on the quiet street that led to the house where he had spent his childhood. There were more houses now than there had been a decade earlier, but he still knew most of them by the families. He saw a fence he had jumped as a boy, a tree he had climbed.

Then, a block ahead of him, College Street made a dead end into Marvin Avenue. And there at the southeast corner stood the two-story house in which he had been born. Across the avenue loomed the dark, empty hulk of Marvin College.

King smiled, remembering his boyhood fear of that building, which he had thought haunted. He had insisted to his father that the front windows and doors looked like the eyes and mouth of a devil.

In his reverie Jeff King pictured his father standing beside the fireplace, smiling softly behind his mustache, assuring Jeff that no ghosts infested the empty building. Walnut shells and a half-cold cup of hot chocolate littered the hearth beside the parts of a puzzle from a Christmas long past. Then, before King could stop himself, he remembered that same fireplace with flowers in front of it.

He tried to break away from the scene, but he was too late. He could turn his face from the flowers, head down toward the purplish carpet, but when he lifted his eyes to the far wall of the parlor, two white coffins lay with their lids yawning open. Against his will, against all his better judgment, the boy in the man's memory walked slowly toward

17

that south end of the room until he was close enough to see inside.

"Here we are, Mr. Jeff. Reckon the place still looks the same as when your folks was here."

King tore his mind free. "Reckon so, Sam. Thanks. And Merry Christmas."

He stood while the trolley rolled away, its tracks turning left onto Marvin to head back downtown. Alone on the curbing, he bent to pick up his leather valise. When its weight came on his upper body, he gasped and let it down again. His bandaged arm weighed forty pounds. He lifted it slowly until the hand was well above his head. *If anyone could see me,* he thought, *they'd wonder who I was voting for.*

He let blood drain out of the arm until it hurt. Then he took up his leather cases and turned along the brick walkway toward the secluded front porch of his home. A thin line of smoke rose from the chimney; a lamp burned in that same front parlor where he had spent his Christmases as a boy.

King twisted the doorbell key. He could hear the voice of a woman talking to children. "No," her voice murmured. "It must be Mr. Foster. Just go on with your work."

He heard a bolt slide back. The door opened. Because the soft lamp light was behind her, the woman stood with her face mostly in shadow.

"Put the—" she began, the words directed back over her shoulder. Then she saw King and the words trailed away.

Jeff King said, "Hello, Rachel."

The woman turned half away from him so that he saw her face. Her lips still moved, but no words came out. Brown hair was wound and braided around her head like a crown. She was leaner than he remembered. Nine years of dry wind and mountain or desert sun had not been kind to her skin, but had pulled it tight and tanned like thin leather across her high cheekbones. Rachel Hollis was overworked, dried out, careworn.

She was the most beautiful woman he had ever seen.

"Rachel," he said again. Her bright blue eyes had gone turquoise with tears.

"Jeff Davis," she said. Then she was falling.

From the kitchen a child's voice sang out, "Who is it, Mama? Is it Mr. Foster?"

King dropped the valise and looped out his long left arm in time to catch her round the waist. She folded limp and helpless across his arm and did not stir. With conscious gentleness, he drew her up beside him and tilted her head back to look into her face. She might have been dead but for the strong murmur of her heart against his chest.

He wanted to say, Oh Rachel, I've so much that I've waited nine years to tell you! Instead he bent his head to her and kissed her softly. She didn't stir. He pressed her face to his throat and held her with the hope that she wouldn't wake up for a good long time.

In the kitchen doorway a six-year-old boy scraped his foot on the sill. "Are you going to be our new daddy?" he wanted to know. He was missing a couple of teeth in the front. His freckled face was made for smiling.

Beside him—taller, tough, proud, aloof—stood his older brother. "Hell, no, he's not," the bigger boy said. He drew a little pistol from his pocket. "Mister, you let my mother go or I'll shoot you dead!" C.D. Hollis, Jr., was almost nine, but his dark eyes glinted with the experience and disillusionment of fourteen.

King ignored him. To the younger boy he said, "No, not your daddy, Travis."

"How'd you know my name?"

"I'm your uncle Jeff."

"That's a lie!" young C.D. said. "Our uncle's dead. Pa sent for him to come help him at Willow Springs, but he didn't come. Ma said he must be dead or he would have come to help. Now our pa's dead, too."

"I know he is, son."

"I'm not your son. Not going to be. Let her go!"

Jeff King put his stiff right arm behind his sister-in-law's knees and lifted her as he might have lifted a doll. He carried her to the horsehair sofa and bent to lay her on it. Then he knelt beside her.

"What have you done to her?"

"Surprised her is all. Your mother's about worn out, Dee. She's swooned."

"Get away from her. And don't call me Dee!"

"No offense meant."

Travis said, "Are you really our uncle Jeff?"

"Hush, Travis. It don't matter who he is. Here." He put the tiny pistol into his brother's hand. "I'm going to get some water to bring Mama around. If he tries to hurt her while I'm gone, you shoot him right in the gizzard."

"Shoot him?" The smaller boy's lip trembled. "I don't know's I can shoot a stranger man on Christmas Eve!"

King smiled and pushed himself up to his feet. "Travis, you come over here and hold your mother's hand. I'll get the water myself."

"You don't even know where to find it!" Dee cried.

"I'll make you a wager I do," King said. He walked past the boy into the kitchen. By the time he returned, Rachel was awake, rubbing her eyes while the boys bent over her.

"I'm fine," she was saying. "Move back and let me sit up. You don't need to make such a fuss." Then she saw King and went pale again.

"No fuss," King said. "You were thirsty."

"Jeff Davis," she said.

"Pay me my dime!" Travis said to his brother.

Rachel Hollis sat up and held out her hand for the water. King gave it to her. Their fingers touched along the moisture-beaded side of the glass.

"He's not a Hollis," Dee replied, "so he's not *my* uncle!"

"Well he's mine!" the smaller boy insisted. To King he said, "We wouldn't really have shooted you. This old pistol don't even work."

King ruffled the sandy hair. "I knew that, Travis. Fact is, your pa gave me that same old gun to play with when I was about your size. It didn't work then either."

Dee said, "He did not! Ma, he's lying. He's not our uncle. And he kissed you while you were asleep."

The color came back to Rachel's cheeks. She looked at King. "It's all right," she said to the boys. "Jeff Davis is your

,daddy's half-brother. B-brothers can kiss sisters. It's the law."

They can, King thought. *They do sometimes, the law aside.* He took the glass and turned quickly away, going back to the kitchen with it.

When he returned to the parlor, Rachel was on her feet. "Dee, you put that old pistol back in your drawer," she said. "You know you're not to point it. You boys go on now. Until I call you."

Dee looked disgusted, Travis, rebellious. King watched them trudge up the stairs like jealous little old men. Then he let his eyes fall on Rachel. "I'm sorry," he told her.

"Why?"

"For not sending word I was coming on Christmas Eve."

"I'm—we're grateful to see you."

"For wasting those nine long years without coming to visit."

"You should have come. You don't even know the boys."

"For being two days too late to stop them from killing Holley."

Her eyes went turquoise again. She pursed her lips together to keep from crying out. Her eyes were a question about the business at Willow Springs.

"Yes," he said. He hesitated a moment, but there was a truth there he didn't want to tell. "I got them," he said instead.

She looked at his right arm. "They hurt you."

"Yes. They hurt me. And I ran here to you for help."

"Then don't be sorry. We'll help you, the boys and I."

"I wasn't sure if you'd be here."

"But you came anyway."

"I did."

"Would you sit beside me?"

He nodded. "But it's cold," he said, "and it's Christmas Eve. You ought to have a bigger fire."

She smiled. "The wood's still where it always was."

King went through the kitchen and out into the backyard. A crescent moon showed through the thinning clouds. Out by the back fence stood a shed. He made his way to it through an untended thicket of small trees and bushes. The latch was where he remembered it. He stepped inside, struck a match, found the old lamp right where it should be.

A meager stack of wood lay in the corner. King had bent to gather up an armload when he heard the door creak behind him. He knew it was the wind, but thoughts of Edwin Spivey spun through his mind. His left hand was awkwardly holding the butt of his pistol when he straightened up.

Rachel Porter came quickly through the door and closed it behind her to shut out the midday sun. She was sixteen. Jeff King had just turned seventeen. She came boldly to him, stretched her arms over his shoulders, and kissed his mouth.

"Jeff," she said so that the word hung heavy in her throat. "Oh Jeff, I do love you."

"You can't love me," he said. "And I can't love you." But he couldn't keep himself from drawing her tight against him and kissing her hard enough to hurt their teeth. "You're engaged to Holley now," he said when he finally pushed her away. "This isn't fair to Holley."

"It isn't fair to us either!" And then she was gone.

For a long cold moment King clung to his memory, almost believing that Rachel had been there beside him a moment before. Then he gathered up his wood, blew out the lamp, and headed for the house. Far off to his right, across the avenue, a quick point of light caught his eye, winking from the west devil's eye of the old abandoned college building. It brought him back to his senses. He had left the front door unlocked, his things on the porch, forgetting entirely that a madman might be stalking him and his. Besides, the building was haunted. He'd always known that.

From the Journals of Edwin Spivey

THEY SAY I'M A MADMAN AND A KILLER, THAT I KILL PEOPLE without reason. That's why I started this journal. This little leather book, it and the others like it, they're proof. For anyone who reads them one day, I've set out my reasons. I've always had a reason for everything, like anyone else.

It was Trueblood and Tex Hollis and that murdering posse who were crazy. They lied about me. I told that to the judge and jury, but they never believed me. So I went to prison, and those who persecuted me ran free. But now I'm almost done with my story. Gentle reader, should you come to the end of the writing while there's still a lot of pages left, you'll know I've found the last of them. There's only Tex Hollis left, and I'm close on his trail.

While I'm still at the writing, perhaps I should set down some events of my youth. I started out alone when I was pretty young, and I've been alone ever since. All my life, I remember being lonely, excepting that brief time with Sallie May. If it hadn't been for her, I'd never have known I was lonely. She showed me the difference, but we had just time for the two little boys.

But already I've gotten my story out of order. I never knew my ma. My pa used to beat me until he died sudden and I was out in the world. Not that God or anybody cared. I had barely turned twenty when they put me in the Wyoming State Prison for next to nothing. I'd found some money that was almost untended. They shouldn't have held it against me just because that rancher was so greedy to keep it he got himself hurt.

I told them so, too, but they kept me six years. That cell might have driven some men crazy, but not me. A preacher, the Reverend Millsaps, came into that prison with the idea that the convicts might be educated. I was just a youngster, but I kept dark what I knew about him and God, and he took a liking to me. Taught me to read and write and cipher a little. That was where I learned about Dickens and Poe and Sir Walter Scott.

When they set me loose, the Reverend Millsaps said I should have a bright future ahead. It wasn't four days after that until I met Sallie May, and in four months, we got married.

I'd by then gotten a job on a ranch near Green River. It paid enough for us to live and eat, just about. When the first boy was born and we knew the second was on the way, I found some pretty nearly untended money. You might say I did wrong. But God was wrong to tempt me did He not mean me to have it.

I took Sallie May and the boy over along the Wind River. That's where I came across Milford Bransdon. I'd first made his acquaintance when we were in prison together. There are few enough people in Wyoming that a man can come across someone he knows almost any time. And there aren't so many people but what the law can make trouble for anybody they take a disliking to.

Milford was running a few horses he'd found. I went partners with him. About that time, there was a big robbery at the Riverton bank, and a couple of greedy people were killed. Then the law came around making trouble for us.

We didn't ask a thing but to be left alone. Milford and Sallie May and young Davey and I, we just wanted to go

about our business. The trouble wasn't our doing, not even about that deputy. Many a man would be alive today if he hadn't mixed in other folks' business.

We picked up and moved again. This time Milford went with us. Our intention was to leave the state and start afresh in Colorado or California. We were almost in sight of the border when we made out a half-dozen riders, armed and mounted so well they had to be a posse. We made our way back north and never came any closer to them. But after all these years, I still believe it was the first time I laid eyes on that damned Trueblood and his pack of wolves.

Chapter 3

JEFF KING BALANCED HIS LOAD OF FIREWOOD AND CROSSED THE backyard in long, quick strides. He climbed onto the back porch still thinking about the unknown specter of Edwin Spivey. He managed the back door with his left hand, slipped into the kitchen sideways with his wood, and heard a man's voice coming from the parlor. Rachel Hollis was laughing at the man's words.

King went through the arched doorway into the parlor. The voice belonged to a nicely dressed man in his early thirties. He looked just about as happy to see King as King was to see him.

"Oh, Jeff," Rachel said as he came in with the wood, "I want you to meet Randy—ah, Randall Foster."

King shoved his left hand out ahead of his load of wood and shook awkwardly. "Jeff King," he said.

Foster had been sitting beside Rachel on the sofa. He was leaner than King and a couple of inches shorter. Dark thick hair had begun to go gray at the bottoms of his sideburns. His small black eyes protruded just enough to give him the

26

alert and piercing stare of an inquisitive blue jay. His smile, however, was quick and warm.

"Glad to meet you," he replied. "Did you say King? I'd thought you were Rachel's brother-in-law. Expected you to be a Hollis."

"No."

"He *is* my brother-in-law," Rachel said.

"Her husband was my half-brother."

"I see."

King put his wood on the hearth and added a couple of split pieces to the fire. He felt like a bull having his pedigree traced. He didn't like it. "Are you related to Rachel?" he asked.

Foster smiled. "No," he said. "Not yet."

"Randy is our neighbor down the street," Rachel said. "He goes to our church."

King said, "I see." He kept his eyes on Foster. "You must be new to Waxahachie."

Foster said, "I bought the old Sanders house. Been there a little more than a month."

Jeff King made up his mind to play this hand as carefully as possible. A little smoothness, he told himself, a little bit of patience. No need to give away his real concern. "Ever been in Wyoming?" he asked.

"Pardon?"

"Wyoming. Ever been there?"

"Well, yes. But I don't see how—"

"How long ago?"

"Have you got some reason to be asking—"

"I have."

King came a step closer to Foster. The smaller man's face changed shades, but he stood his ground. "I'll hear your reasons then!"

"Jeff," Rachel said. She tried to stand between them. "What are you doing!"

King pointed at Foster. "How long have you known him?" he demanded of her.

"Jeff, how rude. And in your own—"

"In my own house? Yes. And in *your own* house." The whites began to show too much around King's eyes. "Now," he said, "I want to know how long you've known this man."

Rachel looked carefully up at King's face. She saw his left hand resting too heavily on the butt of his pistol. Glancing at Foster she saw the color deepening in his face, his eyes protruding like black olives. From the corner of her eye she saw Dee peering through the stair rails at the landing.

"Come into the kitchen," she said quietly. "I'll make us all some coffee. Then we'll talk."

King ignored that. "I want to know."

"Two weeks," Foster said. "I've known your sister-in-law for two wonderful weeks. Does that satisfy you?"

"No."

At the front door the bell jangled.

"Jeff!"

The bell rang again.

"Who'll this be?" King said. "Another gentleman caller?"

Rachel lifted her right hand toward King. He moved instinctively to block with his right hand, but it wouldn't obey. Her slap cracked across his cheekbone hard enough to hurt his teeth. Then she whirled away to answer the door.

A boy stood back in the darkness of the front porch. He stared under the bill of a black leather cap a size or so too large for him. "Telegram for a Mr. King," he said. His voice was changing, and the word *King* came out in a shrill cackle.

Rachel said, "Jeff King?"

Uncertain of his voice in the sharp night air, the boy nodded. The cap fell over his face. Finally he ventured, "He here?"

King stood beside Rachel, rubbing the red spot on his cheekbone. He looked at the envelope that the boy held in both hands. "I'm King," he said.

The boy shoved the cap up, stared hard at King, and grinned. "Are you? Pleased to meet you. Then this telegram's yours."

"Who's that behind you?"

"I don't know." The boy looked over his shoulder at a bulky shadow. "He come along with me."

28

"Why, hey, Jeff," the shadow said. He stepped into the light. "It's only me, old Tom Trueblood."

Rachel Hollis took a quick step forward, looking up at him. "You're Tom Trueblood?" she asked in wonder.

The big man seemed to lean back into the shadows. "Why, yes," he said. "I reckon I am. Have we—?"

"From Wyoming Territory!"

The shadow nodded.

"Well, come in the house," she said. She reached out to take the boy by the sleeve. "Both of you. Come in and get warm."

King smiled. "Sure. Come on in." He stepped out of the doorway and turned to see how Foster would react to Trueblood. Foster was gone.

Rachel was saying Merry Christmas and escorting her visitors into the parlor. Trueblood put out a big hand to shake with King as he went awkwardly on into the parlor. ". . . some hot chocolate!" Rachel was saying. King turned in time to see Randy Foster coming down the stairs.

The boy from the telegraph office waved his envelope in King's face. "Mister," he said, "I thank you, but I can't stay for refreshment. They got it figured how long it takes to walk up here to the college and back."

King took the envelope and tore it open. "Walk?"

The boy grinned. "I got me a bicycle I ride daytimes. You going to send a reply?"

The telegram was from Captain John Slater, Office of the Adjutant General, in Austin. "Hate to bother," King read, half-aloud. "Rev. Wallace Melton missing with orphanage funds. On 12/18 train to Waco. Never arrived. Most urgent you see wife in Dallas. Verify. Merry Christmas."

In the parlor Rachel was introducing Foster and Trueblood. "My husband worked with Mr. Trueblood in Wyoming," she was saying.

"Yes, I'll reply," King said. "You have a form?" He tried to reach his pen and remembered his bad arm. "Maybe you'd better write it."

"Sure. What happened to your wing?"

It reminded King of a dark little man he'd known for a while in Willow Springs. "Got it banged up."

In the parlor Randy Foster was explaining that he had been upstairs to get the boys tucked in again. "They've got the Santa Claus fever," he said. If Foster was concerned about Trueblood, King couldn't tell it. And of course Trueblood would have recognized him in a blink if he'd been Spivey.

"What is it you want to say?" the boy asked. He licked his pencil.

"Slater. Will see Mrs. Melton right after Christmas. King."

"Address?"

"Back where it came from."

"What I was wondering was—well, ain't that the Texas Rangers' headquarters address?"

"How would you know that?"

"Just wondering. Guess maybe I'd someday like to be one of them Rangers."

King smiled. "Maybe you will," he said. He dug in his pocket and handed over a quarter. "Does this cover it?"

"Sure. Thanks. Mister?"

"Yes."

"I was wondering could I see your badge."

"If I was about to arrest you, you could."

"Oh."

King smiled again, pulled at his lapel, and showed the silver badge pinned inside his coat. "Merry Christmas, son," he said. "Tell your boss the same."

He closed the door behind the boy. In the parlor the men were talking about trains and cotton.

"Cotton buyer," Foster was saying. "Went away to school for a while and tried my hand at being a buyer for mercantile stores. Then, recently, I came home to Texas to buy cotton. Settled in Waxahachie because it's the queen of the cotton belt."

"I don't understand what a cotton buyer does."

"I buy cotton."

"Why, hey, if you just buy it, looks like you'd pretty soon have a barn full of it."

"I sell it, too, of course." Foster smiled and turned to King for relief.

King appreciated the opportunity to make amends for having been inhospitable to Foster. "Folks around here mostly raise cotton," he said. "Black field hands pick it, mostly. Ginners bale it. Middlemen buy it at the gin and sell it to those that make cloth of it."

"Why, hey," Trueblood said.

Foster said, "Something like that." He did not seem happy with the explanation.

"Why don't the clothmakers come buy it for themselves?"

"Gentlemen," Rachel said, "Christmas Eve is no time to be talking business. Randy, will you take this, please?" She handed him a tray laden with cups and cookies and a steaming pot. "Won't you please have a seat?"

Trueblood sat on the sofa. King went to the fireplace and put a larger piece of wood on the fire. Rachel brought him a little flowered cup and poured it full of hot chocolate. In his mind he saw walnut shells on the brick hearth. Immediately he looked to the other end of the parlor, expecting to see the two coffins lying on chairs. Instead he saw the Christmas tree, its candles flickering. Above it, on the upper landing of the stairway, two little boys peeped through the railing.

He had a home, King realized. He *was* home. He had visitors. It was Christmas Eve, and he would spend it with Rachel. If that meant drinking hot chocolate with Foster and Trueblood, then he would drink. He sipped his hot chocolate, smiling to himself.

"Jeff? I asked you a question."

He tried to remember. "I'm sorry. I was—thinking."

"I wondered if you knew Mr. Trueblood from the old days in Wyoming?"

"No, I didn't ever know Mr. Trueblood, though I guess Holley must have known him pretty well. The thing is that we met on the train. Tonight."

"Fate smiled," said Trueblood. "It must have been her

31

plan to bring me here to a warm fire and this wonderful cocoa on this lonely Christmas Eve."

"Hear, hear!" said Foster. "We're well met, all of us this blessed evening."

King lifted his cup toward them, took a tentative sip. "Well said." He smiled at Foster. Then he raised his eyes to the stair landing. "You boys," he called. "You might as well come have some hot chocolate. Santa Claus won't be here for a while yet."

"Jeff!" Rachel watched the boys race down the stairs and across the parlor. "Randy just got them back in bed."

King smiled at her. "It's Christmas Eve," he said.

Rachel took the boys in tow. "All right, then. Come on out in the kitchen. Randy, would you put on another pot of milk?"

Trueblood came over to stand by the fire. "That telegram," he said. "They sending you out to work on Christmas Eve?"

"Trying to," King said. "Guess it can wait."

"Just like the government. And you with a bad arm. They must really be shorthanded."

"It's nothing. Man gone missing with somebody else's money. I'll look into it."

Trueblood snorted. "Most likely you'll find him in the nearest whorehouse spending up that money."

"I don't think so. He's a preacher."

"Is he?" The lawman rubbed his beard and frowned. "Well, hey. Still, you can't never tell, not about any man."

"Maybe not."

"Well, hey, what about them ponies then? You got them for Christmas, didn't—"

"Quiet," King said.

"Oh, sure. My apologies. It's been so long since I celebrated among a family. I mean, I forgot."

King smiled. "Me, too." He thought about things his mother had tried to teach him, about Christmas being a time for showing kindness, about hospitality. "Tell you what. I'd like you to help me with them."

"Why, hey, I'd consider it a privilege."

"I'll stop by the hotel about sunup."

"Better be a little sooner. If I know them boys, they'll be awake mighty early."

King looked at the hearth where he had opened Christmas packages so many years before. "You're right as you can be. And you'll want to stay for Christmas dinner."

"Would you?" Trueblood said. His eyes had gone wide with surprise. He wiped at them with his sleeve. "I'd be much obliged."

The boys came rushing in, sipping at their cups and clutching their cookies. "Don't you boys run with that cocoa!" Rachel cried. Foster came in carrying the tray with a fresh pot and more cookies. Rachel came behind him, drying her hands on a pale blue apron. "And don't you spill a drop on Mr. King's carpet, you hear me?"

If they heard her, the boys did not give it away but trotted straight to the fire. Trueblood knelt beside the hearth to look at them up close. Rachel said, "C.D. and Travis, I'd like you to meet Mr. Trueblood. He and your father used to ride together in the Wyoming Territory."

"Gosh," the younger one said.

"Are you a Ranger?" C.D. wanted to know. He stared at the big badge on Trueblood's coat.

"No, son. In Wyoming I'm a special deputy in service to the governor. But hey, that's just a fancy name for a bird dog."

"Did you really know our daddy?"

"Know him? Why, your daddy and me was like partners." He reached out to ruffle the older boy's hair. "Named after him, are you? That's right nice."

"Did you chase outlaws together?"

Trueblood got an arm around each boy as he nodded his head. His eyes glistened in the firelight. "Caught right smart of them, too."

"Bad ones?"

"Some. One especially. But that's no kind of talk for Christmas Eve. Now you two tell me, what are you hoping old Santa's going to bring you?"

Rachel let them list a dozen hopes before she reminded

them again that it was bedtime. "And you know better than to think that Santa can bring all those things," she said. "I've told you."

"You mean about how our daddy's dead and we won't be having as much Christmas as—"

"C.D."

"That's what you said."

"We'll talk about that later. You get on up to—"

But the boy saw that there was some safety in numbers. Emboldened by the company, he added, "And that's how we know there's no Santa Claus or it wouldn't matter whether our daddy was dead or not! And Clete Miller says now our daddy's dead, we'll likely get sent to the orphans' home in Waco!"

"Clete Miller is a bully," Randy Foster said. The blood was showing in his face again as he lifted C.D. off the floor and held him up at eye level. "And that'll be enough sass from you, young man."

"You can't tell me that," the boy cried. "You're not my daddy."

King said, "Put the boy down."

Rachel stepped in to collect C.D., reached for Travis, and headed for the stairs. King took two steps and stopped her with a hand on her arm.

"Let me take them up."

"I'm sorry," Foster said.

"It's these boys should be sorry," Rachel snapped. "I'll get them tucked in for good and we'll all say our apologies."

"I won't!" C.D. cried.

"Why'd you say *these boys?*" Travis wailed. "I didn't do nothing at all."

"Let me," King said again. This time she looked at him fully, blue eyes flecked with turquoise. "I'm sorry I've been rude," he said, including Foster in his glance. "But I need to have a word with the boys. Alone."

Still looking at King, she released C.D.'s hand. "All right," she said.

"You ain't our daddy either," the boy said.

"True enough, Dee. But I am your blood kin. And I have something to tell you once you're in bed. All right?"

Under his direct gaze, the boy squirmed a little. "I'll go," he said. "Don't mean I have to listen."

"Dee!" Rachel warned.

"It's all right," King said. He scooped Travis up and started upstairs, looking back at the older boy. "You coming?"

Dee followed King up the stairs and along the hall in sullen silence. King opened the door of what had once been his room and swung Travis down onto one of the narrow beds there. Dee climbed onto the other, ostentatiously turning his face away. Travis was sniffling and King sat down beside him, ruffling his hair with a gentle hand.

"It's tough, the first Christmas without your pa."

"What do you know about it?" Dee growled.

"I know all about it. I was but a mite older than you when my folks died, right in this house. I remember they were laid out in the parlor downstairs, and me and your aunt Nancy figured we were orphans."

"Golly." Travis sat up, staring at him. "What happened? Did you go to the orphans' home?"

"Nope. Your pa quit his cowboying job out in West Texas and came back. He wasn't much more than a boy, then, but he raised us both until we could do for ourselves."

He smiled down at Travis, then looked at Dee. Unwillingly, the boy had half turned to listen. "That's what I meant to tell you," King said softly. "You two and your ma will be all right. You aren't orphans and you won't be sent away. Not while I'm alive."

"Maybe you can't help it." King recognized the stiffness in Dee, the stubborn set of his jaw. He wanted to believe, but he wasn't taking any chances. "You didn't keep them from killing our pa."

"I couldn't. But I can keep anybody from hurting you. Or your ma. And I will. That's a promise." He straightened from the bed. "That's all. You two get some sleep now."

"Uncle Jeff?" Travis had snuggled into the covers, but he peered up at King. "Will you hear our prayers?"

"Surely."

When King came back downstairs, Foster and Trueblood were deep in talk about Wyoming, while Rachel prodded them with questions. King didn't miss the pause in the conversation when he came in.

"They're all right," he said. "Rachel, could I have another cup of your chocolate?"

Her eyes met his, cool and level. "Of course." She rose from her chair and put out a hand to Foster. "Randy, would you help me in the kitchen, please?"

He followed her, casting a quick, hard-to-read glance back at King. Trueblood cleared his throat, put a hand on the hearth, pushed himself up.

"Well, hey," he said. "Those are fine youngsters. It's a nice family you've got, Jeff."

King had lost his holiday spirit again. "It's a fine family," he growled. "Not mine."

Trueblood strode toward the door. "I'll be at the hotel."

"I'll see you out."

On the porch they stood a moment in the fresh cold air. The clouds had broken up and stars showed through the bare branches of the trees. "I think you and me's more the outdoor kind," Trueblood said with a lazy grin.

King agreed. "A little bit of town life goes a long way," he said.

"Well, I don't envy you, going back into that catfight. I mean, hey, I feel like I got scratched up pretty good, and I didn't even bring a cat." He chuckled, then looked sharply at King. "Take care, now. That's a fine family, like I said. Spivey, likely he'd think so, too."

From the Journals of Edwin Spivey

WE FLED TO THE NORTH, SALLIE MAY AND MILFORD AND ME.
And little Davey. Trueblood's wolves followed us away back.
We shook them off long enough to hide out Sallie May when
her time came to lie in with our second baby. As much as I
hated it, we left her and Davey with some good people in
Sheridan.

With Milford, I rode on into Montana. We made a good
living with nobody much to bother us. But I couldn't go
back for my family because they'd put out a poster on me,
Dead or Alive. It was Milford who slipped back to Sheridan
now and again when we'd found some untended money to
take to Sallie May. And he'd see to the boys.

That was hard, that my boys never saw me to remember.
It all but drove me crazy. People said the boys came to think
Milford was their father. People said—though not where I
could hear it straight out—that Sallie May treated him as if
he was.

That wasn't why I killed Milford.

No. I never believed those lies about him and Sallie May.
But he'd gone over. I could see it by his eyes. He meant to

37

betray me. So I naturally didn't give him the chance. That would've been crazy.

After that, I had to go myself to take Sallie May the money Milford had left untended. I wrote her a letter to tell her my intentions. Then I crossed the border along the foot of the Big Horns where nobody knew my face. I was sure I could get her away safe. And I would have, but for God helping Trueblood and his kind instead of me who never did Him any harm.

But I didn't know better, so I rode to Sallie May and saw my two wonderful boys starting to get their growth and held Sallie May close again. It gave me a start to feel how she trembled in my arms. She was afraid.

It was some woman's instinct. She felt it first. It roused an awful fear in my heart, and I started to ask her what was the matter. Just then Trueblood himself called from out by the corral for me to give myself up.

No posse could take me away from Sallie May. I leapt up and fired my six-shooter empty before I even realized it. Then I found my rifle and commenced to pocking at anything that moved between the house and the barn. Trueblood had upwards of ten in the posse, counting that damned transplanted Tex Hollis who didn't have any business there anyway. I made it hot for them. But then my ammunition started to run out.

I'd left the bulk of my cartridges in my saddlebags, out in the barn. It was worth a man's life to go outside, so I called to ask Sallie May if she had any in the house. She didn't answer. She didn't, and when I turned around *I turned around and saw it was that murdering Trueblood it must have been his shots and Hollis and the posse had shot down my family sallie may dead and Davey the boys killed and alls dead without me even knowing then the lawmen burst in and put me in irons I got loose and beat two of them down but hollis got behind me and broke my head with his rifle butt and that was all i knew*

He'd struck me an awful blow. I've known some men get hit like that who were never right in the head again. In jail, I waited for the trial—for justice against the ones who killed my chicks. But right in open court, before the men and women and God and all, Hollis and Trueblood lied. They flat lied and God didn't say a thing.

They swore they knew I didn't have many shells. They swore they never fired one shot at me, just waited until I'd burned up all my powder. I told the judge it was a lie, but he was stern like God and they all said it and the jury brought in against me! Like I was crazy! But it was a lie!

And here's the proof. If such a thing was true, how did they explain who killed my family? I asked them. I asked each one right before I killed him.

But none of them, no single soul, has tried to answer me that!

Chapter 4

JEFF KING SLEPT UNTIL FIVE-THIRTY. THEN HE AWOKE WITH A jump from a confused and troubled dream. It was the same dream that had followed him, asleep and waking, since he was a child: the parlor with its purple carpet, the two white coffins, the overwhelming sense of fear and loss. This time, it was somehow different, but the difference slipped away before he could focus on it.

He lay still for a full minute before he remembered he was at home in his own bed. Then he rose, shivering from the cold of the bedroom, and went to the window to look down into the leaf-cluttered backyard. The shadows were still too deep for him to see the shed where he had gotten wood the night before, the clotheslines stretched between two poles, the board fences at the perimeter.

Somewhere in that darkness, Edwin Spivey was looking for him and his family. Or else he had already found them and was waiting for his chance to kill them. Or it could be that Thomas Trueblood was entirely mistaken about Spivey, that the madman was nowhere near and not interested. For a moment, King even wondered if it were Trueblood who was mad, if Spivey had never existed and the whole incredible story was a hoax.

Shaking his head, King dropped the problem. It was beyond him at the moment, but he intended to know more about it before he was much older. Meanwhile, he wouldn't alarm Rachel or the boys.

Deliberately, he lifted his right arm, flexing his fingers as far as he could. He no longer had to change the dressings daily. The wounds from which a doctor in Willow Springs had extracted nine shotgun pellets were healing, their scabs giving way to tight shiny scar tissue. And his muscles were gradually regaining their strength. Today, he might hold an apple in his hand without dropping it if he'd keep his palm up.

King turned from the window and found the bandage to wrap his arm. Then he slipped his clothes on, shaved, and combed his hair at the washstand. His movements were awkward but less so than when he'd first had to master the knack of doing everything with his left hand. Because it was Christmas morning, he had intended to leave his heavy gunbelt draped across the back of a chair. He started for the door, then halted, hesitating. He could not risk the possibility that there really was an Edwin Spivey waiting for him—or for Rachel.

He strapped the belt round his waist and tried the gun with his left hand. Again, he was less awkward than he'd been at first, but he felt no confidence. He was pretty sure that with warning he could have the gun in his hand, cocked and ready to fire, within three or four minutes' time. Then the question of hitting anything when he fired would come up.

"Better to carry a club," he muttered aloud. He flexed his right hand again, hard, grinning with the pain as tight muscles stretched and tendons pulled taut. No. It would be his left hand or nothing.

He picked up his bag, went down the stairs as quietly as he could, and spent a few minutes at the Christmas tree. In the kitchen, he got a lid off the stove. He'd improved at using his left hand, but every new chore was a challenge. He found a coal, got a little blaze going, and warmed up the leftover coffee, which didn't taste any better than he'd expected. But the coffee didn't matter; he had to get started.

As soon as King stepped onto the darkened front porch, he felt vulnerable, as if some demon were watching him and awaiting its chance. He drew in great chestfuls of cold damp air as he walked toward the courthouse square. Thomas Trueblood had been right about the appeal of the outdoors. Here and there lights already burned in kitchens or bedrooms. But most houses were still dark; it was the time of day that King liked best.

Street lamps burned at the corners of the square. Standing beneath the lamp by the Rogers Hotel, Tom Trueblood was the first soul King saw stirring. He saluted King, spoke hoarsely, and fell in beside him. They walked across the muddy square to the south and on down the hill beside the trolley line.

Trueblood said, "I don't know how but to ask you."

"What?"

"About the widow."

"Rachel?"

"If you told her yet about Spivey."

"Well, no. I thought it best not to."

"Why?"

"Christmas didn't seem like the time to bring it up."

"You drather see her get her throat cut sleeping?"

"Just as soon not."

"Then you can't afford not to warn her."

"I guess you're right. Maybe I'll tell her part of it."

"Which part you going to tell her—the head or the ass of it?"

"All right. I'll talk to her about it."

"When?"

"Right after our Christmas dinner."

At the corral they found the attendant asleep. They waked him to help catch up the frisky colts. He and Trueblood got the bridles in place. "Listen," Trueblood said. "You want them saddles on these ponies?"

King nodded. "Easiest way to get the gear up to the

house." Keeping two horses in town was not going to be easy; he hadn't put much time into that worry.

"You know which one of these goes with which?"

"No, and I don't figure it matters much."

"Sure it does. Saddles like these? Why, they'll be fitted."

"You match them up, then, if you see any difference between the horses."

Trueblood tried them a few times, decided, and finished saddling the ponies. "Ready to go," he said cheerfully. "Want to lead one?"

"You've got them matched?"

"Right enough."

King took a pair of reins. "Better mark them then."

"Mark which?"

King led the way, moving along the tracks toward the street that rose to the square. "One pony and one saddle."

"Mark them?"

"How else will we know them apart the next time?"

"How do you mean mark them? What are you grinning about? Why, hey, you're teasing me, aren't you?"

"You could paint a spot on one horse and one saddle."

"Shoot!"

"Or you could notch them with your knife."

"Be all right for the saddles. Don't expect the ponies would much take to it."

"Of course, since you've got them marked in your mind now, you can always tell them apart for us, even in the dark."

"Merry Christmas to you, too!"

"I've invited Tom to spend Christmas morning with us and stay for dinner if it suits you," King said. He stood in his kitchen watching Rachel getting the coffee started.

"That's your privilege," she said. "It *is* your house."

"I've apologized for last night," King said. "I'll do it again. The house—and the grounds and the home farm out by Bethel—they belonged to Holley and Nancy and me equally. His part is yours now. It's your home, too."

"I don't know," she said. She shook her head. "Never

43

mind. We'll talk about it later. Tom is surely welcome. Where is he?"

"He's out back. Getting more wood."

A heavy thump sounded above their heads, followed by a yelp from Travis and muffled laughter. Rachel smiled.

"Those boys," she said. "They'll be down here any minute." Her smile faded. "The truth is—"

"What?"

"I don't have much for them."

King stepped close to her and put his good arm around her shoulders.

She said, "C.D. didn't leave a lot. And I haven't yet tried to sell the house in Willow Springs."

"It's all right," King said.

"You can say that." She pressed her lips together. "I'm not a kid anymore. Neither are you. You can't tell me that Santa Claus stuff!"

"Yes I can." He bent to her and kissed her. "Merry Christmas. I give you my promise."

She drew away from him. "I hear the boys!" Her cheeks were flushed, but at least she didn't offer to hit him again.

Going into the parlor, they saw the boys on the landing, saw their eyes gleaming in the firelight as they looked at the Christmas tree. Trueblood banged the kitchen door.

Rachel put her hands to her cheeks. "Oh, my!" she said. "Where on earth—"

"Santa," King said in her ear. He squeezed her arm with his good hand. "Travis, why don't you try that package over by the window seat?"

"The red one?"

"Yes."

"It don't have my name on it."

"Doesn't."

"I expect it belongs to you, all the same."

"How come Santa Claus couldn't have put my name on it?"

Trueblood paused in the doorway, balancing his load of firewood. "It don't do to question Santa on Christmas morning," he said. "Do that, and them presents might just take fire and burn to ashes."

"Aw!" Travis said. But he hurried to tear into the big red package while there was still time. He uncovered a battalion of blue-uniformed wooden soldiers. "Aw," he said again. "I'm too old for these. Santa should have known."

"Who's this one for?" Dee wanted to know.

King said, "Probably it ought to have your name on it."

"What's in it?"

Trueblood laughed. "That's what God give you hands for. Rip into it!"

Dee very carefully untied and opened the package. "Gee," he said. "That's a real pocketknife, just like"—he stopped for a second—"just like Pa's . . . was."

"Let's see." Trueblood reached across a long arm. Holding the knife close to his eyes, he nodded. "It's a sure-enough stockman's knife, all right. You'd better ask your uncle Jeff to teach you about handling it."

"Can *you* teach me?"

"Well, I—" The lawman looked helplessly at King. "Well, I'll be proud to, if'n I'm here long enough. Look there, you've got another little package, and Travis, too."

The boys pounced on two little twists of paper—hotel stationery, King thought—and opened them up. Inside each was a shiny silver dollar.

"Mr. Trueblood! You didn't need to do that," Rachel protested. "It's much too generous."

"Well, hey, I wanted to. I've rid with your husband. Any little thing I can do for his kin wouldn't touch the half of what I owe him!" He shifted uncomfortably. "Anyway, I like kids. And I got none of my own to spoil."

The boys interrupted, clamoring for their mother to open her present. While she admired the flowered robe they'd pooled their money to buy, they looked through the books and puzzles that she'd gotten for them.

"Look, Travis, it's *The Jungle Book*." Dee came running to show it to Trueblood. "Look, it's Mr. Kipling's book. Will you read us some of it?"

"Why, hey, I'm not too much of a hand at reading. Anyway, there's still one more thing," he said. He held out a bright red apple in each hand. "Got one of these for each of you."

Dee and Travis glanced at each other, puzzled, but took the apples and thanked Trueblood politely.

"Wait," King said as Travis started to bite into his. "They're not for eating. We have to take them out in the backyard."

"Out in the *yard?*"

King nodded. "Go ahead, now. I'll show you why in just a minute. You, too," he added as Rachel held back, looking as puzzled as the children. When they were gone, he leaned toward Trueblood. "Why don't you help me with those ponies?"

"No, indeed! This is your gift to them and they need to see that and remember it. I've took a big enough part for one day."

Outside, King went into the shed and led the colts out. They whinnied at the door and leaned toward the boys as puppies would have done. Dee and Travis stared, unbelieving.

Rachel took hold of King's good arm. "You cared this much about us?" she said.

"Not so much me," he said. "These horses are sort of a gift from Holley. It's what he would have done."

"Gee-rod."

"Travis!"

"I didn't think he cared that much about us."

Rachel started to speak again, but she couldn't frame the words. She turned her face away, looking up into the bare branches of the big pecan tree beside the shed.

"Thank you," she whispered, barely loud enough for King to hear.

"Which one is for which?"

"Why, hey, them horses'll sort that out." Trueblood had come out onto the back porch. "Just hold out your apples and let them choose *you.*"

While the boys and ponies were busy choosing each other,

King took a small box from his coat pocket and held it out to Rachel. "This is your Christmas gift from me," he told her, not very smoothly.

She looked at him, turning the box slowly in her hands. Then she opened the lid and looked down at the golden heart-shaped locket that lay inside.

"This was your mother's."

"You remember."

"You didn't think I'd forget? You tried to give it to me once before."

"I still want you to have it."

She looked at it a moment longer. Then, reluctantly, she snapped the box closed and pressed it back into his hand. "No, Jeff Davis," she murmured. "It's too soon."

"I know. Holley's only been gone for a month. But—"

She gave a little shake of her head. "No. It's more than that." She paused, looking toward her laughing sons but not seeing them. "I'd lost him a year or more before he was . . . shot. I wondered why I didn't grieve more when it happened. Then I knew. It was like he was already dead."

"I don't understand."

She put her hand to his lapel and touched the hidden Ranger badge. "It's the badge—or the job or what it does to the man who has it." There were tears in her voice but not in her eyes. "It's late hours and days when I didn't see him and not knowing if he was dead or alive and it's you all shot up from going after his killers." She drew a long breath and closed her eyes. "I don't want to do that any more, Jeff. I don't think I could live with a man who can't put his gun aside even on Christmas Day."

King ached to explain. "There are reasons," he said.

"There were reasons that Holley went armed every day of his life. There are reasons he's in his grave today."

"Could you live better with a man like Foster, then?"

He thought she wasn't going to answer, except by the hurt that showed in her eyes. After a moment, though, she said, "It's too soon to consider any man. But since you ask, I think Randy would love me and the boys. And he'd be home when they needed him—when I needed him." Her eyelashes glistened as she turned away from him. "I must get things straight in the house."

During the long morning, the boys never once left their ponies long enough to go in the kitchen. Their mother brought out some warm muffins and handed them up to the boys in their saddles. It took a few dozen laps around the back yard for the boys to learn to rein the ponies away from the clotheslines and low limbs. In their estimation they were just getting started riding when Rachel Hollis called everyone in to wash up for Christmas dinner.

"Aw, Mom!"

"You heard your mother," King told them. "These ponies will be here when you come back. Go on, now."

Trueblood loosened the cinches and removed the bridles so that the ponies could forage around the barren yard. "Listen, you sons," he told them, "we'll get you some hay and grain here in a little while."

Rachel Hollis called out the kitchen door. "Mr. Trueblood! You and Jeff come on in the house now. Mr. Foster's coming up the front walk!"

Trueblood looked at King and grinned. "Is there any other way out of here?" he asked.

"No. And don't put your spurs on either. Remember this is Christmas Day."

As they came in the back door, Foster was holding open the front one for a tall, slender black woman carrying an enormous silver tray. Though all the dishes were carefully covered, the aromas suggested baked chicken, ham, dressing, and apple pie.

"Oh, Randy, Mary! What have you done? You shouldn't have! Thank you."

Foster said, "Right on through the archway, Mary. I think you'll find everything you need in this kitchen. If not, we'll have things brought over from home. Merry Christmas, Rachel."

She stepped out onto the front porch and drew him aside. "Randy, doesn't Mary have family?"

"Family? Oh, I see. Yes, and she'll be back with them after lunch. Coming over to help out was her idea."

"That's sweet. Of you, too, Randy."

He shrugged, a satisfied glint in his black eyes. "I'd have preferred it to be just you and me and the boys. But it *is* Christmas and you do have guests. I got to worrying that you might run a little short on Christmas dinner."

She smiled again and touched his arm. "You're awfully thoughtful. And you're exactly right. I was worried sick about having enough dinner for all of you. You're a life-saver!"

"That's true," Foster said with mock modesty. "Depend on me. For everything," he added in a lower tone.

Rachel moved back, reaching out to draw him inside. Her eyes fell on the bag of beautifully wrapped packages Foster was carrying.

"You've brought presents, too. I wish we'd waited."

"You've already had your tree?"

"I'm afraid so. But we'll have it again right—"

"No, we won't! We'll have another one after we eat." He saw King and Trueblood, who had come in toward the end. Smiling, he nodded to each of them. "Better all the way round. Dee and Travis will enjoy it all the more. Now let's get this meal going!"

"Cotton buyer," King muttered, following along as Foster and Rachel went to put the presents under the tree.

"What's that?" Trueblood asked.

"No riding lonesome trails. Doesn't carry a handgun. No maniacs looking to kill him. Always around for her and the boys. Maybe he would be better for all of them."

"Hope you don't mind me standing here while you're arguing this out with yourself."

"And a Ranger's pay, too. But it's not the money that matters most. C.D. was in the Rangers when she married him."

"Or maybe you'd rather I just go on in to dinner. Miz Hollis has called us twice. And your friend Mr. Foster's there already."

"Yeah, that's what I was saying." King looked at him. "What?"

"Dinner," Trueblood repeated. "Best we go on along. This has the makings of a real special meal."

"Yes. Today's started out so special that there's only one thing I need to make it perfect. Come on, I'll show you where to wash up."

Trueblood followed silently. But as he came back downstairs, rubbing clean hands together, he said, "What you were saying about the day being about perfect. Near as I can make out your meaning—"

"Never mind," King said. "It's not important."

"But—"

There was a knock at the front door. Then the bell began to gong.

"Somebody's awfully anxious on a holiday," King said. He started down a little faster, frowning as the knocking resumed.

"I'll get it," Rachel called. She came out of the kitchen, wiping her hands on the frilly yellow apron she wore. "One moment. I'm coming."

"No!" King bounded down the stairs, Trueblood close behind. At the bottom, he missed a step, grabbed for the railing to steady himself, caught a sharp breath as pain lanced through his wounded arm.

"Jeff! What on earth—?"

"Let me."

He brushed past Rachel in the hall and reached the door first. The shadow of a man, wide shoulders and hat, arm raised to knock, loomed on the curtain. Pain forgotten, King reached for the handle with his right hand. The fingers of his left were curled around the butt of his Colt as he swung the door wide and faced the man on the porch.

"King!"

Just one more thing, King thought. *Just one thing to make the day perfect.*

The visitor was shorter than King but wider, built square and blocky through the shoulders. He wore a black hat and a dark suit with the circled star of the Rangers shining on its lapel. Dark eyes in a dark face scanned King, looked past him at Rachel and Trueblood, came back to King again.

"Captain Slater," King said. "Come in. I'd just been thinking about you."

"Yes, Captain," Rachel said from behind King. "It's good to see you again after so long. Please, join us for lunch."

Slater touched his hat. "I'm obliged, ma'am. And I have to tell you how sorry I am about what happened to C.D. But I don't have a lot of time just now." He pulled a silver turnip watch from his pocket and studied the dial, then focused on King again. "Jeff, I need you to come go with me right now. We have to be at the station in twenty-six minutes for the Dallas train."

From the Journals of Edwin Spivey

THERE'S SOME PEOPLE WHO ARE JUST PERVERSE. TAKE A MAN LIKE the Reverend J. Wallace Melton, now. Him being a minister and all, you'd expect him to have some trust in his fellow man. But no.

It wasn't so bad, him having his initials embossed in gold on the outside of his valise. No. That was all right. For a matter of fact, carrying that valise made me feel a little more respectable. While I had it, I wasn't poor Ed Spivey, hiding behind a beard and running from his persecutors. No, with that valise I could be Jarvis W. Masters, cattleman, or a hardware merchant called Jasper Murchison.

Then I found he had his whole name—James Wallace Melton, and I wonder why he didn't use the James. If he hadn't died so sudden, I'd like to ask him—his whole name burned into the leather *inside* the case. And that's what I mean. If he'd trusted in people the way a preacher should, he would've had no reason to do that.

I had to get rid of it. It was a pure shame, having to do away with Jarvis W. Masters and Jasper Murchison and Jerome Walter Murdoch, but that's what I did. Some two days after he'd fallen off the southbound train, I threw his valise off a northbound train on the same line.

I'd planned that toss so the case would never be found. But, as the gentle reader should know by now, I'm a careful man. Careful and patient. In the event that someone should find it, I left a little money inside, still in its offering envelopes, to mislead the finder and discourage him from mentioning it to anyone else.

Then I pitched it out the window just when the train was crossing a river that I knew to have some water in it. No sooner had I let it go than it occurred to me that it would float. I should have put a brick inside or a few railroad spikes from along the tracks or even cored some holes in it with that knife. But I never thought until it left my hands and was falling away toward the water.

Trains are good places to think. There aren't many interruptions. I hate to be interrupted when I'm trying to think. The next hour or so of riding I spent in reverie, pondering. Finally, I saw that the mind is a separate thing from a man, a thing that knows ahead of time what's right to do but doesn't tap a man on the shoulder about it until the moment to act has passed. What I mean is my mind must have known from the first I should sink that valise. But it told me only when it was too late. I saw that a man's mind controls him without his even knowing it. Worse than that, a man's mind may delight in playing such tricks on him and then lean back and laugh at him!

Perhaps that little bit of philosophy will not impress you, gentle reader. But if it doesn't, why, you just watch very slyly for a while and see if your own mind doesn't play you just such a trick.

Chapter 5

"Aw," DEE AND TRAVIS HAD SAID, ALMOST TOGETHER. "YOU promised to show us how to saddle those colts."

"I'm really sorry you have to leave before lunch," Randy Foster had said, sounding almost as though he meant it. "That's real devotion to the law. I can't tell you how much I admire the two of you, going out to investigate a crime on Christmas."

"Hard lines," Trueblood had said. "Don't you worry. I'll stay right around close with Rachel and them young'uns till you get back."

"I don't know what else we should have expected," Rachel had said. Her voice and eyes were cold as the first thin edge of a blue norther. "A lawman's family is always alone."

Rolling toward Dallas on the northbound train, Captain John Slater puffed a burst of smoke from his blackened pipe and looked contentedly out the window.

"Surely appreciate you taking that seat," he said to King. "It makes me sick to ride backwards."

"I don't enjoy it myself. But I'd do anything for the privilege of leaving my family on Christmas and riding to Dallas to talk to a woman whose husband's probably run off with the collection money."

Slater's eyes narrowed. His face showed no other expression, but King knew the captain well enough to realize he'd said the wrong thing. The hell with it, he thought. It was Slater's party. If his feelings were all that tender, he should've come alone.

John Slater spoke quietly. "I want to say this next to you only once. I grew up with Wally Melton."

"Did you?"

"I knew his wife before they married. I've kept up with them through the years. He's not the kind to run off."

King looked out the window.

"A farmer's kid found his valise washed up on the bank of Chambers Creek two days ago, over near Blooming Grove. I just this morning heard the news."

"How do they know it was his? Was anything inside?"

"Valise was shut up tight. Had his name burned in the lining. There was a few dollars left, in coin, mostly. Still in the offering envelopes, and all the records were inside. But most of the money was gone, envelopes and all.

"And we know your friend wouldn't have done that."

"*I* do. Hell and damnation, Jeff, look at it the way I taught you. Suppose Wally had run off with the money. He would have kept it right in that valise. He surely wouldn't have thrown it away with his name in it. He might as well've took out an ad in the newspaper to tell everybody what he'd done."

"What you've taught me is to go a step further, to put myself in his place," King said. "I figure that once I'd been gone an hour longer than the trip lasted, all bets would be off. Everybody would know what I'd done. Could be my only hope to cast off the valise so's people would think I'd been robbed and killed."

Slater opened his mouth to answer, then closed it again. He stared at King. "I taught you better than I figured," he said finally. "Just you hold to that side of it. Me, I'm going to comfort the widow of an old friend."

"And you want me to be looking into it just like you always taught me."

Slater nodded. "*I* know Wally wouldn't take a penny from anybody. And I don't figure he dropped his valise out the window by accident. And I know we'd have heard from him by now if he was alive. But that's my feelings getting in the way of my thinking." He pointed the pipestem at King. "*You're* in charge of this investigation, and I'll expect you to bring me the true facts—whether they hurt my feelings or not."

"Yes, sir."

"Trueblood, now. That Trueblood's a queer duck. But there may be something to this Spivey matter."

King blinked, caught off guard by the sudden change of subject. "You learned a lot in just a few minutes at the house."

"It's my business to listen and watch." Slater took the pipe from his mouth, frowned at it for a moment, then put it back. "Yours, too. But there it's *you* that's letting your feelings get in the way of your thinking. Now, I can see Rachel's still a handsome woman."

"I don't see that's any—"

"But I wouldn't worry, was I in your place. We left her and the boys pretty well protected."

"Are you that sure of Trueblood?"

"Well, it's not only him. That cotton buyer fellow—"

"Foster. Randall Foster. I doubt he'd be much help."

"Oh?" Slater removed the pipe again, but this time his frown was aimed at King. "He was packing a pistol under that Sunday coat."

"Foster?"

"You're not paying attention."

King tried to picture Randy Foster, the drape of his coat, the expression in his eyes. "Maybe not," he admitted.

"No maybe about it." Slater leaned forward and tapped King's knee with a blunt forefinger. "Listen here, Ranger.

It's your arm that's supposed to be stove up, not your head. Best you start thinking straight, or you'll have wasted a lot of that Willow Springs doctor's time patching you up."

Adelina Melton was a tall, spare woman. She was built as trim and square as if her plans had been drawn out by a carpenter rather than an artist. She struck King as a person who had been cheerful every minute of her life and was thus very uncomfortable in this moment of apparent tragedy.

"John," she said. Her voice was low and clear. "Do we *know* it's his valise?"

"We're sure, Lina. It has his name in it. You'd know it on sight."

Looking at the man and woman, King saw that they were much the same age, that they had known each other for a long time, that the moment was very difficult for them. King could understand why Slater had needed to do this one himself. Now, after their talk on the train, he understood why Slater had wanted him to be there.

"Did you bring it?" she said at last.

"It's on its way to Austin. We can look at it later if we need to."

King would have bet money that Adelina Melton had never before cried in her life. But she cried then. She cried hard and long, even after Slater moved to sit beside her and hold her. King shifted on the hard ladderback chair, looked at the cheerful wallpaper in the parlor, and wished he were someplace else. But he remembered why Slater had brought him along, and he realized there'd been another reason, too.

When they were on the southbound train, King took his turn staring out the window for a while. At last he said, "Mrs. Melton's a fine, brave woman."

Slater nodded. "She is. And I appreciate it, your riding backwards."

"Lately, that's been the most pleasant part of my job. Where do you want me to start on her husband's disappearance?"

"You'll need a map."

"Probably I'd better talk to the railroad people. Porters, brakemen, conductors—folks like that."

"Not likely you'll find anything there. They would have spoken up by now."

King looked out the window at lights in the darkness. He figured they would be back in the depot in Waxahachie in five or six minutes. "I started off with a captain that told me never to decide ahead of time what I'd find in an investigation."

"You're right. Talk to them. Find every damn one of them that was on that train and get his story," Slater said. "Track down any hobos or tramps that might have been riding free and ask them. First, though, as your captain, I'd like you to study the map to find out where this railway crosses Chambers Creek."

"About ten miles south of Waxahachie," King said. "There's a trestle there. Used to play under it when I was a kid." He grinned. "Thought I'd ride down and see what else got thrown off the train there. After that, I'll talk to the railroad people."

"King, you're insubordinate."

"Yes, sir, I reckon that is so." He looked at Slater, serious now. "Cap'n? Don't you want to go with me to that trestle?"

"Dearly love to. Wally was as good a friend as I'll ever have in this life. I'd like to find his body and cover it for decency's sake. But I have to be in Galveston tomorrow night. Have to." Slater had spoken half to himself. Now he straightened and jabbed the pipestem toward King. "The way you're crippled up, I sure don't want you to go alone. See if you can't get Tom Trueblood to ride down with you. He struck me as sound."

King felt the brakes as the train slowed into the station. His watch read a quarter after ten.

"All right," he said. He rose to his feet, then looked down at Slater. "Captain, if I find him, I'll try my best to do right by him. That's a promise. Then if I can find the gutter trash that would do a thing like that, I'll kill him for you."

Slater smiled. "If it comes to all that, you'd better take some help. Wally Melton could lift the back of a hay wagon while you changed the wheel. Whoever killed him is going to be a bearcat to handle."

The train lurched to a stop. "I'll have Trueblood," King said. "You have a good trip. And see to it you don't ride backwards. Good night." He lifted his left hand to his hatbrim in salute.

"Merry Christmas, Jeff."

When King reached the house, he saw the parlor light still glowing. "Trueblood," he said to himself, "watching over Rachel and the boys." At the thought of Edwin Spivey, he looked across the avenue toward the dark hulk of the college. There were no ghosts waiting at the windows with candles. No, King thought, ghosts would have sense enough to be asleep.

He would have gone into his own house without knocking, but the front door was locked. He was still fishing for his key when Rachel opened the door. "Jeff," she said, "come in. Where's your Captain Slater?"

"He had to get back."

"We saved supper for the two of you. Come to the kitchen. I'll warm it."

King looked above her shoulder and saw Randy Foster standing in the middle of the parlor. "Where's Trueblood?" King asked Rachel.

Foster answered him. "Said he was going to the hotel."

Rachel took him by his good arm. "Come on in the kitchen, Jeff. I know you're starved."

"I can't dispute that. But you stay with your company. I can get my own supper."

"I guess you've had plenty of practice. But you won't get your own supper so long as I'm here in your house to help you!"

"I've been wanting to speak to you about that," Foster said.

Rachel Hollis stopped in the arched doorway and turned

back toward her guest. "No, Randy, it's much too soon to talk that way," she said.

"Normally, I would agree with you."

"Normally, I wouldn't be here. We'd never have met."

"Normally, I make a good chaperon," King told them. "Tonight I'm tired. Excuse me, and I'll go to the kitchen."

Foster looked at him. "No, you must excuse me," he said. "Now that you're back, Mr. King, I'm sure Rachel will be safe. It's late. Time I was going—for tonight."

"Not on my account, I hope," King said brightly.

"Hardly."

"Will I see you tomorrow, Randy?" Rachel asked.

"Of course, if you want to." He looked at King. "Thank you for having me in your house, Mr. King." Surprisingly, he smiled. "Just remember, not *all* its contents belong to you."

"Merry Christmas, Mr. Foster."

King went into the kitchen by himself, leaving Rachel to see Foster out. Coffee was warm on the stove, and he poured himself a cup. Then he heard the bolt go home in the front door. Rachel was with him a moment later.

"I don't know what Randy meant by that," she said.

"I do." He looked at her, admiring the bones of her face, the freshness in her eyes. "You must be tired after such a long day."

"Me? Certainly not. I haven't been out riding a train half the day. Besides, I had a nap in the late afternoon. Now, sit yourself down at the table, and—here, let me have your coat. Sit right there, and I'll heat you up some supper."

He let her slide the sleeve off his injured arm and take the coat. "No," he told her. "Put it on a chair."

"I'll just hang it on the hall tree."

"I'd rather you stayed with me."

"Silly. I'll be right back."

He went with her into the parlor. "It's been a long time," he said.

"Since what?"

"Since I got to watch you walk."

She stopped, turned toward him, holding the coat across her breasts like a shield. "You haven't been drinking?"

"Worse than that." He looked up to the stair landing to be sure the boys weren't spying on them.

"Come sit down. Let's get some food in you."

"All right." He sat at the table and watched her while she put food on a plate and slipped the plate into the oven. "I haven't had a private word with you since I got here."

"Would you like some coffee?"

"There's so much to say. I was thinking about it on the train this evening."

"What are you talking about?"

"That's just it. A man like me can't ever get said what he really wants to say. Life is so short. Most of it drains out of the barrel before we can get the leaks plugged."

"Well, aren't you serious this evening? And quite the poet."

He had his chance and he knew it. Anybody could see that Randy Foster was way ahead of him with Rachel. She was saying things like *quite the poet* because she'd been talking to Foster. There was no time to be wasted. Jeff King knew that he could say *I love you* to Rachel right then and get away with it. But he was afraid. "I—" he said. "I—"

"Yes?"

He cursed himself for a coward, whipped himself up to the challenge, and looked at her squarely. In his mind he said quite clearly *I love you.* It even showed in his eyes. But Rachel didn't see it. She had gone to the stove. She opened the oven and took up his plate with a cloth.

Then she brought his food and put it in front of him. "Don't touch the plate," she told him; "it's too hot. Well, what was it you were going to say? You can tell me now. Would you like some butter?"

King said, "I—I was going to tell you something Tom Trueblood thought you ought to know. But then the captain came, and I never had a chance."

"Now you have a chance." She smiled. "Is that food warm enough?"

King nodded. "Seems like there was a bad hombre that Holley and Tom Trueblood put in Wyoming State Prison when you were up there."

"Isn't it nice to see Mr. Trueblood after all these years? Yes, I believe he and Holley put quite a few badmen in that prison."

"I'm sure they did. But this one escaped."

"That was all so long ago. Do you ever think of things that far back?"

"The escape wasn't so long ago. The word is he headed off down here to Texas to get even with Holley."

"This really is your serious evening, isn't it? Surely he's too late on his errand now."

"I would have hoped so." Now she had him talking like Randy Foster. He didn't like it. "Trouble is—"

"Well then?"

"Trouble is, I've been wanting to see you for a long time." She smiled. "To see me walk, you mean?"

"That, too. Do you remember an afternoon in the shed when—"

"No. But tell me, Jeff. I've long wondered. Did you never find a wife to suit you?"

"I've never married."

"Did you never find a girl to suit you?"

"Once." King hesitated. There had been another time, in Willow Springs. But that had ended. "Once," he repeated. "I found a girl that more than suited me."

"Oh? But you didn't marry her?"

He took a bite of his ham. "She was already taken."

"Oh. Was she pretty?"

"Pretty! Lord, I guess." He spent a minute looking into Rachel's eyes. "She still is. The prettiest woman I've ever seen." Did he have to say it any plainer? Surely he wasn't the only man that ever had trouble telling a woman he loved her.

"Did you—"

"What?"

"Do you—"

62

"Yes. I did. I do."

"You need some more coffee."

"When I was out in the shed getting firewood last night, I saw you there."

She stood at the stove pouring his coffee. "I never left the house!"

"You were there. You came to me. Do you remember?"

"I can't remember *your* memories. No one can do that."

He watched her over the rim of his cup. "Can't you?" The coffee was too hot to drink. He put it down and pushed back the chair. "Let me show you."

"Some things are better left as a memory."

"I want to show you."

She smiled. "We could check on the colts."

He helped her into her coat and let her help him into his. Then he took her arm and led her to the back door and out into the yard. Together, they went down the steps and out toward the shed.

"I don't see myself," Rachel said. Then she laughed a few syllables. It surprised her as much as it surprised him. "I don't see the horses either."

"Maybe they're in the shed with you."

She laughed again.

Her breath and the sound of her laughter washed over him like an August breeze. "I like to hear you laugh," he said.

"Do you? I think I like it, too."

He opened the board door and helped her through it into the shed. "I love to hear you laugh." He looked for matches to light the lantern. The colts moved restlessly in the yard beside the shed. "The horses are outside," he told her.

"Will we need the lantern to see me?" she asked.

Something in the way her voice stopped at the top of her throat made his scalp prickle. He put down the matches. "No," he told her. "I was standing right over here by the wood pile. Then I turned back toward the door. Suddenly it was bright as day in here. It was a July afternoon. You came through that door calling my name low in your throat the way you spoke just now."

"Jeff. We're not seventeen any more."

"You were wearing the blue and white dress Holley had bought for you in Fort Worth. And you—"

She sighed. "—came right to you and lifted my arms around your neck like this and—" She kissed him. He kissed her. They met so evenly in the dark that neither of them could ever be certain who had moved into whose arms.

He kissed her until he feared he was hurting her. Even after that, he kept his one good arm round her for fear she would disappear as she had the night before. But this time she was real. She smelled real. Her body was firm and warm where it molded into his. Her heart thumped against his ribs like a padded hammer. "I—" he said.

"What?" she murmured.

"I—"

"I know."

The back gate slammed as if a gust of wind had taken it, but there was no wind. Because it was hinged to the back wall of the shed, it rattled the whole building.

Rachel's fingers bit into King. Her voice was a tense whisper. "What was that?"

It came to him that she was not at home here. He was. "I'll see."

He drew away from her, ducked through the board door, and started around the shed. He reached awkwardly for his gun, but then had to fight for balance as his boots skidded in something wet and slippery. At the corner he groped for support, caught the edge of the shed, dug in his boot heels, and turned back toward the gate. Then his feet lost purchase. He slipped, reeled backward, and then fell headlong across some very solid object.

After a moment Rachel came round with the lantern. "Where are you?"

King didn't try to get up. He wasn't at all sure that he hadn't undone all the healing in his right arm. A warm wetness was spreading all across his chest and right side.

"I'm here," he said. "Just give me a minute."

She held the lantern over her head, shielded her eyes, and looked down at King. "Oh my dear God," she said.

He got his good arm under him finally and pushed himself up on one knee. "Wait," he said. "Don't move the light. I want to see what the hell—"

But he was already sure. The blood that soaked his shirt and coat wasn't his, but he knew where it had come from. And he was sure that the man who did it had intended to disturb them by banging the gate. He took the lantern and proved to himself that he had stumbled over one of the colts after he had slipped in the puddle of its blood.

He had fallen on the second horse, which lay just beyond the first one. The throats of both gaped open redly in the light, cut up high the way a butcher would have bled them if they'd been cattle. Neither had even had a chance to whinny. The blood was warm and sticky, still fresh enough to steam in the cold night air.

"Spivey," King said. "He's here."

From the Journals of Edwin Spivey

WHEN I GOT FREE FROM THE WYOMING STATE PRISON FOR THE last time—which I say was the *last* time because I am determined to die before I will let anyone imprison me again—I wanted more than anything in the world to lay hands on that murdering Thomas Trueblood and kill him with one snap of his neck.

But I was always the kind of fellow who would eat a helping of greens and fatback and whatever other things were on my plate before I'd ever allow myself a bite of fruit cobbler, not even if there was fresh cream to pour on it.

That is, I can wait for what I want most. Not everybody can do that. I know some that would go first hell-for-leather after what they want most for fear that someone will beat them to it. But I am a patient man.

So when I most wanted Trueblood, I took pride in accounting for the rest of his posse first. All the while, I was waiting for him, knowing him to be the chief of my persecutors. And in the end, he came to me! Fact is, I had to work fast and run my horses hard just to stay a few hours ahead of Trueblood, who was after me for killing the others.

When I was ready all I had to do was let him catch up to me. Then I lay in ambush, snug and quiet while he followed my trail like a crazy man. And I shot him off his horse smooth as you shoot a quail when you've been waiting for him to fly and know right where he's going to be when he breaks cover. The only mistake I made was hitting him in the head. That way, I didn't get to ask him my question the way I had the others.

Though I don't suppose he knew the answer either.

But I was talking of patience. Trueblood caught up to me before I got to Tex Hollis. I hadn't meant him to be last, but he's the only one left. So I came off down here to Texas and bought this new book to write in how I settled last of all with Tex Hollis. And thus one of the worst disappointments of my life was to learn that some West Texas farmer or cowhand or whatever they are out there had beaten me to him. The only thing would have been to find his killer and to take justice into my own hands—except I found out that Hollis had left kin.

A wife. Like Sallie May. Two sons. Like my two poor dead boys. And a brother and sister. I'm not so sure about them—never had brothers or sisters to go by. But I'm patient. I'll work it out. To me—ever since I lost my own—kin are more sweet and precious than anything else in this world.

And that is why I've come here to Waxahachie. I'll bide my time. Since they're the last ones, I'll want to do it right. To sign my name, so to say, to my work. That's not crazy. Anyone would feel the same way.

Then, when I decide the time's right, I'll kill Tex Hollis's kin—right down to the last drop of blood.

Chapter 6

Jeff King had not been in bed nearly long enough when
five-thirty came round the morning after Christmas. He
hoped the boys would sleep late. He closed his eyes and tried
to rest a little longer. But it was no good.

He sat up on the edge of the bed and looked out the
window onto the backyard. Near the fence lay two big
tarpaulins covering the colts King hadn't been able to move.
It was too dark to see them through the trees, but he knew
they were there.

He thought about the banging gate, remembered that the
killer had been right there by the shed, not a dozen feet from
him in the dark—nor from Rachel. The boys had been
asleep, alone in the unlocked house.

With a sound like a snarl, King wheeled away from the
window. He dressed swiftly, put his pistol in his left-hand
coat pocket, and headed down for a look at the alley in the
daylight. It was still too dark. He went back into the kitchen,
careful to bolt the back door behind him.

He made a pot of coffee, had three cups, and went out
again. There was nothing much to see. He looked around for

the knife or sword or axe that the butcher must have used, but he found nothing. A hundred feet down the way he found a scrap of cloth covered with blood. He hoped the killer had cut himself but more likely he'd used the cloth to wipe his weapon clean.

When King came back to his own gate, there was light enough to see a couple of dark, smeared footprints painted in blood between the horses and the gate. He went down on one knee to look at them. A minute's careful study told him two things. First, a cat had stopped at one of them to lap at the blood before it dried. Second, the footprints were his.

Back in the kitchen, he started breakfast. The biscuits he chose to leave for Rachel to manage, but he sliced the leftover ham into half a dozen slabs and laid them in a big skillet. He kept the ham off the fire until he finished scrambling the eggs. He had intended to fry them, but his left hand was too clumsy to avoid breaking the yolks.

Rachel came downstairs in her new robe. Whether she had heard him feeding the fire or had smelled the food, King couldn't tell. He poured her a cup of coffee. Even then, in the early morning fresh from sleep, she was the prettiest creature he had ever seen. He laid his stronger hand on her shoulder.

She put a frail hand on his, smiled up at him.

"Listen," he said, "about last night—"

"It's all right."

"No. I mean it's more than that. It's the way I want things to be."

She looked into her cup. "We talked about that," she said. "Last night was—was—oh, Jeff." She shook her head, her face turned away from him. "But we're not the people we were then. I don't know you, not really, nor you me. And now there's—"

"The horses," King said. "All right." He turned to put the coffee pot back on the stove.

"What are you going to do about the colts?"

"I don't know," he said.

"Please don't be bitter. I'm sorry. I need time—"

"To decide?"

"Just time. It hasn't been much more than a month!"

"All right. Take time." He took a wad of greenbacks from his pocket and laid it on the table beside her.

"What's this for?"

"Groceries. Things a woman or a couple of boys might need."

"It's too much."

"You'd better paint a picture of it then to show folks, because there's never been too much money anywhere anytime."

"I mean it."

"I mean for you to have things you need. When I come home I want to find enough food and ice and hard candy and whatnot to fill this house."

"Where are you going?"

"To find a man that'll come get the horses before those boys wake up."

"Uncle Jeff, those ponies!" Travis cried from the landing. *Too late,* King thought. "What are you doing up?"

"We want you to learn—to *teach*—us to curry them horses and go riding. We've got their names all picked out! Mine's going to be Red Beauty and Dee's going to call his Flame!"

By eight-thirty King had made an arrangement with a man willing to haul the sorrel colts away before noon. Only then did he go by the hotel to tell Thomas Trueblood what had happened. He hadn't looked forward to that any more than to telling the boys. Trueblood had really keened to the little red horses.

"Did what!" the lawman demanded. "Why, the bastard'd do a thing like that ought to be hung without a trial! Where is he? I'll chop off his toes and teach him to trot."

King looked out the hotel window. "I was hoping you might have an idea about finding him."

"Me?"

"It's such an unusual crime, it got me thinking about the man you're after."

"Spivey?" Trueblood leaped to his feet and paced twice

across the narrow hotel room. "Spivey! Why hell, of course."

"You said he'd be hunting Holley's kin. Looks like he's found us."

"Nothing's more likely. And he's the only man I know that might could do a thing like that to them poor helpless little colts."

"This time. Next time it could be the boys."

"I'd like to tell you no. But I can't because you're right. You sure those little tykes are safe right now?"

"Will you help me?"

"Why, hey! You don't have to ask. You couldn't drive me off with a whip. I'm in this right down to the last drop of Spivey's blood."

"Thanks, Tom. I appreciate it."

"Lead on."

"Rachel and the boys are holed up safe over at Randy Foster's house. His Mary's there to watch after them."

"I don't like him."

King smiled. "Well, I'd about decided to adopt him," he said. "Anyway, he's helping us right now."

"How's that?"

"We don't want those boys home to see the man haul off their horses. Later, I'll talk to Myles Brewster—he's the chief of police here—and we'll do something about getting them some full-time protection."

Trueblood sat on the bed. "Well, I don't know we want to do that," he said thoughtfully. "That much ruckus might scare Spivey off. What if he decided to lie low, wait his time? He's a patient man."

"If he gives me enough time, he'll be a dead man."

"We could take them boys somewhere. On a long picnic, say. Mrs. Hollis, too. Just the five of us find a place off down the way. Leave them there till we kill Spivey."

"No. I need you to help me with what I have to do. I'd like you to ride with me."

"Ride with you? That would mean a lot to me—considering how close I was with your brother and all."

"Get your gear."

"I'm wearing it. What else'll I need where we're going?"

By noon King and Trueblood were near Italy, some fifteen miles south of Waxahachie. Around them was gently rolling farmland, low hills crowned with groves of blackjack and post oak, small narrow draws densely overgrown with brush and trees and brimming with water. Mostly the land was fallow for winter, but here and there a patch of rye or winter wheat showed its first green. The road was muddy, and Trueblood made slow going with the light spring wagon King had rented in town.

"I been studying on why you rented us a buggy," Trueblood said when they stopped to rest the horses and brew a cup of coffee. "Alls I can figure is it must be pretty hard on you to straddle a horse, with your arm and all."

"I can sit a horse if I need to, but this is easier." King grinned. "A lot easier with you holding the reins. Truth is we may need the wagon. I don't know whether to hope we do or don't."

"That a riddle?"

"It is." While they had their coffee, King told Trueblood about the missing minister. The man from Wyoming rubbed his chin in silence until they were back in the wagon and headed south. Then he cleared his throat.

"I hate to say so."

"What?"

"Likely we'll find your minister friend killed—"

"I never met him."

"—because killing him is exactly the thing Edwin Spivey would do."

"Spivey!"

"It's the God's truth. I can all but promise you this is Spivey's work."

For a moment, all King's doubts came back. "I value your opinion," he said. "But I can't see how to cash it in. What good's a guarantee like that?" The more King thought about Trueblood's idea, the less he liked it. "You can't be sure. You've got the itch about Spivey because of the horses. Now

I think about it, we don't know for sure that he killed those ponies either!"

Trueblood sighed. "Got a lot of other enemies, do you?"

"A few. And I've been responsible for jailing some people pretty near as mean as Spivey."

As if he were trying to explain gravity to a child, Trueblood said, "Hey. You tell me there's a bag of money missing. That signifies somebody's stole it." He held up his hand, ticking the points off on his fingers. "Now, you tell me the preacher wouldn't have stole it. If'n that's so, somebody else did. And I can tell you Spivey hates preachers bad enough to kill them on sight."

"How does he recognize them on sight?"

"Thunderation, *I* don't know! Maybe he looks for men wearing black."

"I'm wearing black."

Trueblood spat toward the roadside. "They sure as hell grow them stubborn in Texas," he said. "I think you'd argue about arguing."

"I'll take that as a fair comment. But tell me why Spivey'd want to kill a preacher?"

"Something that happened when he was young. Don't know exactly. Heard him get started cussing preachers one time. Didn't make much more sense to me than anything else he said." He rubbed his chin. "Funny thing about it is they'd have hung him if it hadn't been for a clergyman convincing them Spivey was crazy."

"Don't they hang crazy people in Wyoming?"

"Why, hell no. If'n they did, ever tree'd be full! Hee-ha!"

It was the first time King had heard Trueblood laugh. "We got the same law against it in Texas. For the same reason, I expect. Of course, we've got more people."

"You've got more trees! Ha-hee. It'd come out about even. Somebody planned it that way. Oh-ha-hee."

If King had remembered rightly, the road would string along parallel to the tracks long enough to bring them within a hundred yards or so of the trestle across Chambers Creek. He began watching for the spot. A little before two o'clock, he nudged the dozing Trueblood.

73

"Say, Tom, pull up in that grove of trees. We'll leave the horses and walk from here."

"Walk! Wasn't nothing said about that. I might not have spoke so soon about helping you if I'd thought you was going to try to cross the state on foot. These boots wasn't made for serious walking."

King laughed. "Now is when we wish we'd rode horses." He set out to the west, picking his way through the thick growths of brush and tall dead grass. The black dirt was muddy and slick so that he had a hard time keeping his balance. It came to him that a man with a bad arm was worse off than a crawdad with one claw, because the man had to carry and tend to his arm.

The railroad trestle was a fairly short span, not much taller than the flood stains on its pilings, and flat topped with no upper support structure. Beneath it, Chambers Creek ran deep and clean over a mossy limestone bottom. The center channel, dark with moss, was deep enough so King saw not even a hint of the bottom.

"Looks like it'd be good fishing," Trueblood said. He was panting lightly from the walk. "I'd like to drop me a fly into that swirl under the little waterfall there."

"Don't know about the fly, but the fishing should be good. We'll try it one day soon."

"Bring them boys?"

"It was what I had in mind. We'll do it the minute we're safe from Spivey."

"Deal. Where you going now?"

King climbed on up the crossbank to the tracks, waved for Trueblood to follow, and stepped from tie to tie out to the middle of the bridge. He was standing there studying the edges of the water and looking for places a body might have hung up when Trueblood came up beside him. "What do you think?"

"Could be where the valise came from. Anything thrown off here would surely go in the creek. Which way was the train going?"

King pointed. "South. Why?"

"Well, it makes a difference."

King looked at his helper for signs of a smile, but Tom Trueblood was serious as stone. "No, now, let's try this." Trueblood walked along the trestle until he stood above the north bank of the river. "If you saw the river and started to throw a body over the railing, why the train would be farther along before you got it over."

King saw what he meant. He did a little figuring as to how long it would take to lift and shove a body over a railing. Three, maybe four seconds at the least. Depending on the weight of the body and the strength of the killer, it might take twice as long.

"How fast do you figure a train'd be going right along about here?"

They looked along the tracks in both directions. The tracks curved gently in from the north and fell nearly straight away to the south. "How much of a train?"

"Skeleton. Three, four, five cars at the most."

"Sixty miles a hour then. Maybe better."

"If you were running that speed, how long would it take you to cross this span?"

They worked at their calculations for half an hour or more, crossing and recrossing the bridge, counting off the seconds against the screaming thunder of a steam locomotive flying at a hundred feet per second. Once, they scrambled down as a freight plowed through from the south, shrilling its whistle angrily at them. In the end they decided it would be easy enough to throw a valise off a train and hit the creek with it.

"Tossing a dead body in the creek from here would be a different story, though," Trueblood said. He rubbed his beard and squinted toward the trestle. "Most especially if you weren't ready. There's no gospel certainty to it that Spivey throwed your friend in the water at all."

"Captain Slater's friend."

"Maybe Spivey didn't throw that body off the train at all. Maybe he put it in an empty box car, cattle car, or the like. Might be plumb to New Orleans. Nobody finding the body way off somewhere would know who it was."

"I see what you mean."

"By the time they find it, probably nobody could identify it, not even your Captain Slater."

King didn't want to think about that. "All right."

"Or Spivey didn't have to drop the body and the valise in the same place. Could have throwed him off anywhere in the—how many miles you say it is from where he started to where he was going?"

"Hundred."

"Why, hey. We'd maybe have to scout out a hundred miles of track to find out." He looked up. "Course, Spivey might have throwed him off on down the line past where he was going."

"No," King said. "You can't just sit on a body that long. The train stops at Waxahachie, maybe two or three other places. Somebody would see. Come on."

"Come on where?"

"Let's walk this track a ways south."

"I hope I didn't give you that idea!"

"Figure you need to get those boots broke in right."

Here the track was elevated on a ridge above flood level. King kept his eyes on the brush and tall grass at the bottom of the east slope.

Tom Trueblood watched on the other side. "Ain't it a shame what people won't throw off a train!" he said after a while.

King agreed. He'd never paid much attention to the right of way along the tracks. Now he saw that travelers had been throwing things from the windows right out in God's clean countryside. "They must carry a bag of trash with them, or they'd never have enough to last them this far out of a station," he said.

Trueblood pointed. "Oh Lordy, what's that?"

King stepped to his side of the tracks. At the edge of the grass lay a black boot, sole up. "I don't think anybody wore it out walking," King replied. They floundered down the embankment, sliding in the cinders, but keeping their footing until they came to the boot. King had hardened himself to what he would find. He was relieved to discover no foot in the boot, no leg protruding from it, no body sprawled in the deeper grass.

"How big was your friend?"

"Hundred sixty pounds. Five feet, eight and five-eighths of an inch tall. Fifty-two years old. White hair, blue eyes, size nine boot."

Trueblood turned the boot in his hands. "Well, this could have been his. Like you said, it wasn't wore out."

"Bring it along, if you don't mind. Somebody might be able to identify it."

"Lordy me," Trueblood said, "but I hope we don't find a dad-damned anvil with your friend's initials on it."

From the Journals of Edwin Spivey

IT HAS OCCURRED TO ME THAT THE GENTLE READER MIGHT WONder why I'm so forgiving. Why I've limited my retribution only to the men of Trueblood's posse. The jury who convicted me and old Judge Carson who sentenced me, why, I've not harmed a hair of any one of them.

There are reasons for that. I've always had my reasons. Firstly, it's not only my own self I'm concerned with avenging, but Sallie May and the boys. The court did them no harm; it was Trueblood and his wolves.

Again, the jurymen were only doing their civic duty. It was their part to listen to the evidence. They believed the lies they heard told of me, but I can't fault them for that. With all of the posse and those others that lied about my past and God Himself against me, who could blame them?

And last of all, the jury and Judge Carson and that Reverend Barnes that talked to the court did me a great favor. Those jurymen had it in their power to hang me. Instead, they decided I was crazy. They gave me time, there in prison, to think things through. To decide what I was going to do. To study how I could make myself out to be crazy until I got my chance to escape. To make a clean break with no innocent soul killed except that one guard who shouldn't have gotten in the way anyhow.

Yes, I have a lot to be grateful for. When I'm done with all this and I've settled my account with the Hollis family, why someday I'd like to tell them how grateful I am. The judge and the Reverend Barnes, especially. Someday I'd like to thank them in just the way they deserve.

Maybe someday I will.

Chapter 7

Between bites Thomas Trueblood said, "What let's do next is to ride that train from wherever your friend got on it to wherever he was headed."

"The captain's friend."

Rachel Hollis passed fresh biscuits hot from the oven. "My goodness, Mr. Trueblood, wouldn't that take a lot of time?"

"Not so much as to rent a pair of good saddle horses and ride the right of way."

"Me and Dee would sure love to go with you. If we had our horses. I'm sorry, I wasn't to say that. But we'd ride up behind your saddles. We'd like to see a dead body since we've never seen one."

"Travis Lee. Do you want to go on to bed without your supper? The very idea!"

"We'll ride the line on horseback when everything else fails," King said. "Rachel, this is the finest meal ever served."

Travis put an enormous pat of butter on his steaming

biscuit. "I thought you said Christmas dinner was the finest meal you ever et."

"Ate."

"It was at that time, son," Trueblood put in. "But it weren't a patch to this one."

"Wasn't."

"Travis Lee! You apologize to Mr. Trueblood!"

The boy looked bewildered. "But why? That's right, ain't it?"

"Is—" Rachel stopped, scowled at King and Trueblood for laughing, then joined in herself. "Travis, honey, you eat your biscuit and let us talk for a minute, please."

"What let's do, Jeff, is to ride the cars with one of us at a right window and the other at a left one so's we can see both sides at once."

"Sounds sensible."

"Else we could set on the same side and look real careful all the way down. Mrs. Hollis, these biscuits is a meal to themselves! And then ride back on the other side, if needs be, studying it both of us together."

"Would we sit on the right side or the left?"

"What? Why, hey . . . first on the one side going down and then on the other side coming back. What are you grinning at?"

Dee put a double bite of beef in his mouth before he said, "No, you'd have to set on the same side both times!"

"Sit."

"I'm sitting!"

"You mind your sass, son. And next time make two or three bites out of a piece of steak that size."

"You just ate a bite that big."

"Dee."

"He did."

King hesitated. He wasn't sure he wanted to leave Rachel and the boys alone again. Trueblood's point about scaring Spivey away had been a good one, but King wasn't sure. In a few days, Christmas vacation would be over. If nothing was settled before Dee and Travis went back to school, King would have to bring in Myles Brewster and his police, whether Trueblood liked it or not.

"Let's think about it after supper," King said at last. "Coffee'll help us figure it out. Rachel, you did a fine job of shopping."

"Thank you. More steak, Mr. Trueblood?"

"I'm amenable."

"Pardon me?"

"Please."

After the meal, Jeff King said, "If it's not too cold for you, Tom, we might take our coffee out on the porch."

"Never too cold in Texas for a Wyoming man."

"Ever been up in the Panhandle in December?"

"Where's that?"

"I didn't think so."

Trueblood put his steaming coffee cup on the porch railing, took out a pipe, and began a search for his tobacco pouch. Two little boys watched him from the parlor, their noses mashed against the cold pane.

"Them boys want to be out where you are, don't they?" Trueblood said with a smile. "I like that."

"Not with me so much as they want to smell that tobacco. Their daddy smoked a pipe."

"I'd forgotten." Trueblood's eyes clouded for a moment while he stuffed his pipe to overflowing with rough-cut tobacco and got it going with a big match. Bright strings of red and orange coals from the overflow fell on his boots and flung across the porch in the north wind. "Why, hey, I'm going to catch the house on fire. What do you see off over there where you're staring?"

"Nothing. That old college building's been standing empty for years. When I was a boy, I thought those front windows over the door looked like eyes and a mouth."

"Well, so they do, by Joe."

"These boys." He nodded toward the window. "They think they've seen a ghost over there."

"Do they?"

"They imagine they've seen a light at the upstairs windows. I expect they've been having bad dreams."

"Seeing ghosts is a boy's dream, like seeing a dead body."

At the mention of dreams, King glanced quickly at Trueblood. Again he remembered waking that morning from the dream of coffins. For a moment, he almost remembered what had made this dream different from the others. As always, he'd been drawn step by step forward, drawn against his will until he could look down—

"I've seen my share," he said thickly. "Of bodies."

"You'll see more if you live."

"You're really willing to ride the train looking for Melton, are you?"

Trueblood let out a thin, thoughtful stream of smoke, lifted his cup, and drank it all off at once. "'Bout to go cold on me," he said. "Sure I'm willing. But I'm in the traces and you've got the reins. I said too much at supper. I'm ready to do whatever seems best to you."

"You're right about the coffee. Nothing stays warm very long in this wind."

"Might keep a dead man better than in summer."

King still didn't want to think about it. It reminded him of the colts. He was glad when Rachel saved him the trouble of answering.

"Gentlemen," she called from the door. "The boys and I have our dessert on the table, if you're ready to come in."

"You don't have to call a Wyoming man twice to sweets!" They brought their cups, took off their coats, and sat at the table. "Oh my lands, don't that cobbler smell good!"

"It's peach."

"Where did you ever get peaches this time of year?"

"They're only canned. Got them at the store today. They won't be as good as fresh."

"Better," King said with appreciation. "And there's not another woman in Texas that could have spiced them up this good."

"Not nary in Wyoming neither."

"Not nary in the world!" Travis crowed with Dee's

enthusiastic second. Rachel opened her mouth with a correction, smiled, and gave it up.

"Would you care to put some cream on yours, Mr. Trueblood?"

"Mrs. Hollis, you know a man's mind before he knows it himself."

The front doorbell rang. "I'll get it!" Dee cried. He pushed his chair back and started to run for the hall. King caught him with a long left arm.

"We'll get it together, Dee," he said. Rising, he let the youngster pull him along to the front hall. A few steps short, he released his hold. By the time Dee worked the bolt and opened the door, King was standing to his left rear, his hand ready on his Colt.

"It's Mr. Foster! Come in. We're having dessert."

"Thank you, Dee."

Foster stepped inside, removing his hat. As he hung it on the hall tree, he saw King. His eyes shifted to the half-drawn Colt, then back to King's face.

"Ranger."

He took off his overcoat and hung it below the hat. King seated the revolver back in its holster and offered his left hand. Paying attention this time, he saw a slight difference in cut between the right side of Foster's suit coat and the left.

Shoulder holster, he thought. *Suit's tailored for it, so he carries it a lot. Cap'n's right about me.*

"Mr. Foster. Come on back to the kitchen and join us in some cobbler. Glad to have you."

"Glad to be here."

In the kitchen, Trueblood reluctantly stood to welcome Foster. Rachel welcomed him more warmly and got him seated at the table.

"It was awfully nice of you to have me over," Foster said. "That looks good."

"After the way you helped with dinner on Christmas and took care of us today, this was the least we could do."

"Would have waited on you, but we was hungry," said Trueblood.

"As long as you left me some cobbler. Jeff, I didn't see you around today. I would have expected you to stay close to home."

"We rode out south, Tom and me. Not far."

"Did it have to do with the horses?"

"No," King said.

Trueblood swallowed hard on his cobbler. He started to speak, then let it go.

"I see." Foster was silent a minute. He leaned forward in his chair, staring at King. "I had the idea from Rachel that there might be some danger for her and the boys."

"Could be. We don't know who would have come in the yard here and hurt the horses."

"Then I'd think you want to be near to protect them."

King bit back an angry answer. Instead, he looked at Foster, then at Rachel. Her face was expressionless, but her eyes held a touch of the Arctic cold from the day before.

"I was following up on an investigation my captain left me. A missing person."

"Reverend Mr. Melton?"

King put his cup down. "That's right. How did you know? Was he a friend of yours?"

"Two and two. The news is going the rounds in the church here. I notice you used the past tense."

"Habit," King said calmly, glad Captain Slater wasn't there as witness. "I'd appreciate it if you didn't add to the church gossip."

"It was not my intention."

"Would you have some more cobbler, Randy?"

"It is fine winter cobbler, but I'd better not."

Trueblood frowned. "Us in Wyoming never heard of *winter cobbler*. Why do you call it that?"

"Perhaps it is a regional term. I merely meant I prefer cobbler when the fruit's fresh. In winter we have to use canned fruit."

For a moment no one spoke. Then Trueblood said, "I like it this way. You can't put enough sugar in summer peaches to make them sweet. I'll just have me another bowl of this fine cobbler, if you don't mind, ma'am."

"With cream?"

"You bet."

"Can I have more?"

"May I have some more."

"Sure you can. But me and Travis want some, too."

"C.D."

The boy silently passed his bowl.

King said, "I'll get us some more wood for the fireplace."

"I'd help you," Trueblood said, "but I'm still busy here."

King stepped out into the night air. He caught the scent of oak wood smoke from the chimney and thought of a campfire. Town life was all right, but he'd take a little bit of the outdoors. Pretty often.

The shed was as dark as a coal bin, but he knew it as well as the inside of his coat. He gathered a light armload of wood, tapping each piece to dislodge any scorpions, got it balanced across his right arm, and started back to the house. The old college was dark, but then in one of the windows above the entrance a light seemed to flicker and vanish. King stopped dead, staring until his eyes began to water. The light didn't come again.

It must have been a reflection on the window, he told himself; nobody's been in that building in years.

He took the wood in, noticed Foster finishing off a second bowl of cobbler after all, and put down his burden on the hearth to one side of the fireplace. Through the window he had a view of the dark building across the avenue. He saw no light. But he couldn't help thinking that Edwin Spivey would find it a perfect place to hide out. Quiet. Deserted. And handy to King and his family.

Half an hour before daybreak, Jeff King crossed the empty avenue and made his way across the weeded lawn to the entrance hall of the old college. The front door was shut fast, its lock rusted solidly in place. He had expected nothing else.

He stayed close to the walls as he walked around the building to the east looking for open windows. Everything was just as dilapidated as ever. At the back there were two doors. The northeast one hung loose and shaky but he couldn't open it. He would not have found the northwest door if he hadn't known where it was. Mostly, it was hidden by a tree and a tangle of rose bushes that had run wild.

That door, when he forced his way up to it, was in better condition than the others. An arc in the dirt showed it had been opened since the last rain. The knob turned as easily as if it had been oiled, but the door wouldn't open. King searched his pockets with his left hand out of new habit and found a ring of skeleton keys. The first refused to go in the lock, but the next one he tried fitted and worked. The lock, too, had been oiled so that the bolt slid back silently.

King returned the keys to his coat. Then he drew and cocked his long Colt revolver. Balancing it lightly in his left hand, he pushed open the door with his right.

He was not surprised when the old hinges made no noise. Once inside, he closed the door but left it unlocked. He paused there a moment while a thrill of remembered childhood fear coursed through him, leaving his body alive and tingling. Then he moved cautiously forward.

Every noise he made echoed like the inside of a drum. He had heard it before, the curious tomblike quality of an unused building that made it ring as if it were hollow. His eyes needed a couple of minutes to accustom themselves to the darkness.

A quick tour of the first floor turned up nothing more than a couple of long-locked doors and the signs and noises of rats. He tried the wide central stairs, expecting every moment to fall through. But they dated from a time when workmen took pride in constructing things to last. They were remarkably solid and quieter beneath his boots than the wooden floors.

At the landing he stopped. A hint of dawn brightened the upper hall and spilled into the stairwell. He realized that the window that had looked like a nose in his imagination was the one beside him at the level of the landing. From there he could see his house clearly enough through the sparse tall trees.

Once on the second floor, King didn't bother with the west end of the hall. The light he had seen flicker had been in the eastern eye of his demon. He tried the first door on his right. The knob turned too easily, but the door was locked.

Keeping the gun in his left hand, he fished the keys out with his unwilling right. He fumbled with stiff fingers for the one he'd used downstairs. As he tried to fit it into the lock, his hand twisted in a sudden cramp. The ring of keys clattered on the dusty floor with noise enough to wake a dozen killers.

"Damn," King said, but the word was barely a whisper. He strained his ears. On the far side of the door, something rustled. Floorboards creaked. The night noises of an old and empty building, maybe—or the light footsteps of a man.

He should have brought Trueblood along, he thought. There wasn't much use to call out. If Spivey were inside, he wasn't going to come out and give himself up. He would just wait for King to open the door before he shot him to pieces.

With that cheerful thought, King stood aside from the door while he tried several keys. The last one worked as if it had been made for the lock. With the gun ready in his left hand, he turned the knob with his right. He had just enough movement in it to get the door open. It swung in easily as soon as he let it go.

Straight across at the window was a table. Dim sunlight showed a large blackboard on the west wall. Students' desks were stacked and piled on all sides. No more than a dozen men could have hidden themselves in the shadows of the room.

Jeff King stepped past the door and slid round to the dark side of it. He waited, listening to himself breathe. Nothing moved, but as soon as he started toward the window, a dark shape let out a squeak and leapt off the table. A rat. It scurried away into a corner beneath a stack of desks.

When King could hear above the beat of his heart again, he walked softly across to the window. Marks on the floor showed that smaller desks had been shoved aside and the table dragged across to the side of the room. From the window King had the best possible view of his house through the leafless branches of the trees. Someone had chosen his vantage carefully.

The light King thought he'd seen in the window might have come from a candle which had been allowed to burn down and die in a shallow puddle inside a quart fruit jar. The rat had been at a freshly opened tin of crackers. They hadn't been there very long—left by workmen, maybe, he thought, but a moment later he knew better. Beside the jar lay a shiny brass telescope.

King laid his pistol on the table and reached for the telescope, careful to touch it only with his fingertips so as not to erase any marks. Then he heard the least soft tread behind him and realized he hadn't closed the door. The telescope clattered to the table and his hand snatched for the Colt.

"Freeze right there, you gotch-eyed son of a bitch," Tom Trueblood said from behind him. "Just twitch one hair on your ear, and I'll blow you right through that window."

From the Journals of Edwin Spivey

WITH SOME OF THE MONEY THE REVEREND BROUGHT FOR US orphans, I bought a telescope. Shiny brass, of the kind that can be fastened to a rifle. I hadn't found a rifle yet, so I used my shiny new telescope to keep watch on the kinfolk of Tex Hollis.

I've explained that I'm not crazy. I only pretend, so as to ease my way. I've made that clear. But even pretending offers surprising benefits. To take an instance, I have noticed that many people don't seem to see me. They neither look directly at me nor do they speak to me. And they seem quite startled if I address them. Sometimes they don't answer.

If it's clear they don't see me, I don't always speak. Sometimes I only watch and listen. Sometimes they talk to one another like I'm not even there. I find it most helpful.

I must warn you, reader, that pretending to be crazy has its frightening side, too. Now and again, I work so hard at it that I lose track of which is real and which is pretended— the way a watcher through a telescope can forget which end he's on and feel that he's right in the room with the folks he's watching. That scares me. There must be a difference between the real and the imagined. There must be, and it worries me when I can't keep them straight.

But then I suppose it must frighten other people even more to find they sometimes wind up doing and saying just what I've been thinking they should!

Thus I don't suggest any of my gentle readers should pretend lunacy. Not unless your reasons are as good as mine. Because when you lose track, when people who should be dead are alive and the other way around, then you may begin to doubt yourself. You may no longer be sure which is the pretend.

Trueblood. He's one of those changes I was warning you about. I had hardly started watching through my telescope, when lo, there he stood on the front porch of the Hollis home talking to Texas Ranger Jefferson Davis King. I could hear Trueblood telling him all about me, sure as if I'd been among them and they'd been able to see me. I realized I'd lost the element of surprise beyond any hope of recovery!

So please beware of playing crazy. Else, about the time you feel in control of all the people and their actions, and every word they say, you will suddenly have one of them turn upon you inside your own mind, exactly the way the ghost of Thomas Trueblood has turned upon me!

Chapter 8

THOMAS TRUEBLOOD STEPPED OUT OF THE DARK HALL INTO THE predawn gloom of the abandoned college classroom. His eyes glistened as he stared at the shape of a man standing by a front window. Trueblood kept his pistol pointing in the middle of the man's back.

"Just twitch as much as a hair on your ear, you gotch-eyed son of a bitch, and I'll blow you right through that window. That's good. Now you turn round here slow to me," Trueblood said, "so you can see the face of the man you left lying for dead in Wyoming."

The figure by the window turned slowly around to face Trueblood. For a moment they stood with their eyes locked and their guns pointing so nearly the same that the bullets might have met in midair if the men had fired.

Trueblood's face went lax. He lowered his gun. "Why hell, Jeff," he said, "you mighty near got yourself killed!"

"So did you." King held the pistol steady, gripping hard with his right hand. "How does it happen you found this place at the same time I did?"

"How does it *happen?* I don't understand you." Tom Trueblood slid his gun into its deep holster. "Couldn't sleep. I was out taking the air, watching, keeping an eye on your place. When I caught sight of you sneaking across to this old building—excepting it was too dark for me to tell who *you* was—I just followed along." He laughed. "Why, hey, I was mortal sure I had Spivey dead to rights."

"I was watching pretty careful, myself, Tom. I didn't see you following me."

Trueblood looked at the pistol in King's hand. His smile drew out into a tight line. "Didn't intend you should see me. Up in Wyoming they don't train us to follow a man like a calf bawling after his mama."

"Then you didn't know anything about this rat's nest until now?"

Trueblood shook his head, looked disappointed. "I wouldn't have thought you'd ask me a thing like that. Hell, I don't know anything about it yet, but for what little I can see in the dark here." He paused, looking at King and his Colt. "Here, let me show you something."

The man from Wyoming took off his hat and tossed it aside. Then he bowed his head, putting up his hand to draw back the long hair behind his left ear. King saw a wide jagged scar, ridged as if the skull beneath it was misshapen.

"Got that from Spivey. Shot from ambush and left in the road. Likely he'd have come up and scalped me, hadn't some folks in a wagon heard the shot and turned back. Still, I expect he's sure I'm dead. I'd hoped I was about to prove him wrong."

King at last lowered the pistol. He turned it in his hand, then laid it on the table. "Well, come and look."

Together they pored over the table. Someone had laid in a little bit of food and had apparently been looking at King's house through a telescope. "I guess you figure you know whose nest this is," King said.

"Don't you?"

King shook his head. "I don't. I don't even know it was my house he was looking at through this telescope."

Trueblood pushed his hat back to let his cowlick fall across his right temple. "Sure. I expect all this stuff was left here when the college shut down. And I imagine that them ponies had the misfortune to run into your clothesline and cut their own throats."

"All right," King said. "I see what it looks like. But I can't say I'm sure what it really is."

It went through his mind that Randy Foster could have been in this same room peeping at Rachel through the new brass telescope. He turned away toward the window, putting his back to Trueblood.

Trueblood picked up a cracker, took a little bite off the corner. "These is pretty fresh for forty-year-old crackers."

"They were good enough for the rat," King said.

"Rat?" Trueblood looked at the signs on the desk. Then he threw the cracker onto the floor. "I can eat off the same plate with bugs and spiders and maybe a occasional snake. But I draw the line at rats."

King turned again to the items on the desk. He hadn't had time to study them before Trueblood distracted him. The corner of a piece of paper showed under the jar that held the candle.

Trueblood saw it at the same time. "What's that?" he asked, reaching toward it across the desk.

But King already had it. "It's an envelope," he said. King held it up to the weak sunlight. He had seen others like it in church. The name on this one had been penciled by a strong but shaky hand.

"Envelope?"

"Offering envelope," King said. He read from the blanks. *"Giver's Name*—Edna Dugan. *Amount*—Ten cents."

"Why, hey, ten cents ain't going to shake the earth much one way or another."

King went on looking at the envelope. "No," he said. "I don't suppose the widow's mite has ever done that."

"The what? What says she's a widow? Anyway, there's no saying how long that old envelope's been up here."

"It's dated—this Sunday'll be three weeks ago."

"You're funning me again."

"Not about that." King handed him the envelope.

"I wouldn't've believed he'd been holding Sunday School class up here. Why, hey, would you look at this! The dime is still sealed up inside." Trueblood squinted, stretching out his arm to bring the print into focus. "They's some other writing on it," he said. "What's this part mean, this 'For— The Methodist Home'?"

King took the envelope back and put it in his inside pocket. "It means that's where we're going to deliver that dime and a lot more when we get it back from the man that murdered Wallace Melton."

Jeff King didn't like any of it. He didn't like it that some stranger had been sitting up in that room watching Rachel dress. He didn't like it that the telescope had little clamps on it—he hadn't used a telescopic rifle sight, but he knew what one could do. And he didn't like it that the man who'd been at the college wanted to be damned certain that King knew who he was.

King thought it through while he and Trueblood made a gun-in-hand search of every room and cupboard and broom closet in the entire Marvin College building. They didn't turn up as much as another rat, not even in the basement. King did not feel any better. His man, be it Spivey or not, had gone to the trouble to sneak around oiling locks and shading candles and hiding in an abandoned building like a shadow in the night; then he'd left lying right out on the desk a piece of evidence that would hang him in any court.

"Edwin Spivey's not worried about being brought to trial," Trueblood said.

"What?" King wondered if he'd voiced his thoughts aloud.

"He's not worried about it a bit. He expects to be killed or else kill everybody that could bring him to trial. Most likely the latter."

"Why hasn't he killed us then? He must have had chances enough."

"You ever see a cat catch a mouse? He don't kill it right away. He plays with it."

King nodded. "All right," he said. "But Spivey didn't waste any time playing with those sorrel colts. What good did it do him to kill them?"

"It's like I told you to begin with. Ed Spivey is just plain goddamned mean."

Walking would have been faster, but King saddled Pistol to ride down to Myles Brewster's office at the jail. The roan needed exercise, King told himself, and the work of getting saddle and bridle on him would be good for his own injured arm.

The morning had turned off fair, with sunlight but no warmth and only a few thin clouds high in the north. King greeted a couple of other riders, tipped his hat to the Widow Granby, and raised a hand to Sam and Ahab and Jezebel as the yellow streetcar trundled past on its way up College. Then he turned right and drew up before the massive walls and tall, metal-capped turret of the Ellis County jail.

When he was a boy, he'd made believe the jail was a castle. He and his friends had been Robin Hood and Little John and Alan a'Dale, plotting against the evil Sheriff of Nottingham—though it had troubled King to think a sheriff might be evil. He knew better now about a lot of things, and he smiled a little at the memory and the lost innocence. Then he thought of Dee and Travis and he stopped smiling. They still had that innocence—or they'd had it a few days ago.

"Spivey," he muttered, half aloud, as he dismounted and passed his reins to a hard-eyed guard in a shiny new silver beaver hat.

"How's that?"

"Nothing much, Newt. Just thinking. Is Myles around?"

"You know the answer to that. Back in his office, same's he always is. Chipper and cheerful, same's he always is."

"Thanks. Take care of Pistol for me?"

"Sure thing." The guard looked him over, half frowning. "Good to see you back. We'd heard you were dead."

"I was. I got over it. You ever think how this place looks like a castle?"

Newt started a laugh, stopped when he saw that King wasn't smiling. "Looks like a cage to me," he said. "Same's it always does. We got nobody lined up for hanging, but business is pretty brisk otherwise." He raised a hopeful eyebrow. "Figure you'll be bringing us some more?"

"Can't tell yet." King turned slowly, managing to walk without a limp as he headed for the heavy oaken door. "But I'd better talk to Myles."

Myles Brewster was a thick man, tapering a little only at the head and neck. When he stood, he was like the trunk of a mature tree cut off head high in its prime. Frost-gray hair gave way to completely white sideburns in front of his delicate ears. The flat stare of his pale blue eyes and the pallor of his skin gave him the nickname that Waxahachie's children whispered in awe: Walking Corpse.

He sat behind his desk like a post oak stump, his expression unchanging as he watched Jeff King step through the tall glass-paneled doors of his office.

"Morning, Myles," King said. "How are you today?"

"Tolerable. I've been better."

Brewster's voice was a harsh croak. Coupled with his pallor, it gave the listener the feeling he might not live out the day. He was thirty-eight.

King waited a moment, but Brewster seemed to be finished. "Myles, I've got a couple of unusual circumstances," King said. "Figured it was time I let you know about them."

"More dead horses?"

"You heard about that then?"

"I do hear about what goes on round here—despite my fellow lawmen choosing not to tell me."

"I'm telling you now, Myles."

"Not fast enough, you're not. But I wish you would before we're both in the grave."

"I brought home a couple of colts for Rachel's boys. Had them here for Christmas morning."

With what seemed a great effort, Brewster flapped his hand at King. "I know all that," he croaked. "Tell me what I don't know, before next Christmas morning."

"Christmas night I found them dead in the backyard. Still warm with their throats cut."

"I don't see how you could have reported it any sooner than that."

"No."

"Nor how you could have failed to report it to me any *later* than that. Who did it?"

"I don't know."

"Doomsday!"

"I have an idea."

"Death won't wait!"

"I met a fellow on the train coming in to Waxahachie, Tom Trueblood—"

"My God, is this going to be your autobiography? Do you think this Trueblood fellow did it?"

King stopped and drew a deep breath. He'd reported things to Myles Brewster before, he reminded himself. And Brewster was a good peace officer.

"No. I don't think he did it. He told me a Wyoming fugitive named Edwin Spivey was looking for the family of C. D. Hollis with the intention of killing them."

Police Chief Myles Brewster creaked at his knees and hips as he stood straight out of his chair in the shape of a heavy yule log. He put on his hat, came around the desk, held out a big left hand in deference to King's injury.

"Good morning," he said. Life seemed to course through his arteries, giving him a color much like that of real flesh. "I liked C.D."

"You've often told me so," King said as he shook hands.

"No harm's going to come to his wife and sons in my town. Not unless it comes after I'm in the grave. Where is this Spivey? Let's go get him." He found his Smith and Wesson revolver in the drawer of his desk, checked the loads in its cylinder. "I mean 'let's go *get* him.' Taxpayers aren't so self-righteous about a trial in a case of this kind."

"Hell," King said. "I didn't come down here for that. I'd

be bringing him to you over his saddle right now if I knew where to find him."

"You don't know where he is and you've left C.D.'s family by themselves at his mercy?" Brewster's eyes were pale as diamonds staring at a new sun.

"Of course not. The man I met on the train, that Wyoming deputy, is watching over them. I don't even know what Spivey looks like."

"You've never seen him? Heart's blood, man! Well, here." Brewster moved across the room like a huge cat, grabbed up a piece of paper, shoved it at King. "Take a look at him."

Jeff King took the poster. It promised a thousand dollars for Edwin Spivey, listed his crimes, and offered a shadowy drawing of the face of a man. A heavy beard hid his cheeks and chin. The eyes reminded King of Randy Foster.

"Why would they send you a poster on a man from Wyoming?" he asked.

"Don't know. Didn't pay any attention. Maybe they thought he might come down this way."

"Who sent it?"

"I did notice that. It came from the office of the governor of Wyoming. Most likely, they circulated it to every department west of the Mississippi. No respect for taxpayers' money." He threw out an arm toward King. "Well, don't take root there. Show me what you've found. And I want to meet this Trueblood, ask him why he didn't come to me when he arrived."

"Wait," King said. "How long've you been sitting on this?"

"Came last month—before Thanksgiving, it was. Didn't mean anything till you spoke the name. Come on. Let's get out of here, walk around the square, drink some coffee, find our man."

Brewster swung through the office door and padded away along the dim hall. King caught up with him at the street. He didn't figure they were going to find Spivey right then, but he wanted some coffee and he wanted to tell Brewster the rest of the situation.

* * *

Half an hour later he had shown Brewster the desk by the window in old Marvin College and explained how he and Trueblood had stumbled over the place and each other. Brewster snorted his contempt, but he took a deep interest in the brass telescopic sight.

"He made a mistake here. I'll put a man to checking the gunshops for who bought this telescope," Brewster said. He moved around the room like a hound on the scent. "Doomsday, some storekeeper may even remember who bought these crackers and candles. But you said there was something else."

"There's this envelope. Do you remember the case of Wallace Melton?"

The chief turned the envelope in twig-like fingers, peering at it closely. "Wallace used to be my pastor," he said, "a long time ago. By God, I want to kill this Spivey myself!"

"You'll have to stand in line."

"I just wish you'd explain to me why he'd be stupid enough to keep this envelope, let alone leave it right here for us to see."

"Maybe he was that sure we wouldn't find his nest."

Brewster pulled at his lower lip. "Maybe. Or maybe he wanted to be good and damned sure we knew it was his."

From the Journals of Edwin Spivey

THE NEXT GREAT SURPRISE AWAITING ME WAS THE EASE WITH which Jeff King and Nine-Lives Trueblood found my writing spot and confiscated my telescope. It annoyed me to lose the telescope. And I knew at once that I would never find another such vantage from which to watch the King place.

But they didn't find my journals, which were right under their noses. And that was the luckiest day any of us would have for quite a spell. Lucky for me because I did not lose my journals nor have my thoughts compromised by being read. And lucky for them because I'd have killed them flat, even though I hadn't at that time finished thinking through my plan for killing.

I was mired instead in memories of killings from the past. Most of all, I was having trouble keeping it straight in my mind how Thomas Trueblood could be alive among us. Recall my warnings, gentle reader, concerning pretended lunacy—lest you too should suddenly find yourself confronted with a ghost pretending to be alive!

I have related, in an earlier volume, the particulars of killing Thomas Trueblood in Wyoming. I was so cocksure he was dead—lying there in his own blood with his skull showing through his hair—that I didn't waste a valuable extra bullet on him as I should have.

So I believed it later when I got wind—from keeping company with a group of yeggs I'd gotten to know while riding the rails—of Trueblood alive and showing his Wyoming badge on several Texas trains. Asking about Edwin Spivey!

No one knew that name in Texas, of course. But that was when I went underground, so to speak, and began to lie in wait for Trueblood so I could kill him again.

I tell you, my friend, patience always finds its reward. My chance came about one day in early December. As fate would have it, we both were riding the same train down below Hillsboro. I saw a tall man at a distance, and I was morally certain it was him. He didn't see me nor would he likely have recognized me if he had.

He got off the train at some little town short of Waco. I followed him until he was walking along the bank of a river staring at his reflection. Then, while there was nobody else around, I stabbed him three times in the back before he fell.

Until the day I got my telescope my great regret was that I still didn't get to ask him my question about who killed my family. And I didn't have the enjoyment of his knowing who killed him.

But now that he's come back, I have to ask myself very seriously whether I might not have killed the wrong man. It's either that this new Trueblood's a ghost or that the one on the river bank was another poor soul who got mixed up in my pretending and never saw nor heard of me at all.

Chapter 9

THE FIRST THING THURSDAY MORNING, JEFF KING WENT OUT TO the shed with a rag soaked in coal oil. When he finished wiping and polishing the green buggy, he rolled it outside and hitched up the carriage horse he'd borrowed from Myles Brewster. Tom Trueblood sat on a sawhorse and watched, whittling idly on a twig from the pecan tree that shaded the backyard. Beside him, Dee sat, brow furrowed, working at another twig with his new stockman's knife.

"Wish you'd let me help," Trueblood said for the third time. "No call to be so uppity just because you're stove up."

"I can manage." King fumbled at the straps with a right hand as stiff and lifeless as the pecan twigs. He paused, thought out a way to do the job left-handed, and set about it. "I need to work this hand a little, that's all."

Trueblood pursed his lips, started to answer, changed his mind. "That lawman you showed me to—that Brewster feller—known him long?"

"Ten years or so. Good man."

"I reckon. Is he always that peaked looking?"

Dee forsook his whittling. "Sometimes he's a lot worse," he said. He leaned toward Trueblood, lowering his voice. "All the kids say he's really—"

"Dee," King interrupted. "Where's Travis?"

"Back of the grape arbor, playing with those soldiers he's too old for. We made a fort. We're playing Spaniards and rebels, like Uncle—Mr. Foster read us from the newspaper."

"Go fetch him, please. I don't much want you boys out of sight for the next little while."

"Because of the horses, you mean?" Dee asked. "And what that Spivey did? Do you think he might come back? Right in daylight?"

King looked up, surprised. "Spivey? Where'd you hear that name?"

"I don't know. I just heard. Will he come back?"

"I don't think so, Dee. But go get Travis."

The boy closed his pocketknife, then scampered away. King frowned after him. "Kids hear everything," he said. "Never any point in trying to keep a secret."

Trueblood nodded. "Hell of a thing, too, those boys having to worry about a lizard like Spivey. It ain't right."

King nodded. "Sure you don't mind?" he asked.

"Why, hey," Tom told him, "I wouldn't have it any other way. You go right on and have a good time and don't spare a thought about these boys. I'll watch over them like they was my own!" He concentrated on a careful cut in the twig. "Still think you should tell me where you'll be. Just in case."

King hesitated, then shook his head. "Sorry, Tom. It's nothing against you. Myles made me promise I wouldn't say a word to anybody."

"Your business." He slid off the sawhorse and stood up, folding the big Case knife into his pocket. "'Morning, Miz Rachel. We're getting things ready for you."

Rachel laughed. "So I see," she said and smiled at King.

He stepped to meet her, giving the gray carriage horse a pat with his numbed right hand. Rachel wore a long-sleeved blue traveling dress that matched her eyes and brought out golden highlights in her hair. For an instant, King saw her again at seventeen. Then he saw her as she was, with a black mourning band on her arm, with marks of years and care and joy and sadness in her face and eyes. Beneath it, she still wore the beauty he'd loved at seventeen.

"Hello," he said. "You look nice today."

She laughed again. "You've seen me already," she said. "At breakfast. But maybe you didn't look at anything but the flapjacks."

"Mighty good flapjacks they were, too, ma'am," Trueblood put in.

"Are we ready?"

"Ready for what?" Dee wanted to know. He and Travis had come up quietly. Each held an armful of the blue-coated wooden soldiers.

"Uncle Jeff and I are going"—she glanced up and caught King's eye—"on a sort of picnic today, honey."

"You told us it's too cold for picnics," Dee said. "And it's getting cloudy. Are you going to bundle up good?"

"Can we go?" Travis asked at the same time.

"Well, hey, I'd view it as a favor if you two could stay with me today," Trueblood put in. "I'd been thinking this would be a good time to look into that book you two got for Christmas. What was it?"

The Jungle Book. Could we?"

"Surely enough."

Rachel went back into the house and returned with a basket and a green-and-red plaid blanket. King put the basket into the back, then handed Rachel up into the seat and arranged the blanket across her lap. Trueblood shook King's hand as hard as if the man and woman were leaving on a cruise.

"Now, you don't worry about a thing. The boys and me, we'll be right here safe."

"Thanks, Tom. We should be back by suppertime."

King drove slowly down College to the square. It was still filled with rubble that had been the courthouse. A few workmen were busy in the southeast corner, loading stone blocks onto a heavy ox-drawn sledge.

"Do you know what's happening here?" King asked.

"They're supposed to rebuild. But the city council is having some kind of fight over who has the contract for cleaning up. I don't understand it." She frowned over at him. "Where are you going?"

"Don't you remember?"

He had swung the wagon left on Franklin Street. Snapping the lines, he urged the gray horse into a spanking trot for a tour of the square. Merchants and passersby gaped in surprise as the green buggy rattled past.

Rachel's laughter trailed behind them. She held tightly to her hat with one hand. "I remember," she said. "I haven't seen anyone do this since I was a girl."

"You're still a girl."

"No, but you're still a boy."

"You might be right." It came to King that he wanted to pass beneath Randy Foster's office window. He wanted Foster to see the green buggy, to see Rachel riding where she belonged. "That being the case," he told her, "why don't we just take up where we left off ten years ago."

"As boy and girl?" She bit her lip and shook her head slightly. Her gloved hand rested on his right arm, tightened a little. She watched the store fronts and the people round the square.

Jeff King felt her grip like a smoking brand. At first he thought he only imagined the weight and warmth of her hand. But then a lean, unkept little white dog dashed yapping out into the street just in front of King's horse. The gray shied and kicked. Before King could rein back, the dog got itself tangled in the hooves, tumbled back beneath the buggy, and ran away with pitiful yelps. Rachel cried out and squeezed King's arm.

He felt it. He looked down, saw her knuckles white with the effort, knew that he was going to get his arm back. "You, up!" he said to the horse.

The fresh tone of his voice surprised him as much as it did Rachel and the horse. They fairly flew to the corner, swung south on Rogers toward the railroad tracks, and raised dust all the way down the hill.

"What's the matter with you?" she wanted to know.

King grinned broadly enough to hurt his chapped face. "Not a blessed thing," he said. "You, horse! Up, let's go!"

They clattered across the iron-framed bridge south of the depot. Beyond, the road ran east for a mile, then south an hour or more. Its surface was roughly graveled with white caliche rock. To either side, deep black soil lay fallow and prickled with rows of dead stalks left from the once green fields of cotton. Thickets of oak and pecan, the oak leaves blackish-green and shiny, capped the low hilltops. Below them, the fields seemed flat, but King knew they sloped gently down everywhere to running water. Water gleamed in the ditches along the roadside.

"It's been a good autumn for the farmers."

"For the farmers," Rachel agreed.

King tried his arm again. It hurt. The pins-and-needles feeling came and went but never quite to the dead numbness he had grown to dread. It wasn't ready for horseshoe pitching, but it was better.

At Five Points they turned west between the Bethel Church and its tabernacle by the creek. The clouds had gradually thickened until not even weak sunlight showed through. The road ran for a way beside the black iron fence of the old Bethel Cemetery. Rachel turned her face away, but King looked beyond the fence at the tall gray granite markers. He picked out the one where his parents lay and for a second saw again a cozy parlor with two white coffins before the fireplace.

"The things that happen when you're young," he murmured, half to himself. "You never forget them."

Rachel shivered. "The ponies," she said. "Dee and Travis will never forget that, will they?"

"Sure, they—" King stopped, angry with himself for letting gloom drape itself over the day he'd planned with Rachel, angry at the lie he'd been about to tell. "No. Probably they won't. But they'll have better memories, too. As we do."

"As we do," Rachel repeated. She smiled. "Remember how we used to ride out here together, back before— before?"

"And how your friends were so scandalized because you wouldn't ride sidesaddle?"

"And my mother found out. 'Rachel Elaine Porter, your grandmother would turn in her grave. I've raised you as a lady, and you're behaving like common trash!'" Rachel shrugged and drew the blanket up. "She didn't know!"

He raised his hand to touch her, then stopped. His arm had begun to tingle. Feeling ebbed from his fingers. He clenched his hand, willing himself to feel the pain of his nails digging into his palm.

"What's wrong?" Rachel asked.

He wondered if his face gave away his thoughts as easily as that. "Nothing," he said, dropping his hand to his side.

"There is. Just now you were bright and young and—and hopeful."

"Sure. I still am."

She looked steadily at him. He stared straight ahead. Presently the road curved back south. They rode in tense silence for another mile until they came to the fenceline of the old Hollis farm.

"There," Rachel cried. She pointed off to the west. More than a hundred yards from the road, the tall white house stood empty.

King watched it as he drove, wondering if it would be safer than the house in town. From a distance, the farmhouse had stood up better than he had expected. He found the gap in the fence and drove up the rutted lane that ran beside the woodlot.

"Nancy and Will and the girls stayed here through the cotton season. Looks like they left the place standing."

Rachel stared along the road ahead of them. "It doesn't matter how nice you paint an empty house," she said. "It's still empty."

"We'll fix that," King said cheerfully. But the earlier mood didn't come back. Neither of them found anything more to say until they drove into the yard. King stopped the buggy at the rail in front of the house and stepped down to tend the horse. His right arm was tingling and quivering too much to be of any real help.

"Are you all right?"

"Sure. I'm fine. Let's walk some."

"Let's do." She took his left arm and strolled along beside him toward the barn. She smiled and swung her free arm in an arc. "The last time I walked along here I was barefoot!"

"Well then, we'll pull our shoes off."

"Silly, it's too cold. I was remembering, that's all."

"Remembering is a lot."

They studied their shoes as they walked.

He reached across to put his wooden hand on hers. "I was just remembering," he said.

"Yes?"

"Seems like somebody fell out of that loft." He nodded up at the hay door and the rusted pulley hanging beside it.

"I never heard of it."

"Maybe it was some other loft."

"Or some other body!"

"I thought you were hurt. I picked you up and carried you inside, back where the new hay was stored. Remember?"

Rachel's cheeks were reddened by the sharp breeze. "We were children," she said. "We didn't know what we were doing."

"Didn't we?"

King leaned down and kissed her. She started to draw back, then didn't. Her lips were soft and eager, but after a moment, she did pull back. "Don't." She looked at him seriously. "Do you mind?"

"No. Mind what?"

"If I just let it all go for today?"

He didn't understand. "All right," he said.

"Let me float out and fly free. I haven't been alone, not for a moment since—"

"All right." The north wind cut through his coat.

"No. I don't want you to leave me. What I mean is I don't want to be a mother today. I don't want to be a widow. I only want to *be!*" She drew away from him and went through the tall creaking doors into the darkness of the barn.

"All right."

He followed her inside. His right arm was trembling like a

fresh frog leg. After a moment he found her in the darker shadows by the stalls. She was cold, trembling like his arm. He had only started toward her when she let her hat fall without notice and rushed back to him.

She plunged blindly into his chest, slid her arms inside his coat and round his vest until she held him tight.

"Listen," he said.

"Don't talk," she said in a whisper. "Put your arms around me like you mean business and hold me."

He put his arms around her like he meant business and held her. She was not crying but he could feel the heat from her face where her cheek crushed against his coat. He bowed his head and let his lips press against her hair until he felt the warmth of her scalp. She smelled of lilacs.

If this was what she meant by being herself, King hoped she would never be anyone else again. He thought how to say that to her in words and then gave it up.

Without moving or breathing she said, "I do."

His patience was a question.

"I do love you." She said it as simply as that. "I always have."

King's spine quivered like willow. He cleared his throat. "Well, God knows—" he said.

"But I'm not ready to talk about it yet."

"But I—"

"I'm cold."

"Cold!" Her touch burned him. "You're cold as a fresh pot of coffee."

"I'd like that."

"What?"

She led him out of the barn and back along the furrowed path to the kitchen door of the farmhouse. It was not locked.

"It's never been locked. But it ought to be."

"Look," Rachel said. "Someone's been here."

The kitchen was smaller than King remembered, crowded with the big stove and pie safe and a tall cabinet with many drawers and doors. Opened tins and dirty silverware littered the kitchen table. Someone had eaten a can of beans and a can of tomatoes.

"Nancy wouldn't have left a mess like this," Rachel said. "A hobo must have stopped in."

"Maybe," King said. "There's not an empty house in the county that doesn't draw transients—at least not a house this close to the railroad. But with Spivey around—"

Rachel shook her head. "No. He couldn't know."

"I'm not sure you and the boys would be safe here."

She smiled at him. "I always have been," she said. "I could never be afraid here." She moved away. "It's cold. How about that coffee?"

"Right." King checked the wood box by the stove. "They left us some kindling, but there's not a single stick of stove wood."

"There's not much coffee either. Looks like enough kindling and coffee for one pot."

King surprised himself by using both hands as he built a small fire in the stove. Rachel pumped water until the rust was out of it, filled the pot, and set it on the stove to boil. Then she wanted to look through the house.

Small and sturdy, the house was unimaginatively square. Next to the kitchen was the front parlor. The fieldstone fireplace took up much of the west wall. On the north side, tall windows flanked the front door, opening onto a porch that ran along the front and the east side of the house. Both south rooms were bedrooms. Their windows revealed wide, bare flower beds and gaunt leafless pecan trees.

"The furniture's still here," Rachel mused. "It all looks just the same."

"It is," King said. "Will and Nancy didn't bring their furniture out here. Took it off to Fort Worth with them when they moved. Most of this has been here since we were kids. Probably longer."

"It'll do fine," she said. "The boys and I will love it. The water's boiling. Come back to the kitchen."

King was thinking about keeping them safe out there all alone. He stared out a kitchen window toward the barn. He wondered whether a guard in the barn would have time to get to the house in case of trouble.

Rachel stood beside him, put her hand on his arm, and

looked out the window with him. "It's going to rain," she said.

"That," King said, "or bring a new norther." Watching the clouds, now grown low and dark, King wished that the weather would isolate them, shut them off from the rest of the world so that they could be alone for a day. A night.

"I wish it would be an ice storm," he said. He tried to lift his arm to embrace her.

She held the arm and put her other hand on his. "How is your arm?"

"What?"

"Your hand. Is it better?"

"Better, thank you. It does better whenever you touch it. You pretty nearly healed it this morning in town."

"Did I?"

"Like a miracle."

"You'll be able to go back to work then?"

There was an edge in her voice King hadn't noticed before. "I'm working now," he said.

"You know what I mean." She touched the handle of the Colt in his belt. "You never mean to take off that gun?"

King tried to smile. He began to think he knew what she meant. "Well, sometimes when I take a bath," he said.

"It's not a joke. You do intend to go back?"

"Yes. That's what I intend."

"Even if your hand doesn't get well?"

"It'll get well if you keep healing it."

She ignored that. "Even though you might get yourself killed any day?"

"That goes with living."

She took her hands off his arm. "That's a lie! You—"

He pawed at her with his right hand, took her by the elbow, cinched his grip. "I'd been wondering who taught your boys to talk like that," he said. His voice had gone so low and rocky that neither of them recognized it. "It might be bright of you to notice that the three of you are the only ones in the world I've allowed to call me a liar. You've now used up that privilege."

"Don't!" she said steadily. "Let me go."

He let her go and turned away to look out the window above the sink. He now thought he ought to get her in the buggy and back to the noise of civilization.

She rubbed at her elbow for a moment. For several moments while she made the coffee, she said nothing at all. When she had poured two steaming cups, she said, "There's no sugar or cream."

He took one of the cups. Something in the way he'd been raised made him say, "Thank you."

"Listen," she said.

He shook his head.

She put down her cup without tasting the coffee and rounded on him in sudden anger. "Can't you understand? Isn't a man able to understand what a woman's up against? It's always the *him* that chooses what *he* wants to do! The woman has to follow along like a mare in harness."

"I understand some of it. I've seen it happen. A woman who doesn't want to be a storekeeper's wife. Another woman who doesn't want to be a preacher's wife. I've seen it."

"Well, then. Can't you understand what you've seen?"

"What I've seen is women who don't love their men."

Rachel started to answer. Then she stopped and shook her head slowly. "No," she said. "If that's what you believe, there's no point. We'd better go back."

"Am I wrong?"

"Yes, you're wrong." She stood up and came to face him, looking up into his eyes. "Now I *am* ready to talk. I said I love you. I loved Holley, too. He was like you, only older, grown up. He knew things we didn't. And I was too young to take time to think.

"I followed him for almost ten years." She made a face. "A lawman's wife. I don't want to go through that again." She stopped. Almost in a whisper, she said, "I don't want to bury another husband."

"Any soul's likely to get himself killed any day. It doesn't matter if it's a policeman or a railroad man or a woman working in a shop."

Rachel laughed without humor. "Don't forget, I have

experience with the law. Almost as much as you." Her voice was low and angry. "It does make a difference. It makes a difference when you pin a star-shaped target on your chest and stand in front of other men's guns every day until you get killed. But it's the woman who's left alone."

"What if the man gave up his job? Did what the woman wanted?"

"She'd love him."

"What if they had a child?"

"She'd love it—them."

"And then they were going to have another baby, only she died in childbirth? Then it's the man would be left all alone."

"He'd have the children!"

He studied her eyes, waited.

"All right." She relaxed, her voice dull. "I have the children. What is it you want me to do?"

He put his arms around her from behind, drew her to him. "Marry me," he said.

"I can't do that."

"After a decent time."

"No."

"You said you love me."

"That's a different thing."

"Is it?" He pulled her closer.

"It is."

She turned in his arms and lifted her face to his and kissed him, neither shrinking nor pushing. He put his hands in the middle of her back and held her against him, pressed against her lips, beginning to lose in her embrace all memory of his loneliness. Unnoticed outside the window, the north wind whirled big flakes like dry leaves, dusting the house with a fine, soft, silent layer of snow.

From the Journals of Edwin Spivey

I WISH SOME ONE OF YOU MIGHT EXPLAIN IT TO ME HOW TOM Trueblood can be alive here in our midst. If it's God's doing, then it's not right. He's always sided against me, and me never doing a single thing to cause it.

It's my belief that Trueblood is a ghost. But that doesn't worry me. I've killed that cat twice, and I'll kill him again as many lives as he turns up in.

I'm not afraid of him. I'm sure you can see it isn't that. But what if others of the dead start coming back to life, too? I mean those seven or eight besides him and that guard and Milford and some others that shouldn't rightly count because they were greedy or unreasonable. What if they come back?

Then there's Hollis. He's one I didn't kill. But then this Jeff King who claims to be his brother looks enough like him to be Hollis. He may be a ghost I hadn't noticed. He may be hiding his true self the way I have done at times. Pretending.

O what a tangled trail we wend when first we practice to pretend. Don't say I never warned you, gentle reader!

King's case calls for more reflection. I'm glad I haven't

had to kill him before I'm sure about it. Then again, if he's a ghost, he may be harder to kill.

I wouldn't trouble my mind over any of them. I can keep killing them every single one again and again over and over. I've had to do that in my memories all along. It's gotten so I can scarcely get any worthwhile thinking done at all except when I'm lost in this journal.

I've read that the pen is mightier even than the sword. I haven't myself done enough work with a sword—unless you count this knife—to demonstrate the truth or foolishness of that saying. But I've done enough work with the pen to know its power to help a man think.

At the bottom of it all are my loved ones. What about Sallie May? And the boys? It's them I have to think about. I've dreamed them back often enough. None of the others really matter. But what if God should send back Sallie May and the boys?

What price would I have to pay for such a miracle as that?

Chapter 10

JEFF KING SAT UP IN HIS OWN BED, RUBBED HIS RIGHT ARM AND elbow for a few minutes, then willed himself up and over to the upstairs window. Shivering in the predawn chill, he looked down past the curtain, searching for any movement. Below him, the backyard lay in frosty darkness. Off to the east, the sun was nothing more than a purple promise tingeing the low, dark clouds. He judged sunrise was an hour away.

King smiled. He looked forward to the dawn. It always meant a fresh start that would wash away the failures and losses of the day before—or give him the chance to build on its successes. Beyond that, each dawn rose as a promise that he would get through the day alive. When he died, it would be at night; he knew that. But he would have called it superstition in anyone else.

He held out his scarred right hand and tried its grip on the heavy pistol. The hand worked as smoothly as a marionette with tangled strings. When at last he had his fingers locked around the walnut grip, he turned again to the window. For some little time, he studied a nest of shadows near the back gate. Then he grinned, laid the pistol aside, and began to dress. By six-thirty, he was ready for the day's business.

"And what is that business?" Rachel wanted to know. She poured his cup full again.

King finished a bite of scrambled eggs. "Tom and I're going to take a train ride."

She stood at the stove, her back stiff. She didn't look at him. "Must I ask you why?"

"No," he said. "I'm a little slow getting it out. We're going to ride down to Waco and watch the right of way for any signs of the Reverend Melton."

"For his body, you mean?"

"That's right." He drained off half the coffee, looked up at her from the corners of his eyes. He had sensed the change in her from the first morning greeting. She seemed a different person today, as if their drive to the farm had never happened. "No need for you to worry."

"Oh, no. Of course not. None at all."

"Myles has his men watching the house to keep anybody out. If you need anything, one of them will go with you. Or go for you."

Rachel's back stayed stiff. "It's not me I'm worried about."

"I know. But I meant all of you. They'll watch the boys, too."

Rachel turned now to face him. She shook her head. "I'm worried about *you*," she said.

His surprise was genuine. "Well, you surely don't need to be worried about me. All I'll be doing is riding a train and watching the scenery."

"All C.D. was doing was 'closing things up for the night.' That was the night they killed him!"

"Rachel . . . I'm not C.D."

"Aren't you?" She laughed, but there was no joy in it. "I wish you knew. You're exactly like him—like he was ten years ago, when he asked me to marry him. Even yesterday, when we—"

She stopped abruptly, biting her lip. King felt the words like a blow under his heart. He looked at her, almost expecting to see the shadow that had fallen between them, but Rachel turned away toward the window. He looked at the back of her head, the rigid set of her shoulders.

King waited until he could trust his voice. "It doesn't change anything," he said softly. "Not for me."

Her shoulders slumped a little. "Damn you," she whispered. She whirled back toward him, sudden anger sweeping across her. "You can't understand. What I see is the next ten years. Like it was with C.D.—a husband gone half the time, away on his business, with a rifle on his saddle and a pistol that was more a wife to him than I was."

King started to speak, but Rachel wasn't finished. "Even in Willow Springs, after he'd settled down as sheriff, it was the same. Sure, he'd have time to take the boys fishing—as soon as things quieted down just a little. Sure, he could quit spending his nights at the office—as soon as his little scrape with the judge got settled."

She faced King without blinking. Her eyes were bright with unshed tears.

"I never said any of this to him. Maybe I should have. What I did was wait, like a good, dutiful little wife." She drew a deep breath. "Do you know what it's like to wait? To sit up nights and wait to see if it was C.D. coming home or somebody who'd tell me he'd been killed? Then, one night, that's who it was."

King rose and went to her, putting his hands on her shoulders, looking down into her face. "Rachel," he said. She shook her head. "Rachel, it's different. Nothing like that is going to happen to me."

"No." She laughed and touched the bandage that wound around his right arm. "No, I can see that. Nothing's going to happen to you."

"But—"

She twisted under his hands, turned her back. He could feel the sobs begin to shake her shoulders.

"Can't you see I've heard it before?" she said. "I know all about it. I'm an authority!"

"Well, listen."

"I've listened! More than once. I know when to worry

about my man getting himself killed! The only thing I don't know—"

She gave way at last to a burst of sobbing. King put his left arm around her and drew her closer.

"What?" he said softly. "What don't you know, sweetheart?"

She tried for a moment to pull away. Then, as if against her will, her muscles relaxed and her body nestled back against his. "I don't know why I let myself . . . let myself . . . forget—why I let yesterday happen!"

He held her with an iron arm. "I'm sorry if you regret it," he said. "I don't. It was what I wanted—"

"I could tell!"

"—as you are what I wanted. What I want."

"Turn loose of me."

He didn't. He felt her muscles tense again, saw her hands clench into fists and her knuckles grow white. But she didn't move. If she struggled, it was a struggle against herself, deep inside herself.

"Damn you," she said again, just louder than a breath. "I had it all thought out. I'd be true to C.D.'s memory for a year. Then I'd marry a carpenter or a lawyer or a storekeeper or a rancher—anybody who wasn't another damned lawman. Anybody who'd be a father to the boys."

"I would," King said. "I will."

She might not have heard. "You know the funny thing? I'd even decided what I'd say when I saw you again." She made a sound like a laugh. "I knew you'd come. But I'd tell you it was all over between us. Years ago."

"Was that really what you wanted, Rachel?"

"Yes!" She turned of her own accord, pressing her face against his chest. Her hot tears burned through his shirt. "Yes! I wanted it to be over! Right up until I saw you."

They were standing together, King holding her and Rachel sobbing helplessly against his chest, when the door from the parlor burst open. Dee and Travis piled through, then stopped dead, staring at them.

"Are you making our ma cry again?" Dee demanded. "I'm about to have enough of that."

King felt Rachel's shoulders shake. It took a moment for him to realize that she was laughing in the middle of her sobs. In a moment more, he placed the phrase. He'd heard it often from C.D. when King was growing up with his older brother as a harried guardian. He grinned.

"Why, hey, there's nothing about it to laugh at," Dee snapped. "You leave her go."

Rachel freed herself, wiping at her eyes with the back of a hand. "Sweet Lord, he's growing into another one," she murmured, so softly that only King heard. Aloud, she said, "I'm all right, boys. Uncle Jeff was helping me, that's all."

Travis sucked back a trembling lower lip. "Funny way of helping," he said.

"That's enough of that. Let's see your hands, both of you. I thought so. You go and wash right now, then come in to breakfast."

She shooed them out and pulled the door closed. Holding to the knob with one hand, she turned to face King. Her lips were pressed tightly together, but after a moment, she laughed again.

"That's how it is," she said ruefully. "It's hard to have a good fight with kids in the house."

"I never knew. But I'd like to learn."

The laughter died from Rachel's eyes. She shook her head. "Nothing's changed, Jeff," she said. "I was too weak to carry it through the way I meant to, that's all."

"But you said—"

"And I meant it," she said. "I meant the rest, too. I won't be a lawman's wife, still less his kept woman. From today, it's over."

King started to speak. The door rattled under Rachel's hand.

"Hey, open up," Dee hollered.

"Go on, Jeff," she said. Her voice caught and she clenched her jaw to keep from crying. "Go on. Catch your damned train."

King let go, wrote it off, turned away. "I'll thank you for the breakfast," he said. He strapped on his gun, took up his hat, and went out the back door. Behind him, he heard indignant questions from Dee and Travis as Rachel let them in for breakfast.

At the alley fence near the shed, King stopped and opened the gate. "Newt," he said.

"Right here, Ranger," a voice answered him quietly from the alley. "Kincaid's watching out front."

"I know you're right there. Take off that damned white hat."

"What?"

"I could see that hat out here as early as six o'clock. Kept my sights on it a full minute trying to decide who was wearing it."

Newt came up, an uncertain half smile on his face. "Hell, Jeff," he said.

"If you think our man might not see that hat, you can build a fire to get his attention."

"I don't care if'n he sees me. He surer'n hell won't get past me."

"Newt. We've got at least one man dead. The man you're watching for has killed closer to a dozen if we can believe Tom Trueblood."

Newt opened the gate and looked carefully at King. "You reckon that's any of it true?"

"Can't say. But even if he hasn't killed but half that many, it might be healthiest to see him before he sees you."

Newt's smile closed down a little. "You think I ought to be afraid right out in the open," he said. "He don't scare me!"

"Glance over here in the yard," King said.

Newt said, "I already saw that. Was that where the horses were?"

"Right there," King said, "the man you're watching for killed two ponies without either of them giving a whinny. Chances are I was right inside the shed when he did it."

Newt stared again at the dark slag of dried blood on the grass. Then he shook his head, shivered, and took the silver beaver hat off his head.

"I'm sure they're both of them good men," Thomas Trueblood said when he heard about it, "but I'd feel better about that poor widow and them boys if I was right there with them myself."

At the bottom of the long hill, the two of them turned to the east, away from the brick-turreted passenger depot. A stubby green teakettle of an engine stood on the siding at the freight depot. The spout of the water tower nosed down to its dirty tender. Behind the teakettle, a half-dozen boxcars and a peeling red caboose straggled like a flock of baby ducks.

"That's the one," King said. "Local freight. Runs from Dallas to Waco, down and back once a day. If it stays on schedule, we'll be back for supper."

Trueblood looked the train over without enthusiasm. "You sure know how to show a greenhorn a good time," he said. "If'n you hadn't told me different, I'd've took it for the Midnight Flyer. Next you'll be telling me they don't serve tea and crumpets on board."

From the Journals of Edwin Spivey

SOMETIMES I WISH I COULD SPEND THE REST OF MY LIFE ON A train. I think of the train as a clean river running through the nasty sty of humanity. Off the train a person is likely to get tangled up in all kinds of ugliness and evil. On the train there's so much less opportunity to fall into error.

In my own case, I've not been tempted by evil but once or twice on a train. I never had to kill but one or two near the rails. As I write this down, I see that it is even truer than I had thought.

But I will leave aside the philosophy a moment to reminisce among my railroad memories. It is not the engineers and conductors and brakemen and firemen I came to admire so much as the yeggs and hobos who rode along among them like fleas on a running dog.

To tell the truth, I spent some of the happiest times of my whole life sitting out under the night sky beside those gentlemen's fires eating their tinned beans and singing their songs. They called me Long Spike because I was the tallest of them.

But after a time, they began to talk about the legend of

Long Spike around the fire with me sitting right there and them not knowing it. At those times, if I spoke or sang, they didn't see or hear me at all.

But that was toward the sad end of my sojourn among them. It must be remembered that for a good long time—two, three weeks—I lived like a happy king among their merry band.

At the end, then, I got out. When I was dead among them, I left. I believe it is better to be the only living soul among ghosts and know it than to be a ghost among the living and know it not. Not like that slow-witted Thomas Trueblood who goes swaggering right along among us now without even knowing he's been killed twice already! But, as I've promised, enough of philosophy.

Chapter 11

KING WALKED ALONG BESIDE THE TRAIN. A MAN WAS STANDING ON the catwalk of the water tower listening to the water flow into the tender's reservoir. He didn't glance down as King and Trueblood passed. The locomotive's engineer was perched on his metal stool, his forearms resting on his knees, his long jaws working steadily on a cud of Red Man. He wore a striped railroad cap pulled down so that the bill touched the tip of his nose. On the steps behind him sat a young black man, shirtless in the cold. His upper body glistened with sweat and the wide, flat muscles of his chest gleamed like polished wood. He looked up and grinned at King.

"Morning, Mason," King said. "Morning, Cletus."

"Hell," the engineer growled. He pushed the cap back, revealing faded blue eyes and a few straggling strands of gray hair. He looked down for a moment at King and Trueblood, then pursed his lips and spat onto the brick walkway between them. "You Rangers are down here damn early for Rangers. Must figure we've got some damn dangerous contraband on board."

King didn't doubt for a minute that Mason Irons was smuggling his usual cargo of moonshine whiskey, but he wasn't interested. "Not today," he said. He looked at the fireman. "Cletus, aren't you cold?"

"Nah, sir. Never get cold." Cletus nodded toward the engine's firebox. "Keep plenty warm enough feeding this old lady."

"Cletus, you hush," Irons growled. "Or else speak with some respect when you talk about this damn engine." He patted the iron flank of the cab. "Fine piece of machinery. They don't build them like this any more."

"Ain't for about fifty years," Trueblood muttered. Irons fixed him with a beady stare.

"We got us a damn schedule to keep here. What's your business?"

King didn't laugh, though he knew the local hadn't run on schedule during his lifetime. "We need a ride," he said.

Irons gave a short, toothy snort. "Hell. You ought to know better. It's against the damn law for me to take passengers."

"Think of us as contraband," King said.

The engineer pursed his lips. No humor showed in his blue eyes. Finally, he gestured toward the back of the train. "Take the first damn passenger car you come to."

"Thanks." King moved on along the tracks. "Come on," he told Trueblood.

But Trueblood was still standing by the cab, looking up at the engineer. Irons stared down on Trueblood, grinned narrowly, and pursed his lips.

"Understand, now," said Trueblood, "you and me ain't starting off even, because I already don't much take to train people. If you next go and spit at me again, I'll come up there and notch your ears so's decent people'll recognize you for what you are."

"Tom," King said.

Mason Irons opened his mouth to grin down at the man from Wyoming. Cletus straightened from his place on the steps and reached for the coal shovel.

"I'll be along," Trueblood said without taking his eyes off the engineer.

Irons laughed.

King studied Tom Trueblood, saw a hard light in his eyes that hadn't been there before. Then just as quickly Trueblood went slack, smiled thinly, turned, and walked away. By the time he caught up to King, the hardness had disappeared from his eyes.

"Why, hey," he said, "I didn't mean to get crossways with your friend."

"It doesn't take much premeditation."

Trueblood grinned as if he'd never known a moment's anger in his life. "Warty kind of bastard like that could take the fun even out of a hayride."

Half a dozen men in crews of three were unloading two of the boxcars; as regularly as a metronome might have tocked, one man would come out the door with a forty-pound bag of concrete on each shoulder. At the same moment a second man would be stacking his bags in a row at the wagon side of the platform, and a third would just be going back into the boxcar for another load. The second crew was unloading nail kegs in a likewise regular fashion.

"There's our new courthouse," King said. Trueblood looked puzzled but followed silently along past the last boxcar to the caboose. They found the brakeman stretched on one of the built-in bunks reading the *Police Gazette*.

"Howdy, George," King said. "Any chance of a cup of coffee?"

The brakeman swung his legs over the side of the bunk and sat up. He was a squat, muscular man with a round face. His thick drooping mustache didn't hide the way his mouth pulled down at the corners at the sight of King. He nodded with no special warmth.

"Pot's on the stove. Cups ain't any too clean."

"That's all right. This here's Tom Trueblood."

Trueblood started to smile and offer a hand, but George ignored the gesture. "He a Ranger, too?" George asked King.

"Nope. Special deputy from Wyoming."

"Lawmen's lawmen."

"Mind if we deadhead for a few miles?"

George stood up. He was easily able to stand erect, even under the low roof of the car. "Can't stop you," he said. He pushed between Trueblood and King toward the door. "Settle in. I got to check the train."

He banged the door behind him. Trueblood looked at King with raised eyebrows.

"Nice fellers on your railroad here. You this well liked everywhere?"

King shrugged. "We had a little trouble this past summer," he explained. "Railroad strike. Not ordinarily much Ranger business, but some folks wanted to burn railroad property, tar and feather some of the agents, things like that. It got pretty rough, out toward El Paso, especially. We broke a few heads. I expect these boys remember."

"Likely."

"I heard the strike was pretty much all over the country. How did you all manage in Wyoming?"

"Oh—well enough, I suppose." Trueblood picked up the *Gazette* and leafed through its bright pink pages, stopping to study the pictures. "Educated fellers, these railroad men. I wasn't hardly involved in the strike. Don't spend much time where there's railroads."

"I would have thought—" King began. The bleat of the teakettle's whistle cut him off. "We'd better get set."

"Sure enough. Say, you ever seen the like of this? She'd get mighty cold in a Wyoming winter, dressed that way."

"Maybe you ought to subscribe."

"Could be. I'll surely look into that, do I get back home." He tossed the magazine back on George's bunk. "That rear platform's going to be the place for us, I'd judge. We can see everything from there."

"Well, it might be a little windy for that today."

"Windy?" Trueblood looked startled. "Why, hey, you call this little dab of breeze a wind? It ain't even snowing! And there's hardly a smidgen left of that snow from yesterday."

King hesitated, then sighed. He buttoned up his sheepskin coat and pulled his hat down firmly to his ears. "All right, the back platform it is. Don't know what I was thinking of."

Ten minutes later, the teakettle chuffed up enough pressure to spin its tall driving wheels. The freight lurched ahead one car at a time, stopped, tried again. Finally it began to roll, swerved through a switch, and swung south along the main line. Trueblood and King stood at opposite corners of the platform and watched the town dwindle to scattered houses and sheds before it gave way to open country. King burrowed deeper into his coat and shivered in the icy wind.

"If there was a body anywhere along heres close to town," Trueblood said, "every trainman in the state would have noticed it by now."

"And every stray dog," King said. It gave him a thought. A man in the tall cab where Mason Irons rode would just about have to see a man's body if it lay anywhere along the right of way. Of course, a man like Mason Irons might see the body and never mention it.

"Let's you and me be looking for ditches, thick brush, anyplace the body could have gotten out of sight."

In the first few miles below Waxahachie, they noted two or three shallow ravines with enough brush to cover anything larger than a rabbit. King was just marking the second one on his map when the train squealed and groaned to a stop. King looked back through the doorway of the caboose in time to see George duck out at the other end of the car. In a few moments, the train jerked forward again, shunted sharply through another switch, and trundled onto a siding.

"What in blazes—?" Trueblood muttered. He leaned far out over the railing of the car's platform to peer forward along the tracks, then jerked back as though he'd been pulled by a lasso. An instant later, the locomotive of a longer, faster northbound train roared past them on the main rails.

"Why, hey," Trueblood shouted over the rhythmic rumble of its wheels. "If there was a mouse hopped between them trains he'd've had his fur shaved off'n both sides."

King watched the express thunder by. "Seems they did cut it pretty close."

"Pretty close? That blamed engine might near took my hat off, with my head still inside! Is all them railroad people crazy? Where are we anyway?"

"We've come about ten miles." King showed him the map. "Pretty close to home, for me. The old Hollis place is a half mile or so west along the creek."

The caboose of the express flashed past. Trueblood looked out across the main track in the direction King had pointed. "Pretty enough country, I guess," he conceded as their train began edging back onto the track. "Not for me, though. Too many trees and people and whatnot to get in a man's way."

King smiled, remembering the farm, remembering Rachel. "Each to his own," he said softly. "Let's step inside and get some coffee before we get rolling good."

The train stopped at Forreston and again at Italy, picking up a carload of bawling cattle at the first stop and leaving behind a boxcar at the second. By the time they reached Hillsboro, King had logged three more unlikely gullies and two very likely water crossings that would be worth closer examination. The clock was pushing noon. They ate lunch in Hillsboro and then split up to walk around the railyards asking about any objects that had been seen along the tracks. No one would admit to seeing anything.

"Why, hey," Trueblood said. "They was a couple that I talked to wouldn't have known a dead body if it fell on 'em."

"I must have visited with that same pair. What we're going to have to do in spite of everything is to get on horseback and ride those tracks."

"Mind me giving my opinion?"

"Hang on to it a minute."

"What?"

"See that fellow down there?"

"Who? That little round bindlestiff? Looks like he just crawled out from under the Santa Fe boxcar."

"He did. Come on."

The man had seen them. He darted away with a speed surprising for his portly shape. Cutting between two cars, he leapt over the coupling, turned right, and disappeared as cleanly as a rabbit gone down a hole.

"Where the hell?" King wanted to know.

Trueblood pondered the cars. "You stand right here and keep a watch both ways. I'll see can I flush your bird."

Before King could answer, Trueblood whirled, ran back to the far end of the car they'd just passed, and turned the corner. For a minute, nothing happened. Then King heard scrabbling on the roof of the boxcar. A moment later, the hobo came scrambling down a ladder. Above him, Trueblood stood stiff as a lightning rod, pointing his gun downward.

"Now you go right to that man there and stand as still as death while he questions you, hear? Else I'll shoot your heel off so's you'll never chase another train."

The hobo stopped, looked at King, looked back at Trueblood. "That," he said, "will scarcely be necessary. No violence, please." He pulled a very expensive but well-worn hat off his head and bowed toward King.

"Sir," he said, "I am Warner Wilson, at your service. Had I realized that you wished to speak with me, I should certainly have obeyed your shouted summons." He shrugged, one man of the world to another. "Unfortunately, I feared you meant to rob me. So I fled."

"Rob you of *what?*" Trueblood growled.

King said, "You'll be able to answer my question, I think."

"Perhaps. But I wish we might move this discussion elsewhere. Standing in the open this way invites attention."

"Sounds like you're hiding something."

"Only myself. Certain—ah—members of the railroad fraternity object to my informal use of their facilities. Sometimes, they're inclined to—" He looked past King and his eyes went wide with apprehension. "Oh, dear."

A yardman strode around the end of the far car. When he caught sight of King and the others, he began to run, slipped on the ballast, lost his hard-billed cap, and came on toward them brandishing a heavy stick. "Hold that damned 'bo!" he yelled.

Warner Wilson came up on his toes like a bird ready to fly. King shot out his left arm and grabbed the smaller man's collar. "Just hold on," he told Wilson. Turning to the yardman, he said, "That'll do. We're trying to have a conversation here."

The railroad man stopped. "I'll give you conversation!" he said. "Ain't none of you got any business here. You're on railroad property." Then he looked more closely at the tall man who had spoken to him. The other tall man had a gun in his hand. "Hey, what the hell?"

Without looking at him again, King opened his coat far enough to let the sun glint on his badge. "Texas Ranger," he said. "You're about one short step away from interfering with an official investigation. I'd advise you to go back inside the depot."

The railroad man bristled. "Listen," he said.

King said, "Tom."

Trueblood leveled his revolver at the trainman's belt buckle. "You can start by putting down that switch," he said.

The yard bull glared at him, weighing the stick in his hand. A couple more men were coming from the direction of the freight depot. King thought one of them was George, the brakeman from their freight. The yardman looked their way, then back at Trueblood.

"You wouldn't shoot me. Not now there's witnesses."

Trueblood thumbed back the Colt's hammer and fired, all in a heartbeat. The big bullet hit the yardman's club, shattered it six inches above his hand, and smashed through to bury itself in the side of the boxcar behind him. With the roar of the pistol, the three newcomers stopped dead for a moment, then broke into a run toward King and the others. The yardman dropped the stub of his stick, shaking numbed fingers and staring in disbelief at Trueblood.

"Why, hey, we settled that," Trueblood said. "Now just you turn round and walk back toward those fellers running at us."

The yardman hesitated, still gaping, until a jerk of the gun barrel got him into motion. Clutching at his injured wrist with his left hand, he hurried back the way he'd come. Trueblood followed close behind.

King released Wilson's collar. The little man stood as rigid as a statue of a hobo. His face, gone pale as marble, would have completed the illusion except for his wide and frightened eyes. He pulled his gaze from Trueblood's retreating back to stare at King.

"You're a Ranger!" he said. "I didn't do it. I swear upon my honor that it wasn't me!"

King had no idea what he was talking about. "That's what they all say," he said.

"It wasn't!" Wilson's voice rose toward a squeak. "I'm not a violent man. You can see that. Please."

"Well . . ." King let the word drag out. He took Wilson by the arm and steered him toward the depot. "There's no denying it looks bad for you. But maybe I could do something."

"You'd have my eternal gratitude if—"

"But if I'm going to help you, you'd better tell me all about it. And if you lie, God Himself can't save you."

"I'd never dream of it," Wilson breathed. "Do you suppose you might release my arm?"

"Just don't run again. I don't feel like chasing you."

"And would you, like your friend, propose to 'shoot my heel off'?"

"I would shoot you if I had to," King said without hesitation, "but I'm not confident I'd hit your heel."

Warner Wilson regarded King fearfully. "Very well. I see your point. I assure you, I shall entertain no further thought of flight." He took off his hat and mopped his forehead with his sleeve. "I might have known you'd come after me. I should have been in California by now."

"We would have found you."

"But it was such a shock. And I was half asleep at the time—it was very late, you know. I was tired from my travels and hungry." His face brightened. "Perhaps we could discuss your business over a cup of coffee? And a piece of pie? I'm momentarily short of funds, but—"

"Later," King told him. "If you've told me the truth. The truth first."

They had crossed the tracks and reached the low fence that bordered the railyard. King stepped across, then helped Wilson clamber over.

"All right," he said. "We'll wait here a minute for Tom. Meanwhile, suppose you tell your story. And remember—"

"—the truth," Wilson finished for him. The little hobo made a face. "It's difficult, telling the truth to a law enforcement officer. I have so little practice at it."

"Try."

"Very well. There's not an enormous amount to tell. I was—ah—'riding the rods,' as the vulgarism goes, on the night train to Waco. I was half asleep when a sound from the end platform above brought me up short. The train had just begun to cross a trestle, and that was when it happened!"

Wilson paused for dramatic effect, looked at King's face, and hurried on.

"It was quite sudden. All at once, a gentleman I'd seen boarding the train earlier came flying—floating, as it were —off the car and out over the edge of the bridge."

"You're saying he jumped."

Wilson waved a hand impatiently. "No, no. He couldn't have jumped so far. And—"

"Then he was pushed."

"Not that either." He stopped, staring with rounded eyes at King. When he went on, his voice was hushed. "I tell you, Ranger, he *flew*. Someone *threw* him out into the air, out over the edge." The hobo shuddered. "There was the most awful sound—I hear it still in the night sometimes. I think he must have struck the iron framework of the railing, and then he was gone, out into the night and the train was past and it was as if nothing had happened."

"Except that a man was murdered." King's voice was cold.

"But—"

"And you saw it. But you didn't report it to anyone. Not to a lawman. Not to a living soul."

"Well, no. But—"

"Tell the rest."

Wilson spread his hands and shrugged, looking down at the sandy ground. "That's all," he said. "Upon my honor, I don't know another blessed thing."

"Now you're lying," King said slowly. His face had lost its expression. His eyes might have been a pair of pale stones set in teak. "Maybe your whole story's a lie about someone throwing a man in the air. Maybe the truth is you did it yourself."

Wilson stared at him. Blood drained from the little man's face, but King didn't notice. "No, now wait!" Wilson cried desperately. "I'm not your man. You've seen, I am not a violent person. Besides, I haven't the strength for such barbarity. Whatever savage did it was stronger than a mere mortal, more cunning than a b—"

His voice choked off into a croak. With his slower hand, King had taken a bulldog grip on the tie at Wilson's throat. He twisted his hold and lifted the smaller man up on his toes.

"Maybe you didn't do it yourself," he said with that same awful slowness. "Best that can be said is you saw murder done and didn't tell the law. I call that the act of a beast." He drew Wilson's purpling face up close to his own. "You've used up my patience. Now I want to know who killed that harmless old gentleman. You can tell me like an honest man, or I'll lift you another inch and hang you for a murderer right where I stand."

Nothing of King's face had moved but his lips, and nothing in his stone eyes hinted of mercy. Wilson clawed at the rigid arm, trying to speak. Finally, he managed to nod his head enough to show willingness. King let him down. Wilson gulped, sucked hard for air, tried to swallow.

"Merciful God!" he said hoarsely.

"You're just a shade away from finding out."

"No, no. Listen to me now. I was under the car. I never had a glimpse of the murderer, I swear. Please let me sit down!"

King half dragged the rotund tramp over to the depot platform and pushed him down on a bench. A couple of men standing nearby looked, started toward them, looked again at King, and moved away. In the distance Trueblood was catching up to them in long, determined strides. Behind him the little knot of railroad men shouted epithets.

"You saw the victim," King said. "What did he look like?"

Wilson got his breath. "I saw him right enough. Real as Hamlet's ghost. I've tried to forget him! But I still can see his white hair, his white shirt, and all that blood."

Tom Trueblood had come up to stand so that he threw a shadow over the hobo. "Blood?" he asked. Wilson stared up at him.

"We've found a witness," King told Trueblood. "We'll go over it again. Right now I want the rest of it."

"There was a vast quantity of blood. Even in the darkness, I *saw* it. It sprayed back from the platform. Here! See this. See this blood on my coat? That was some of it."

"Could have got that pretty easy by killing him yourself," Trueblood observed.

"No! No, I tell you!" Wilson was almost sobbing.

"Did you know who the man was?"

"No. I had seen him get on the train."

"Where?"

"In Dallas."

"Why, hey. Is he talking about your preacher?"

"And you never saw who pushed—*threw* him off the train?"

"No."

"Don't trifle with my patience."

"I never saw the one who did it. When the train stopped in Hillsboro, I saw a man get off—just the backs of his legs. I can't even say he was the one."

"Did you hear anything he said?"

Wilson looked startled. "I hadn't thought to call it that," he said. "But yes. He made a noise. There were no words, only . . . a snarl. Like an animal. I told you, he was a savage, an animal rather than a man."

"But he wore trousers, boots? You saw that."

Wilson nodded.

"What can you remember about them?"

"It was dark. The clothes were dark. Wet most likely. I believe I'd mentioned that it was raining."

"Where was that bridge?"

"Where?" Wilson considered it. "Well, it was on this line."

"Coming south out of Dallas?"

"Yes."

"Had you come to Waxahachie?"

"Maybe."

Trueblood snorted. "Why hell! You've rid this line enough to know ever crosstie, and you want to tell us you don't know where you were?"

Wilson hung his head. "I'd been asleep. Inebriated, if you must know. We were past Waxahachie, I believe, but I'd be lying if I told you more."

"Not as far as Waco?"

"No."

King looked at Trueblood. The Wyoming lawman shrugged and tapped at his temple. King reached down to take Wilson's arm, not roughly.

"Get up then. We're about to take a trip back to Ellis County."

"May I ask why?"

"I'm going to put you up where you'll have a bed and three regular meals a day."

The little hobo's shoulders slumped. He seemed to deflate so that he no longer filled his clothes. "And four stone walls around me. Is that it?"

"That's it."

"Then you think *I* killed that poor man!"

"No," King said. "But I'm not sure. And I want you to be comfortable until I've made up my mind."

From the Journals of Edwin Spivey

THERE RISES IN MY MEMORY LIKE A GHOSTLY SCENE ONE NIGHT before we had to leave poor Sallie May. A night on the high prairies of Wyoming back in the Red Wall country when we camped out in the open. Trueblood and his wolves were behind us somewhere, but for the moment we were at peace. It was nearly as nice as those camps among the hobos.

We ate. We got Davey bundled off to sleep—that was before our second child had come. We got Milford Bransdon out on the perimeter wrapped in his poncho to sit and watch for any interruptions.

Sallie May and I stripped off our togs and lay in our own blankets hot as rabbits. And Milford shuddered in his poncho and watched for us while we strove with each other by the fire.

The best of all things in the world is that God can't rob us of our memories. And those memories have come to my aid. It is only lately I have seen at last that my hope—I almost said my prayer—has been realized. Sallie May and the boys have willed it to live again and return to me.

Seeing it now, I can't understand my blindness. The truth

is so obvious. Truth always is, when once we come to look for it.

Sallie May is alive! And my dear sons. And they've chosen such a clever joke for their return! A joke on me, for they've chosen to live in the persons of Rachel Hollis and Dee and Travis.

Pondering this, gentle reader, you will wonder why it took me so long to notice. I can only plead that in the middle of all my pretending, I was distracted. Give me this at least— that I didn't go to my grave without seeing clearly the living loved ones among the ghosts.

Chapter 12

MASON IRONS TOOK THE LOCAL FREIGHT OUT OF HILLSBORO TEN minutes early and headed for West, the next town down the line.

"That Ranger King and his friend, they're gonna be mighty unhappy when they see us gone," Cletus observed. Irons didn't answer, but he came close to grinning when he saw his morning's passengers coming back into the yard as the green locomotive rolled onto the main line. Leaning out the window of his cab, he pursed his lips and spat a string of brown juice in their direction.

Trueblood shook his head, watching the train shrink into the distance. "I'll say it before God, I want them ears of his!"

"You can notch the left one. The right one's mine."

"After this, now he's left us here afoot in Hellsboro, I'm not thinking any longer of notching. I want them *ears.*"

"It's *Hills*boro."

"Tell it to yourself. I know where *I* am."

"If I may interject a word," Warner Wilson said hesitantly. He gave back a step when both men turned on him. He couldn't give more than that because of the handcuff chain that connected his right wrist to Trueblood's left.

"What is it, Warner?" King asked.

"Well, I'm something of an authority on the schedule for this particular line. The next train to Waco—"

King had been thinking. "Never mind Waco," he cut in. "How about the next one back to Waxahachie?"

"Three-thirty-two," Wilson said. "Mixed freight and passenger. Local, one other stop. Arrives Waxahachie at five-fifteen." He looked sideways at Trueblood. "If you wish to pursue your quest for ears, Mr. Irons should return to Waxahachie at eight o'clock, more or less, bound for Dallas."

Trueblood raised his eyebrows. "Why, hey, ain't that a wonder! Little feller, I might better take you back to Wyoming with me. You could keep track of all my traveling."

"Deeply as I'm honored by your gracious offer," Wilson began, "a more salubrious climate—"

"Except I misdoubt I could get used to you always talking like you were the encyclopedia or somebody. Jeff, are you thinking of going back?"

"Thinking about it. If Warner's story happens to be true—"

"Huh!"

"I assure you—"

"—we could save ourselves a lot of steps. There's only two or three crossings to check between here and Waxahachie."

"Huh!"

"You'll see," Wilson said. He looked hopefully at King. "According to yonder station clock, we have something in excess of an hour before our conveyance arrives. You gentlemen would probably enjoy a cup of coffee while you wait—and perhaps some pie? I'm momentarily without funds myself, but—"

King sighed and motioned to Trueblood. "We might as

well," he said. "We can always chain him to the hitching rail out front if he keeps on talking."

On board the three-thirty-two, with Warner Wilson securely chained to a pipe in the mail car, Trueblood brought up his question again.

"Even if we believed the rotten little tramp, we still don't know which bridge to look under."

"We know enough to find the body if it's at any water crossing south of Waxahachie. And we believe Wilson because he volunteered his story before I asked him. Hell, I believe he knew what we wanted the minute he laid eyes on us, before you ever caught up to him."

"Maybe." They gave the conductor their tickets, watched him move along the aisle. "Thing is, I'm mightily concerned about Miz Rachel and them boys. I can't rest easy until we get home and find them safe."

King nodded. He hadn't spent much time thinking about what Rachel had said that morning. Now the memory came back to him with the impact of a falling rock.

He hadn't thought about the thing from her side before. Now he could see how it looked to her. She'd barely more than buried one murdered husband; it wasn't surprising she shied away from the idea of another who seemed to be riding the same trail. King couldn't doubt she loved him—she'd given ample proof of that—but love might not be enough to swing the matter his way. She had Dee and Travis to consider. And the continued threat from Spivey, vague and shadowy as it was, couldn't be helping her to think straight.

"Spivey," King muttered.

"How's that?"

King shook his head. "Sorry, Tom. You caught me thinking," he said. "You're right about Rachel and her boys. Even with Myles's men watching, I don't feel good about them." He clenched his fist, surprised to find that it closed strongly. "Tom, we've got to find Spivey. We've got to put an end to this business."

"Why, hey, I was just now thinking that very thing." In sudden excitement, Trueblood reached across and gripped

King in a strong, bony handshake. "It's dragged on long enough and more. The time's come to put an end to it, once and for all."

In Waxahachie they rode the streetcar up to the square and walked from there the two blocks to Myles Brewster's jail.

"Jeff, Trueblood." Brewster greeted them with a ghostly handshake. "I'm glad you made it back here in this lifetime. Is this the scurvy little gravedigger that killed Wallace Melton?"

King shook his head. "Not the killer. He claims he was there when it happened. Let's call him an ear witness."

"Call him a what?"

"Never mind. Name's Warner Wilson—so he says, anyway. Can you find him a room until we clear things up?"

"I expect so." Brewster rose with painful slowness and shuffled to the door. "Curly Kincaid! Curly, fill out some papers on Mr. Wilson here and put him in number six. Vagrancy and suspicion."

Kincaid frowned. He was young, not much more than twenty, and he wore his badge with cocky eagerness. "Suspicion of what, Chief?"

"I'll decide later. Get along, man, get along, before you grow old standing there." He stumped back to his desk and peered at King. "Deputies today. No urgency—act like they'll live forever. Now, tell me about this Wilson's witnessing."

When King got home, the first thing he saw was a yellow envelope waiting for him on the sideboard in the hall. He put his hat on the rack and was reaching to pick up the telegram when Rachel called out from the kitchen.

"Jeff Davis? Is that you?"

"Sure enough," he said. "We just—"

He got no farther. She hit him like a whirlwind, skirts flying, arms cinching tightly around his neck. Almost before he could react, she had kissed him hard on the mouth, then pushed back to arms' length to look up at him.

"Oh, Jeff, I'm so glad to see you but I thought you were going to be gone all night what happened?" she said all in a breath.

"We meant to go on to Waco," King said automatically. "But we got busy in Hillsboro and missed the train. And we arrested—"

"Spivey?"

"No, but someone who's seen him—we think." He put his hands on her shoulders and frowned at her. "Sorry, but I need to get my bearings. Aren't you the same woman who told me this morning—"

She put her hand over his mouth. "No," she said. "No, I'm not that woman. That was some different woman. After you left, I got to thinking how unfair she'd been, blaming you for C.D.'s death and making you choose between me and the Ranger service, and"—her voice threatened to die out, but she swallowed and kept going—"and how I'd feel after I'd sent you away like that—if something—if something really *did* happen—and you thought—"

She was an inch from crying again. King reeled her in by the grip on her shoulders until he could hold her close.

"I'd never think anything bad about you, Rachel," he said. "But I did reason out that I'd been unfair, too. It's too soon to expect you to take me as I am. But it's a thing we'll work out."

"Will we?" She leaned back in his arms and looked at him. "There's a telegram for you. From your captain."

"I know."

"Are you going out again?"

"I haven't opened it yet." He let her go, reluctantly, and used his jackknife to slit open the envelope. "Arriving evening train," he read. "Be home. Slater." He shrugged. "Doesn't tell us much. I hope he doesn't mean another trip to Dallas."

"Or anyplace," Rachel said softly. She turned away. "Better get washed up. The boys will be in for supper soon."

He followed her into the kitchen. "Have you been all right today?"

"Yes. I've been able to see a policeman out of any window I wanted all day long."

"We need to make some better arrangement," King said. "I've been thinking. You all might go away for a while. Until this is over."

"Away where?"

"Austin City, maybe, where Captain Slater could keep an eye on you. Or farther. Don't you have family back East?"

"How are we to get there? By train? That didn't help your Reverend Melton any." She shook her head, warding off his answer. "No. I've been thinking, too. Our first idea was better. The boys and I are going to move out to the farm. Right away."

"Not alone."

She picked up a cloth. Stooping, she took a pan of biscuits from the oven. "Yes. Spivey can't know about it. We won't tell anyone. And you or Myles can take us out at night, drive around until you're sure we aren't followed, whatever you think best." She set the pan on the kitchen table and turned to face him. "I've talked to Myles about it. I'd intended to be gone before you came back, but—"

"But I came back early?"

She shook her head. "But I couldn't do that," she said. He didn't answer, and she came to him, putting a hand on the wooden lath of his arm. "Jeff, it's best—for now. Don't you see?"

"I see."

She looked a moment longer into his eyes, then moved to the cabinet and began to set the table. "The boys are outside," she said, her back to him. "Newt's watching them. Will you call them, please?"

"Sure." He started out, paused at the screen door. "I like the one of you that met me in the hall the best," he said and pushed on outside before she could answer.

Texas Ranger Captain John Slater came to Waxahachie in the early winter night. He swung down from the streetcar, turned back to thank the driver, and stood for a moment looking up at the bright cold stars in the twilit sky. Then he huddled his shoulders into his heavy blanket coat and trudged up the walk. King met him at the front door.

"I got your wire."

"Glad you did. Where's your helper?"

"Tom? Up at the Rogers, I expect, complaining how tough Texas steak is. He'll likely be along later."

Slater nodded. "Good. I'll want a word with him." He took King by his wooden right elbow. "Let's walk," he said. "I'm pretty much sat out from riding the train. You can show me where your rat built his nest."

King got his coat and fetched a lantern from the kitchen. *Maybe I ought to set up in business giving tours of the place,* he thought. *Ten cents a head. As popular as it is, it might beat a Ranger's pay.* Slater beside him, he crossed the avenue toward the old college.

"Don't be lighting that yet."

"Why'd you ask about Trueblood?"

Slater took his pipe from the depths of a coat pocket and fiddled with it. "He didn't seem right to me. I had to wonder how he just happened to turn up at the same minute your rat turned up."

"What are you getting at?"

They came to the old building and swung round to the side. Slater didn't answer until they had reached the shadowed back door and King was fumbling with his keys.

"Look at it like this. All of a sudden we had a man from Wyoming telling us you were in danger from another man from Wyoming."

"Cap'n—" King said. He was trying to open the oiled lock.

"All we saw was *one* man from Wyoming, and we didn't have any way to know that he was really what he said. I didn't care much about the whole story."

"Cap'n, one of Chief Brewster's police found the shop-keeper that sold the telescope."

He got the door open and stood aside to let Slater enter.

"Now, you don't say so."

"I heard that from Myles today."

"Well, can he tell us what your rat looks like?"

King shrugged. "He identified a wanted poster picture of Edwin Spivey," he said. "But I've seen that poster. It's mostly beard and eyes. Trimmed down, he could be Trueblood. Shaved clean, he could be Randy Foster or Warner Wilson." He shrugged again. "Or me or you, for that matter. The room's up those stairs."

"You'd better light the lantern then. Who's Warner Wilson?"

"Tell me about Trueblood first."

Slater started up the wide stairs to the second floor. "Well, hell. I guess he's on the square after all. I fretted until I sent me off a telegram to the governor of Wyoming asking him about your new sidekick. Seems like a nice fellow, the governor."

"Yeah?" King found the classroom door and pushed it open. "Go on in."

"Got me a reply right off, straight from the governor himself. Told me he'd sent their best man off down here to collect their worst criminal. Asked us to take extra special good care of Chief Investigator Thomas Trueblood. Made him sound like a Wyoming Ranger. This the place?"

"Yep. Right over by the desk." King smiled enough to show his teeth. "You satisfied then?"

"I also asked what Trueblood looks like."

"Well?"

"Governor says he's forty-nine years old, a big tall man with brown hair going gray."

King grinned wider. "Narrows it down some."

Slater laughed. "Anyway, I wanted you to know I'd looked into the matter and come out sheepish for being so suspicious. Also proves his story, which means Spivey's as real as the typhoid." He put his hands on the desk and looked down through the shadows toward King's house.

King watched the house over his shoulder, saying nothing. A light appeared in the parlor window. The thought came to him that it was time to take down the Christmas tree. He was still holding that thought when Slater straightened and spoke again.

"Something I want you to do for me, Jeff."

"What's that?"

"Forget about Wallace Melton. I'll put somebody else on that. Forget everything except Rachel and those two young'uns. You keep them safe, hear?"

"Warner Wilson," King said.

"What?"

"We maybe have a witness to Melton's killing," King said. Quickly, he told Slater about arresting Wilson and about the hobo's story. "Myles has him down at the jail right now," he finished. "Figured you'd want to see him."

"No doubt of that. You believe his testimony?"

"I've got reason to. I'm sure he didn't do the murder himself. I don't even believe he knows who did. I'm holding him for his own protection and in case he remembers something else."

"Well, let's go down—" Slater interrupted himself to point to the window. "Say now, look there. Who's that going up your front walk?"

"It's the boy that carries telegrams all over town."

The wire was for Captain Slater. Rachel handed it to him. "It must be pretty important if they tracked you to our house," she said.

"I don't know," Slater said but looked as if he did. "Smells like you have some coffee brewing. I'll step out to the kitchen with this if I may."

He was back before King and Rachel had time to do more than look at each other. "You mentioned Trueblood," he said. "Best I go on down to the Rogers and find him."

"Oh, Tom's here," Rachel told him. "In the parlor with the boys, I think. He came while the two of you were out creeping around in the dark."

Slater raised his eyebrows, almost smiled under his straight mustache. "Well, let's us have a little talk with him," he said.

Dee and Travis were sitting on the tapestry-patterned sofa on either side of Tom Trueblood, who was reading to them from *The Jungle Book*. The Wyoming lawman looked up and rubbed his long nose when the door opened.

"Cap'n Slater," he said. "Never thought you'd be back this way so soon." He put the book down and rested his hands on his knees. "What's on your mind?"

"Just a little bit of business, Tom. Dee, Travis, do you reckon your uncle and me could borrow Mr. Trueblood for a while?"

"Yes, sir, Captain Slater," the boys said almost together. "Have you killed that Spivey yet?" Travis added.

"Travis!" Rachel brushed past to corral both boys. "Time to get dressed for bed, you two. Come along." Looking back from the doorway, she added, "You won't be needing me. The woman only enters in when you've come to tell her how her man was killed."

For a minute after she left, no one spoke. Slater crossed the room and stared into the fireplace, his hands clasped behind him.

"There's something in what she says."

"We have a fresh pot of coffee in the kitchen, Cap'n," King said. "Had you rather talk in there?"

"No. Two things." Slater turned and looked at Trueblood. "First one is I've had a wire from your governor."

"Sure enough, now?"

"Sure enough. He seemed mighty glad to learn you're still alive. Says he hasn't heard from you since you hit Dallas, five weeks ago."

"Why, hey, I guess he's right." Trueblood picked up the book, turned it in his hands, and put it down on the table beside the sofa. "You know how it is—you get busy. And I'm not much of one to write so's anybody could read it."

"Send him a wire."

Travis, in pajamas, darted through one doorway, scampered across the room, and disappeared into the kitchen. Dee followed a moment later in pursuit.

"Can't do that. Won't do to waste state funds sending

telegrams all across the country. I'll write soon as I get back to my hotel tonight." He lumbered to his feet. "Here, you boys. Don't be running in the house."

Slater held up a hand. "The other thing. One part of it's over."

King said, "The telegram?"

"Yes. From Asa Talley down in Waco. They've found a body in the river."

Trueblood raised his eyebrows. "Why, hey, you think it could be your friend?"

"There's every chance. He could have floated down there from a railroad crossing, just the way your hobo said."

"He had to be thrown off south of Hillsboro then," King put in. "Else the creeks run the wrong direction."

Slater waved the objection away. "I have to go view the body to see whether it can be identified. Tom, I'd like you to come with me, can you spare the time."

"I'll go," King said.

"No." Slater turned again toward the fireplace, reaching out his hands toward the flames. "Give your time to the living, Jeff, to the living."

The captain's words reminded King of Myles Brewster. "But Cap'n—"

"Why, hey, Cap'n, why do you need me?"

"You'd know Spivey's face, wouldn't you?"

Trueblood gave a snort of laughter. "Why, I expect I would!"

"Talley's made an arrest. A tramp. Fits Spivey's picture. Had a big Bowie knife and put up a real fight when they tried to take him in."

"Why, hey—"

"Listen, John—"

Slater raised a hand. "Easy now. We don't know it's Spivey. Don't make me order you to stay here, Jeff. Here's where you're needed." He smiled suddenly, the smile emphasizing the lines in his face. He looked older than King had ever noticed. "How about some of that coffee now? It's going to be a long trail to Waco."

King led the way to the kitchen and set out three cups.

"You can't go tonight, John. No more trains. We have an extra room."

"Wouldn't want to be a bother."

"No bother." King poured coffee, set out a pitcher of cream from the cooler. "Glad to have you."

"Hadn't you better ask Rachel first?"

King started to shake his head, then stopped and looked closely at the captain. Slater was rubbing his chin, his hand hiding his mouth. Trueblood, busy spooning sugar into his coffee, seemed oblivious to the two of them. "Maybe I had," King said.

"I was rude," Rachel said. "But I'm not sorry."

"No need to be. About John——"

"You may do as you wish. It is your house."

"It's yours, too." King touched her shoulder lightly. "In fact, if that's really Spivey in Waco, there's no need for you to move to the farm."

She moved away. "Yes," she said softly. "Oh, yes, there is." She turned to face him across the room. "I'll make up the spare room. Please tell Captain Slater he's welcome."

"All right."

"Until the time he comes——"

"You've about worn that out."

"I know. But I can't help thinking about it. And I'd think about it every minute while you were gone." She shook her head. "Oh, Jeff, what are we going to do?"

"Damned if I know."

When he came back down the stairs, someone was rapping loudly on the front door. King stepped into the hall as Trueblood appeared from the kitchen, his cup still in his hand.

"I've got it," King told him and went to open the door.

"I've been looking for you," Randy Foster said.

"Nice of you to come," King said. "Step inside. There's coffee in the kitchen."

"Maybe you'd better come out here instead." Foster took

a pace backward and stood, tense and angry. "I've been here several times today. Your police guards turned me away."

King stepped onto the porch and drew the door half closed behind him, conscious of Trueblood still watching from the hallway.

"Not my police," he said.

"Your orders?"

"No." King walked over to the edge of the porch, turned, grinned at Foster. "But I don't think it was such a bad idea. What was it you had to say that couldn't be said inside?"

For an answer Foster pivoted on his right foot. He swung his left fist in a hard overhand punch that brushed past King's slow-responding right hand and knocked him off the porch.

King hit on his chest and right shoulder in the black cold earth of a flower bed to the left of the walk. The shock sent a flame of pain down his arm all the way to his fingertips. As it faded, it left behind a burning wetness, bothersome but not disabling.

Even as his mind inventoried the damage, he rolled to get his knees under him and came up again. Sweeping away his surprise and the pain from Foster's blow was the huge, hot glow of joy that roared through King like a prairie fire. For days, ever since his return to Waxahachie, he'd struggled against shadows and phantoms. Finally, he had a live, solid opponent, one he'd get the greatest pleasure from pounding into the ground. He grinned, bleeding lips skinned back from his teeth, as he got started to lever himself up.

For a second, his right arm gave. He half fell back, then came to his feet as Foster hurtled off the porch and crashed into him, knocking him backward again. Gasping for air, he hit and rolled, up so quickly that the cotton buyer's next punch barely skimmed the side of his jaw.

The roaring in King's head sounded like a babble of voices and his vision was blurred. He moved inside, in the direction the blow had come from, and struck back by instinct. The knuckles of his left hand split against Foster's mouth, and a solid jolt in his shoulder told him his right had landed someplace. This time Foster gave ground.

153

In his eagerness, King plowed straight after him. But the cotton buyer had learned some boxing someplace. He danced back, snapping in two fast left jabs that stopped King's rush and cleared some of the blind anger from his mind. King brought his hands up, feinted with his left, waited for the jab again, and came over it with an overhand right backed by all his weight.

If his right hand wasn't ready to do needlework, it still made a very satisfactory club. It caught Foster on the temple as he tried to slip aside and sent him down on his back in the middle of the yard. Quick as a cat, the cotton buyer twisted, sprang to his feet, dropped back to one knee for an instant, then went for King like an arrow leaving the bowstring.

He didn't get there. A burly figure pushed into King's line of vision, intercepted Foster, held him back.

"No!" King cried. He bulled forward but found a leaner, taller man blocking his way. He lashed out, connected, then felt his feet swept out from under him. A pair of strong hands broke his fall at the last instant, then pressed him down on his back in the flower bed. There must have been a puddle there, he thought hazily, because his sleeve was wet and bitterly cold on his arm. He blinked up at the night sky, and one of the clouds gradually became the long face of Tom Trueblood.

"Why, hey," Trueblood said. The man from Wyoming released his hold and put one hand up to waggle his own jaw back and forth experimentally. "I hadn't seen it before. Seems you get right active when you're upset."

King started to rise. Trueblood let him sit up but stopped him there.

"Nope. Best you wait just a second."

Blinking, King saw Slater still holding Randy Foster and talking quietly to him. Newt, the guard at the front, was watching in astonishment from the walk beside the big pecan tree but hadn't left his post. Dee and Travis peered wide-eyed from the front door. Rachel was on the porch. Some of the buzzing in King's ears resolved itself into her voice.

"—sense enough to stop, either one of you! Couldn't you

see he's hurt and was too caught up in damned pigheaded male pride to admit it?"

"I didn't hurt him all that much," King muttered thickly. He tried again to push himself up, felt the cold in his arm turn to hot, stinging pain. Glancing down, he saw where the wetness had come from. Where it wasn't torn away, his right sleeve was soaked in blood.

From the Journals of
Edwin Spivey

IT WAS AT THAT POINT I UNDERSTOOD WHY I HAD FOUND MY-self wanting to watch Rachel Hollis through my telescope. Why I had wanted to be where she was. Why I wanted to be near those boys who had grown so much during their absence!

It was at that point I began to recognize the ghosts and usurpers woven into the tapestry. I saw that Milford Bransdon was a ghost in the form of Randall Foster. I saw that Jeff King was either the ghost of his brother or a joker God had slipped into the deck to separate me from my loved ones.

It was at that point that I knew the things I must do to be worthy of having my loved ones back. To bring them back to life from the deaths given them by Thomas Trueblood and Tex Hollis—by whatever names they called themselves—and by Milford Bransdon, who wasn't there to keep watch when he was needed.

Dear gentle reader, take one further lesson in philosophy from one who has seen the truth. Let it not go unnoticed

156

that a man may best be measured by the way he fulfills his job when he is needed most.

It was at that point that I saw how other strong men had failed. And I saw how I must succeed in order to be worthy.

Chapter 13

JEFF KING HAD HIS BREAKFAST WITH SLATER AND TRUEBLOOD AT the Chinese restaurant across from Myles Brewster's jail. Then he walked the other two lawmen down to the depot to wait for the Waco train.

"I still don't think it's right to go dragging me all over the country," Trueblood complained to Captain Slater. "Making me check out of that fancy hotel and all. I'll swear it ain't Spivey in jail. He ain't about to let himself be taken again. And if that's so, here's where I'm needed most."

Slater raised his eyebrows. "Well, I'm not arresting you," he said. "But you're the only one can identify Spivey for certain. I'd think it common courtesy to assist another officer this way."

Trueblood dug a toe at the fancy brickwork on the depot's apron. "Why, hey, seeing as you put it that way, I can't hardly say no. You've done more'n the same for me, letting Jeff work with me."

"We'll say no more about it then. And you can tell your governor that the tickets are on the state of Texas." Turning to King, Slater said, "Jeff, you get back about that assignment I gave you yesterday." He smiled a little. "And try to be careful of that arm, hear? Remember what the doctor said."

"I remember." King ignored Slater's smile and Trueblood's amused chuckle. "Send me a wire on what you find."

He helped get the baggage on board and watched until the train's smoke was only a dark smudge against the feathery clouds to the south. The streetcar had already pulled out, taking the arriving passengers uptown, so King walked up College to the courthouse square. His breath steamed in the brisk morning air. Pausing at the corner, he looked up above Thompson's Hardware at a second-floor window. Gold-painted letters proclaimed it to be the office of Randall Foster: Cotton Buyer. The window remained dark. King flexed his right arm, gauging its wooden feel against previous mornings.

"Nothing much to it," old Doctor Simmons had said the night before. "Reopened a couple of these old wounds. What was it, buckshot? Hmm, remarkable, you really should be dead. I've put in a stitch or two and bandaged it." He peered at King, watery blue eyes alert above his bow-rimmed spectacles. "You might want to not roll around in the dirt for a while."

"I'll do my best," King said. He sat in a straightbacked chair in the kitchen, his arm laid out like a lamb chop on the kitchen table. Foster had gone home a little earlier, sheepish but unrepentant. King felt the same way.

"Best thing for that eye would be cold compresses for half an hour," Simmons said. He chuckled. "I can remember giving you that same advice off and on, starting when you were about as old as Travis. Seems to be a recurrent condition."

From where she stood by the kitchen counter, Rachel gave a smothered laugh. King looked at her carefully with his good eye. Her eyes sparkled, but she held her face and voice expressionless.

"Chronic," she said. "Is there anything you can prescribe to make him grow up, Doctor?"

"Afraid that's out of my line." Simmons stood up and snapped his bag closed. "Jeff Davis, you take care, and that's without any joking. With proper time to heal, there's every chance you'll regain full use of that hand and arm. Keep abusing it the way you've been doing, and I can't make any promises. No, Rachel, I'll find my own way out. Good night."

King flexed his right hand, decided it was stronger than the day before, and strode down to the hardware store. T. C. Thompson was just opening his door for business. "Morning, Jeff," Thompson said. "Looks like you stood too near somebody's fist. Come in out of the cold."

"Morning." King went right on back to the big Windsor stove in the middle of the store. "What's the weather going to do?"

"My mother says it's going to clear off, warm up."

King laughed. "I expect it will, one of these days," he said. "She say when?"

Thompson shrugged and spread his hands. "What are you looking for this morning? Need some ammunition?"

King was enjoying himself for the first time since he could remember. "I do," he said. "Colt's forty-five, two boxes. And two boxes of twelve gauge. Double-ought buck."

"Coming up. What else?"

King considered for a moment. "Come to think of it, there is. I need to see the air rifles."

"Air rifles? Air rifles. I've got your Chicago rifle, your improved New Daisy, and your King." He grinned suddenly. "King. I guess you'd want the King!"

"Sounds good. Let's see them."

When King got home with his package, Rachel was taking down decorations in the parlor. She wore a long dark green house dress with a black mourning band on the left sleeve. Her hair was wrapped in a bright flowered cloth. "So you've been out shopping this early. I was worried when you weren't here for breakfast. I missed you. What do you have in your poke?"

"What?"

"What's in your package?"

"No. Before that you said something else."

"At breakfast . . ."

"Yes?"

"I missed you." She could not have said it more softly. "The boys are up. They're around here somewhere."

He came close to her, took the feather duster out of her hand, drew her to him, lowered his own voice. "I missed you," he said. "And I missed the way you make breakfast."

He kissed her just as Dee came flying down the stairs and stopped short at the landing. Right behind him, Travis tried to stop, couldn't, ran pell-mell into his older brother, and sent them both tumbling down the second flight. "You boys," King said.

Dee said, "You leave our mother alone!"

Travis said, "She's not asleep now!"

Rachel said, "Come here a moment." She knelt on the braided rug and opened her arms and drew her sons close. "Don't be worried, now. Your uncle Jeff and I care for each other. It's all right for us to share an embrace."

"Are you going to marry him?"

"I don't know."

"Was he asking you?"

"No."

"What are you kissing her for if you haven't asked her to marry you?"

"Will you marry me?"

"What? Not in front of the boys."

"That's why Mr. Foster kissed her. Because he asked her to marry him."

"Did he, now?"

"Travis!"

"Gee, Mom!"

"I do have a really special question to ask your mother, boys. I'd appreciate it if you'd go out in the backyard for a few minutes."

"Gee-rod!" Travis went running, but Dee withdrew slowly, pausing to give King a black look before he slammed the door behind him.

Jeff King stood beside Rachel and put his good arm around her waist. "Will you?" he said.

"No. Not now." She touched the black band on her arm. "You know why."

"Later then."

She bit her lip. "Nothing's changed," she said. "Not since we talked before. I can't give you an answer."

"Is that what you told Foster?"

"You said you had another question."

"Not a question so much. I was thinking that this thing may be over. There's no real need for you to move out to the farm."

"Yes, there is. I want to think—and I can't think when I'm around you. I have to sort out how I feel about you and about Randy, even about C.D. and the boys." She looked up at him and her voice softened. "Myles offered to drive us out there this afternoon. But I wish you'd do it instead."

"If that's what you want," King said. He considered a moment. "I have some business out that way anyhow. Maybe Dee and Travis could come along with me if the weather stays nice. We could ride along by the river. Make camp in the evening. Do a little fishing."

"Business," Rachel repeated, her blue eyes questioning. "Ranger business."

"Yes. But nothing dangerous."

"I'll think about it. Something like that might be good for the boys. C.D. always intended to take them. But of course he never had the time."

"We ought to take the time."

"Why do you say we?"

"I'm asking you to go."

She moved away, outside the circle of his arms, and began unwinding the string of tinsel from around the tree. "Can you take this out when I'm finished?" she asked.

"Surely."

Rolling the tinsel into a tight ball, she laid it in the

ornament box. Then she looked at King. Her face was serious, but there was a hint of a smile in her eyes. "I'll think about it," she said.

King took his package up to his room, put it where the boys would not be likely to get into it, and went back down to get the Christmas tree. After he'd manhandled it outside, he judged it not quite dry enough to burn and left it near the woodpile to season a little more. He thought of saddling Pistol and taking the horse out for some exercise but instead decided to walk back downtown. At Herring's Drugstore, he bought a *Waxahachie Enterprise* and a *Dallas Morning News* and drank a strawberry phosphate while he leafed through them.

The *Enterprise,* a weekly, had gone to press too early, but the Dallas paper had a bylined story from Waco. A sheriff's deputy had found the body believed to be that of missing Dallas minister Wallace Melton, who had disappeared before Christmas while bringing the district's offering to the Methodist Home. A suspect in the murder was under arrest. The rest of the article centered on the history and operation of the home, and King scanned it quickly. Then he folded the paper, tipped his hat to Mrs. Herring behind the counter, and went across to the jail.

"Well, Jeff," Newt greeted him. He rubbed his eyes and yawned. "You and Miz Rachel have been keeping us all-fired busy. Hard to get much sleep. No, Myles is out someplace. Can I do something for you?"

"I want to see the prisoner I brought in. Wilson."

"Sure thing." Newt heaved himself up and led King back to the cell row. "Right comical feller, Warner is. Nice to get a better class of inmate every once in a while. You don't want in there with him, do you?"

"Not today," King said. He waited until Newt left, then walked over to the door. Wilson was lying on his bunk with his hat over his face, but King was sure the little man was awake. "Warner. Nobody here but you and me. I could tell you didn't feel free to talk before. Feel free now."

"I spoke with your captain," Wilson said from under the hat.

"I know."

"He suggested releasing me." Wilson sat up and faced King, distress in his voice. "Marshal—"

"Ranger."

"—you're not going to permit that, are you?"

"There somewhere you need to be?"

"No, no, far from it. If I didn't like it here, I would have taken my leave already. Actually, if you could see your way clear to it, I wish you might extend my stay a bit longer. It's been quite cold out, I note, with the threat of snow."

"I'll talk to Myles if you'll tell me where the train was when Edwin Spivey threw Melton over the rail."

"Spivey? Melton?"

King had wanted to try the names on Wilson. Neither seemed familiar to the hobo. "We think those were the men involved. Spivey's a fugitive. Melton is—was a minister."

"My goodness. A man of the cloth! And his blood—" Wilson looked at his coat and shuddered. "And the other name was Spivey?"

"You've heard it?"

"Somewhere. But my memory fails me as to the precise circumstances. You think he was a 'bo?"

"I'm asking you."

Wilson folded his hands under his chin and frowned for a moment. Then as if he were a conspirator, he leaned toward King and lowered his voice. "I will venture you this much. For a time I heard of a 'bo they called Long Spike. I thought him a legend among our little fraternity, a bogeyman. He was said to be tall, to dress in black, to have tangled brown hair and beard, to kill without warning. The strangest thing was that he would ride either way."

King didn't understand. "You mean he didn't care which way the train was going?"

Warner Wilson laughed. "I suppose that none of us are too discerning about the direction. No, I meant that when he had the money, Long Spike would buy a ticket and ride with the gents. I think now he's not a legend, but the man I saw that night."

King salted it away. "You forgot my real question."

"No," Wilson said, "I cannot name the creek nor give you mileage from any marker to the crossing. However, we were below Waxahachie and above Hillsboro. There's always water there, the year around. That's where the unfortunate Mr. Melton flew over the railing."

"I'm grateful that you remembered that."

"It's a product of the fine cuisine in this establishment. I hope you'll remember I'm a desperate criminal."

"Now, it would be worth my keeping you here until you are ready to leave—"

"Until *I*—"

"—if you were now to remember those legs you saw the back of."

Warner Wilson closed his eyes tightly, gripped the bars, thought about it. "They were the legs of a tall man. Yes, I can see them now! The trousers were checked, I believe. Even wet, they showed a pattern of some sort. Dark. I would call them gray, perhaps gray and black. The boots are black."

"Any silver on them? Any fancy stitching?"

"No. I don't think so."

"Spurs?"

"No, but there must have been spurs at one time. The boot heels were marked as if they'd carried spurs for quite some time." Wilson opened his eyes and fixed them on King. "I really don't remember anything else about him."

"Yes, you do. You know where he got off the train."

An hour later King finished packing his saddle bags, rolled a blanket, and shoved his short double-barreled shotgun in a saddle boot. All those things he laid across the kitchen table. He was pouring himself a cup of hours-old coffee when Rachel came down from her room.

"Two of Myles's men helped load the wagon," she said. "We have everything, even firewood. But I'm afraid it's going to be a cold ride."

"It's going to clear off, warm up."

"When?"

"Ask T. C. Thompson's mother."

"What?"

"Never mind. Let's get things under way."

King checked the wagon, topping the load off with food and blankets and surprises like King's package. Then the four of them rode out to the farm as cozy and warm as mice in a nest. Jeff King was happy. He clung to the feeling, let the horse loaf, tried to make their pleasant ride last.

T. C. Thompson's mother knew her weather. Just at sunset the sky began to clear, and the temperature rose a bit before the sun went down. By the time he had the horse in the barn and fed and rubbed down and covered with a blanket, there was a high, cold moon staring down on his farm.

King built them a fire. Rachel had brought a sort of picnic for supper. Afterward, she made hot chocolate while King unpacked a tin of cookies. She got the boys into their warm flannel nightshirts. There was a bowl of nuts near the fire. King thought at first he couldn't remember the last time he had been that contented, but he could.

Looking into the orange flames of the fireplace, he was able to separate those two Christmases in his mind. First came the one when his parents had been there to love him and keep him warm and the next one when they had been there in coffins. He set the coffins aside in his mind and came back entirely to the present and the children and Rachel as she was on this evening.

When they had the boys tucked in, the two of them sat before the fire saying scarcely a word but remaining lost each in his own thoughts until there was nothing left of the fire but bright coals.

Finally he said, "I'll bank the fire while you are dressing for bed."

She looked at him with the old distrust. "And you?" she asked. "Did you think that you and I—"

"I did not. Not even if you wished it." *Too,* he didn't add.

"We have those boys to consider and plenty enough to explain to them already. I'll bed down on this sofa."

"Just so you don't think—"

"I don't. But I'd like to tuck you in. That will be less delicate if you get dressed for bed while I finish in here."

"It's cold in the other room."

"All right. I'll see to things in the kitchen while you dress by the fire. You can let me know when you're ready."

He went into the kitchen, closed the door, began to straighten things in their grub box. The moon gave him enough light to work by. After a moment Rachel opened the door. She had laid aside her coat and taken down her hair so that it fell around her shoulders.

"Let's leave all the doors open," she said. "Else the whole house will be too cold in the morning." She went back to the parlor and blew out the lamp, stood for a second in the warm light of the fireplace, and began to unhook her dress.

King thought he should turn away. He tried to busy himself but could not. When he raised his eyes again, she had laid aside the dress. Openly now, he watched as she removed chemise and underskirt and pantalets. The fire's glow outlined her slender body and the moonlight from the kitchen window frosted her back with a faint dusting of silver.

She bent to take up her flannel gown, turned her back to the fire and her face to King, found his eyes in the bright gloom, and held his gaze for what seemed a long time as the moonlight sought the shapes and hollows of her body. At last she lifted the robe above her head, stretched her arms to their full length, and allowed the nightgown to slide down over her.

King released the breath he'd been holding. Rachel smiled at him, her eyes very wide. Then she wrapped herself in a long woolen robe and went into the southwest bedroom where King had already laid out a heavy down comforter. He waited a long count of ten before he followed her in. That room was dark. He found her, caressed her hair, bent toward her pillow, and kissed her gently on the mouth. Her hand brushed his cheek and moved away.

"Good night," he whispered, not wanting to show the hoarseness in his voice.

"Good night." Her whisper was full of drowsy mischief. "Remember to leave the door open."

"All right."

"You aren't going to sleep in your clothes?"

"I guess not."

"Don't."

He returned to the warm memory of the fire, took off his coat, boots, trousers, shirt. The moonlight seemed bright as midday sun. He stripped off his underwear and stood for a moment, looking into the darkness where Rachel might be watching or might be already asleep. In spite of himself, he grinned, thinking in the moonlight that a naked man would always look more naked than a naked woman. But the idea did not make him unhappy as he rolled in the nest of blankets awaiting him on the sofa.

From the Journals of
Edwin Spivey

I LIKE TO REFLECT NOW AND THEN ON THE ONE HAPPY EVENT during my long exile from Sallie May and my boys. I had the happy idea of meeting them one Christmas season. I calculated the law would mostly be home by the fire leaving the rest of us alone for the minute.

For our reunion, I found a cozy little ranch house remote from prying eyes. It sat down on the shoulder of the Big Horns in a beautiful spot all girdled about with tall pines and less than an hour's ride from the border. Best of all, it was untended except for one old man who had no business being so selfish with it at the season of giving and sharing. A man so perverse and greedy as that, why, he shouldn't trouble anyone's conscience for a minute.

Anyway, I got the place ready for the holidays while Milford Bransdon went to bring my family for the happy reunion. I laid in enough firewood to keep us warm for a month probably. I killed a six-point buck the morning of the day they were due and hung it in the shed for Christmas dinner.

It was only the winter season that kept me from picking

fresh flowers. But then I did have some pieces of Mexican silver jewelry for Sallie May. And I had a very special surprise for those boys. By the time Milford arrived with the dear ones, I had the place looking like a real home.

It is my belief that Sallie May felt that way about it when she arrived. I remember it for a fact that she delayed half a day kissing me hello because she was being coy. She was pretending, as was I, that we had just met and were shy with each other.

Milford stayed out on the porch smoking and staring at the snow-covered hills most of that first day, which was Christmas Eve. At first I thought he was probably reminiscing about some holiday memory from days gone by. Then I at last realized he was keeping watch for us all. That's how Milford was before he turned—as good a friend as a man could have, to sit out on that cold porch while I was in the bosom of my family. Now and again Sallie May would take him out a cup of coffee. She would chat with him for a minute and look back through the window at me just as if to be sure I wasn't going to leave her again.

The whole thing was going really well right up to bedtime. Then the youngest boy, who was maybe three, overturned the coffeepot and scalded his arm and hand so bad that it scared me. I grabbed him up and whipped him ragged before Milford and Sallie May dragged me away from him.

I'm sure that she must later have regretted some of the things she said to me then. She was always excitable. The thing that sticks in my mind is her asking me, "What difference do you think it makes that you give the boys a paint pony if you're going to beat them the only time you see them in two years?"

Then she cried, even knowing how mad it always made me to see her cry. I didn't hit her so much for the tears, though. It was for her spoiling the boys' Christmas surprise by letting on about the pony.

Chapter 14

JEFF KING WAS UP BEFORE THE FIRST DISTANT ROOSTER. HE found kindling, uncovered a few coals, built up a fire in the front room. Then in the kitchen he got the old enameled stove going without waking the household. He cut bacon, covered a skillet bottom with fine fat strips, and put on a pot of water to boil for coffee. Finally, he cut into the middle of the loaf of bread, sawed out half a dozen thick slices, and stacked them to the side until it was time for toast.

He set the butter on the stovetop to soften alongside a jar of cold molasses. When the bacon was ready, he forked the strips onto a platter, then broke eight eggs one at a time neatly into the bacon grease. The last three he left sunny side up.

It was time to call the others when Rachel appeared through the front-room door. She came straight to him, stood on tiptoe to kiss his bristly cheek, and turned away to make coffee with the water he had boiling.

"Listen, about that business of yours. What you're supposed to be doing is recuperating. You're not fit to go off alone."

"Then come with me. With *us* if the boys are going."

"That's not what I mean. Where do you intend to go?"

"Not far. I want to go back out to the railroad trestle over Chambers Creek." He grinned. "Should be good fishing along there, even on a day as cold as this one's starting."

"I didn't know you cared that much about fishing."

"I'm supposed to keep my mind off this arm."

She came to him, put her arms around his neck. "Please don't go," she said.

At last he understood. "It won't take long. And there's no danger, or I wouldn't think of taking Dee and Travis." He bent and kissed her lightly on the lips. "Maybe when I get back, we can talk about my questions some more."

At last she understood. "You *have* to go, don't you? Did Captain Slater order you to?"

"He ordered me not to. But you're right. I have to."

"You have a good reason?"

"Yes." King hesitated, then said, "It's right you should know. A witness told me that's where the Reverend Melton was thrown off the train." He felt her tremble and put his arms around her. "I think that's a mistake. They've found his body in the river down by Waco, so it couldn't have come from there. And Trueblood and I looked the place over once before. But I want to have another look anyway. I won't feel right until I do."

"Poor man!" Rachel put her head against King's chest for a moment, then raised it to look into his face. "It's so . . . ugly. Is everything you do that way?"

King thought about it. "Not everything. A lot of it is. But there's others in the world like Spivey. Somebody's got to stand between them and"—he searched for the way to say it, then spread his hands in a gesture that took in the cabin, Rachel, the sleeping children—"and this."

"Do you have to be the one to do it?"

King released her and went to scoop up the eggs. "We should call the boys. Everything's ready."

"Put it in the warming oven. Do you?"

"Somebody does. I'm good at it—good enough to do it."

He laughed shortly. "I'm a pretty fair manhunter but not much of a hand at anything else."

Nor ever tried to be, he thought. He'd never given the future much thought. Now, with Rachel just a reach away, he wondered where he might be at forty—if he lived. A captain of Rangers like Slater? A county sheriff living from election to election as C.D. had been before his death? Dee and Travis would be men grown by then. Would they follow the same trail?

"They could do worse," he said half aloud.

Rachel didn't question it. She might have read his mind. "Travis, Dee," she called. "Come to breakfast. You're going fishing today with your uncle Jeff."

There was enough hot chocolate left for the boys' breakfast. They straggled out of the bedroom as King and Rachel were finishing. Rachel corralled them long enough for a quick blessing, and then she and King cleared away the dirty dishes. Rachel put on a big pan of water to warm for the dishwashing. Dee picked at his eggs.

"It's too cold to go fishing."

"No, it isn't," Travis protested. "I wanna go."

Rachel smiled at King, reached out to touch his hand, glanced at the boys, and moved away. "Would you mind too much if I let you men go on to the creek without me?" she asked him quietly.

"I figured," he said. He lowered his voice. "Looks like I might have a job ahead of me, talking straight man to man to those boys."

"I thought—I might go over to Bethel to church."

"Better not to. People will find out where you all are soon enough." He looked out through the kitchen window. "We shouldn't leave you here alone."

"He can't know. Leave the shotgun. I'll be all right."

"You know how to use it?"

She turned toward him, shaking dishwater from her hands. She laughed. "You've forgotten who you're talking to. I could always outshoot you!"

"We were kids then."

"I haven't forgotten."

"You're telling secrets again," Dee accused from the table. He stood up and threw down his fork. "I'm going outside to wait. Come on, Travis!"

"Dee!"

He slammed the screen door behind him. Travis looked from the door to his mother and back, then got up and hurried after Dee. King went over to close the door.

"Yep. Looks like I've got a job."

King put on his long heavy-denim duster and strode down to the barn. His breath made a cloud of steam, but the sun showed every promise of warming the morning. The horse heard him coming and started talking in a loud, deep series of nubbing whinnies. King led him out of the stall, rubbed his neck on both sides, and ladled out a fresh bait of oats for him. Then he put the collar and harness on so that the leather would be warm by the time he hitched him to the wagon.

"Better get inside and get your coats, boys," he said without looking around. "We'll be going soon."

"You ain't our pa." Dee's voice came sullenly from the farthest stall. "You can't tell us what to do."

"I can tell you you'll get da—awfully cold sitting in the barn in your shirtsleeves."

An hour later, King bundled the boys into the wagon seat, waved to Rachel, and flicked the reins across the horse's back. They headed up the lane toward the road.

"What are we going to use for bait?" Travis wanted to know. "What do fish eat in the winter?"

Dee said, "You know it's too damn cold to fish. He intends to drown us."

"That was my first idea," King admitted. "But I don't see how I could do it without your ma finding me out."

"And that's another thing," Dee said, "you leave our damn mother out of it."

King drew back on the reins, asked his horse to wait a moment. "C. D. Hollis, Junior," he said, "I know your pa explained that well-bred young gentlemen could speak two, maybe even three sentences in a row without using such words. There's nothing smart about talking that way."

"How do you know what our pa taught us? You weren't ever around."

King let it go. He urged the sweaty horse, who did not need to be told twice, to get moving again. They rode in hard silence for a mile or more. The weather changed. King noticed it first when the boys threw off their lap robe. The wind quit blowing down his collar. The temperature rose. The clouds scattered to leave a much brighter sky. King unbuttoned his duster and laid it aside in the fresh warmth of the sun.

"Will the fish know it's warmer?" Travis wondered.

"We'll ask them."

They turned east onto the road that paralleled the creek. Its banks were thickly lined with trees, most of them showing bare branches against the pale clear sky. Both boys stood up to see the water. Travis let out a whoop.

"Why can't we stop right along here and go over to the river and fish?"

"We're going to a special spot," King told them.

"Why?"

King explained part of Warner Wilson's story. Even Dee looked impressed. "Then that man—the reverend—he could still *be* there?"

"The police found a body down the Brazos they think is his. But there might be something there that'll help us or that the widow would want."

"Gee-rod. We're going to look for clues?"

"That's right. Catfish, too. It's not far now to where we'll camp."

Thirty minutes later King saw the spiderweb tracery of the railroad trestle less than half a mile ahead. He turned the wagon down a pair of ruts leading to the river, then back through heavy brush close along the bank. When the brush opened out, King drove the wagon into the same grove of trees where he and Trueblood had stopped. He got down to see to the horse. The boys had hit the ground running, upstream and under the bridge, shouting all the way.

"Uncle Jeff! Over here."

Dee muttered, "Shut up! You don't need to tell *him* everything."

King heard but let it go.

"We got to tell him," Travis insisted. "Uncle Jeff, come over here!"

Walking the thirty yards over uneven ground convinced King not to sleep on any more couches. He was sore from top to bottom. A new stiffness in his arm suggested he must have slept on it long enough to cut off whatever circulation was left in it. He swung the arm in an arc, opening and closing his fingers, as he came under the bridge. Travis gestured from over by a wooden piling.

"Somebody was here. See? He left this."

An irregular circle of rocks held the remains of a small fire. King knelt and fished with the blade of his knife in the cold ashes. He brought up a black and flattened tin can, then another with the label still partly intact.

"Tomatoes," he said.

Dee snorted, but King noticed the boy glanced quickly up and down the bank for any sign of the person who'd left the rough camp. "That wasn't Spivey. Probably just some old hobo!"

"Likely," King agreed. "This fire's from last night. I doubt he's still around." He was about to leave it there, but he noticed the undisguised concern in the older boy's manner. "All the same, we'd better keep our eyes open."

Travis came over and grasped King's hand. As casually as he could manage, Dee sidled closer as the three of them went back to the wagon. King decided he wasn't likely to find a better time to make friends with the boys.

"Suppose you young gentlemen take a seat here on the tailgate," he told them. Then he reached into the bed and pulled out his package. Opening one end, he took out a couple of targets, gave one to each boy. While they were staring, he found a five-pound bag of shot and set it between them.

"You'll need your knife to cut the strings. Don't let all the shot fall out."

"Are we going to throw these at the targets?"

"In a way." He drew out the first of the long, shiny silver air rifles and handed it to Dee.

"Gee-rod," the older boy said.

King put the second rifle in the younger boy's hands before disappointment could set in.

"Mine? Thank you!"

King was pleased. The thanks was more than he had expected. "You're welcome. Your mother and I decided you're men enough to learn to shoot these."

Travis was turning the rifle in his hands, looking at it closely. "Look, it's a King. It says King right on it! How'd you get them to do that?"

"Well, it may be another family," King admitted. He put out a hand and pushed the muzzle down so that it pointed at the ground.

"Be careful now how you point it. That's the first lesson, even before you learn to load." Both boys looked at him, all attention. "You never—and I mean *never*—point your rifle at any human being. Not when you want to tease and not when you're angry. Not even if you *know* it's unloaded. Understand?"

They looked at each other, then nodded with wide-eyed seriousness.

"Yes, sir!"

"You bet!"

"All right then. Let's see you look down the barrel. Point it up into the tree. Good. See the front sight?"

"The straight one?"

"That's it. Now move the barrel until it lines up with the valley of the back sight. Good."

"Gee. Can we shoot them?"

"Let's load them first. That's good. Remember, watch where it's pointing. All right. See that can floating in the creek?"

"Yeah!"

They both shot at it. Shot again. The can gave back a loud ping.

"I got it!"

"No, I did! Uncle Jeff?"

"Dee hit it, Travis. You didn't even shoot that time."

"I would have hit it!"

"I expect you would. Try it again now."

He shot, missed. Shot again. They all heard the solid thunk of the lead shot denting the can. It tilted, turned, took on water, and sank. "Why, hey!" Travis shouted.

It was an hour before either boy would put his rifle down long enough to eat a box of Cracker Jacks. King was beginning to feel a new kind of happiness, one he hadn't known to expect. As he watched the boys, he thought he understood why he hadn't expected it. His own father had died before the two of them had gotten to do things of that kind. Or things of much of any kind. And C.D., eighteen and with a younger brother and sister to raise, had been too busy. As he'd been too busy for Dee and Travis.

King made up his mind right then to do things with these boys no matter what it cost him, no matter how things turned out with Rachel. For a beginning, he unpacked his fishing gear, cut a long pole, and had a rig ready within a few minutes. He baited the hook from a packet of chicken gizzards, then walked along the bank until he found a spot where the channel ran in close enough to reach with the pole. He let the weight swing out and bite the surface of the water as quietly as a wink.

"Gosh!" Travis said.

"Bet you can't do that again," was the highest praise he got from Dee. But King had no complaint. He got his first bite almost instantly, a pan-sized sunfish. The flapping fish brought two boys on the run.

"Gee."

"Can I try that?"

"Sure, but I wish you'd put those rifles in the wagon. It's a poor practice to lay a gun in the grass. When a man needs it, he wants it to be in good shape. Bring back those other two poles. Let's catch some fish."

Before sunset, they had four nice channel catfish, plus the big bony sunfish. Three trains had passed on the nearby trestle, two northbound and one southbound. King watched them and wondered. He was about ready to call it a day when the line on Travis's pole moved upstream so sharply that it sizzled in the water; then it made a rainbow of his pole and all but dragged the boy into the water.

"Pull!" King shouted.

Travis pulled in self-defense. Nothing moved but his arms. The pole bent into the shape of a horseshoe; the contest was even.

"Help your brother," King called out. But Dee had already thrown down his own pole and moved over to take hold of the other. The two of them moved up the bank a step at a time, but the pole did not relax. "Keep going," King said. Finally they backed far enough away from the water to drag the big catfish up onto the bank.

King clamped a gloved hand on the fish so they wouldn't lose it. "That's the biggest one so far," he said. "We—"

That was as far as he got before Dee's cork went under like a stone and something dragged his unattended pole down the bank and into the icy water.

"Damn," Dee said.

King let it go.

The boys forgot the pole they'd been holding and dashed off after the lost one. But it never surfaced again.

"Why, hey," said Travis, "don't it have to come back up sometime?"

King said, "You'd think. There must be snags down there."

"What's a snag?"

"Anything that a line or a pole or a boy could get hung on down under the water. A snag could be a rock or a big limb or even a hook on an old trot line."

Dee looked skeptical. "How would a boy get hung on it?" he asked.

"If he went swimming in this river. Think about it next summer before you jump in." King shrugged and bent to get the stringer with their fish. "Come on. Time for supper."

King got a fire going under the lee edge of the creek bank

and told the boys to get the wooden box of gear out of the wagon. Then he released the perch and the two smallest catfish back into the water for another time and showed the boys how to gut and clean and skin a catfish.

"The first trick is to hold this top fin down so it doesn't stick right through your hand."

"This? Gee-rod, that's sharp as an ice pick."

"It is. That's what the Indians use it for."

"Aw."

While King rolled the fish in cornmeal and dropped them in the skillet, the boys found plates and silverware and even napkins to set three places on the tailgate. Within a few minutes King had the fish half burned on the outside and just done enough to eat on the inside. He forked the pieces onto their plates.

"Watch out now for the bones."

The boys ate as if they had never tasted fish before. King put a pot of water on the fire, finished his meal while it heated, and scooped a fistful of coffee into it when it was ready to boil.

"That smells good!"

"You don't drink coffee, do you?"

"Sure we do!"

King didn't believe it, but he poured a couple of swallows of coffee into their tin cups. "Let it cool now, or you'll burn your tongues."

They waited almost long enough, burned their tongues on the bitter coffee, and said they really liked it. But they didn't want any more.

They made the back of the wagon into a bed with quilts for a mattress and blankets for cover in the sharp cold of the clear, starlit night. From the warm nest of blankets, they stared at the coals, watched the sharp stars of Orion, talked a little, and thought a lot until sleep overtook them one by one.

An hour ahead of dawn King slid out of the wagon bed, made sure the boys were covered, found his hat, and put on his boots. He wanted to be ready for the dawn when it came to release him from the phantoms of death.

He lit a lantern and walked down for a better look under the railroad bridge. Hobos had used the area in warmer weather, but no one had been around during the night. King went along the tracks south of the bridge, then came back, crossed the wooden span, and walked into the wind fifty yards up the tracks. If there were any signs at all, he did not find them. He had picked up a few sticks and one good-sized piece of driftwood for a breakfast fire when he heard Travis scream.

King dropped everything and ran. Without his realizing it, his bad hand found the Colt, had it out and cocked, by the time he found Travis. The boy was running up from the creek bank straight toward King, eyes wide and unseeing with panic. King knelt and caught him up with his free arm. Travis went right on screaming.

King held the boy closer, drew him mostly inside the big, fleece-lined coat, comforted him down to a tremble. Finally, he took him down the bank to the river. Dee was there, standing frozen in place beside a cedar stump. His eyes, wide and empty as Travis's, stared at the dark water.

"Son," King said. "Dee?"

The boy didn't move.

"Dee, what's happened here?"

Dee didn't answer nor look up. He remained quite still. A heavy throw line fell drooping from his hand down into the water.

"Son?" King said again. Travis quivered against his chest. King reached out with his wooden arm, still holding the pistol, and gathered the older boy in as well. Only then did Dee begin to quake and then to cry. He allowed King to pull him up close, but still he kept his eyes on the water. With his free arm he gestured toward the line.

"We got a bite," he said.

"It's all right," King told him. "Nothing's going to hurt you. You got a bite on what?"

"We had this old throw line tied to the wagon spoke." The

boy sobbed again. "Big piece of gizzard on the hook. Just a minute ago it gave a tug that shook the wagon."

King waited. The dawn waited. The three of them remained motionless, waiting. Finally King said quietly, "What did you catch on your throw line?"

Dee went on as if King hadn't spoken. "It took us both to pull it up. Like yesterday. Only when we did—when we did, then—he—*it*—"

Disregarding his own rule, King laid his pistol on the grass. Then he reached across and gently pried the line from Dee's rigid fingers. He felt the live fluid strength of the fish on the line, a blue channel cat as long as his leg, he figured. Maybe it had come close to pulling them both into the water.

He wrapped the line once round the cedar stump and took up a little slack. The fish pulled hard enough so the heavy line cut the water with a hiss. King took up a little more slack. He didn't want to lose their fish for them, and he wanted them to see that there was nothing frightening about their phantom. But the fish didn't come. And there was something else, a strange, heavy drag when he tugged.

"It's okay," he told the boys. Travis kept his head buried inside the big coat. The older boy had stepped behind King and wrapped both arms around the man's neck. "Don't you worry, now," King said. "I'm going to see what this thing is."

He put his back into it and took two feet of line up in a long turn round the stump. The line was dead weight now and much heavier; he could no longer feel the fight of the fish. King braced the soles of his boots against the stump, unwrapped the line, and pulled one to one against the weight. The line drew out hard and solid, tiny drops of water leaping from it as it quivered. An ounce short of breaking strain, it began to come in, slowly, then faster as King overcame the drag.

From the dark center of the channel, the dark specter of a man rose halfway out of the water. He seemed to stand facing King and the boys, stiff in his muddy black suit and a torn and stained white shirt. Long strings of white hair twined with moss and water plants clung to his swollen face.

"Lord save us," King breathed. In the sick moment before he could release the line and let the body slide back, he realized Warner Wilson had been right; this was the place where the Reverend Wallace Melton had died.

From the Journals of Edwin Spivey

I WAS ANGRY WITH THEM ALL. I WON'T TRY TO HIDE IT. WITH THE boy for his clumsiness. With Sallie May for defying me. With Davey for siding in with them. With Milford when he put in his opinion of my disciplining my family. He had sand. I've never said he didn't. But it was nowise his place to interfere, good a friend as he then seemed to be.

He fought me to a standstill. We made peace by saying *mucho hombre* to each other, but I went out and slept in the shed with my buck to show them I wouldn't kowtow to any of them.

Come the following morning early, having slept but very little in that cold shed, I headed down to the barn with every charitable intention of bringing my Christmas surprises up to the house. But I saw a light in the kitchen window and went up to peek in to see if coffee was on.

Milford and Sallie May were sitting at the table. They had those two poor little tykes dressed and wrapped in red blankets ready to travel. I saw it right away. They'd thought to leave before I was awake.

Some who have read this journal will likely think my

patience and forbearance are far beyond the traits of a reasonable man. But I have my faults and failures as well as any other. I want all to know that in that moment I was a natural man. I cast patience to the cold north wind. I went down to the barn as if I hadn't seen a thing of what they were up to. The paint pony nickered at me.

It was no fault of mine. If he hadn't done that, I would simply have saddled up my own mount and ridden out. But in my state of mind, I thought it sounded like he was laughing at me. And I've never been able to abide being mocked.

I led my Christmas surprise out into the yard where they could all see him from the kitchen window. He pranced and threw back his head and tried to pull loose from the short rein. But I was patient. I waited until the next time he nickered.

Then I put my pistol in his mouth and killed him with one shot.

Chapter 15

Jeff King felt the strength of the big fish the boys had caught on their throw line. The fish must have run far enough to get fouled in an old cross-channel trotline. Earlier on, the minister's body must have been hooked by the same trotline. However it had happened, the boys' line was important because it was the best hope of recovering the body.

Travis was perfectly still, probably asleep. Dee had not slacked his hold on King's neck.

"Come round here," King said. He felt for his pistol, found it, slipped it back into its holster. "That's a really good fish," he said. He tied the line off on the cedar stump. "I'm sorry we can't bring him in."

"That's all right."

Dee slid around without letting go of King's neck. His voice was level and lifeless. He looked at the water where Melton had been.

"I hate it you had to see him, Dee. If I'd thought we'd find anything like that, I'd never have brought you along."

"That was the preacher—the one you told Ma about?"

"Yes."

"The one Spivey killed?"

"We think so. We're pretty sure."

"Then it's all right."

Dee put his face against King's shoulder and began to cry. King sat helplessly for a minute, trying to balance the two boys. Finally, he got an arm around Dee and heaved himself to his feet, managing to lift them both. He carried them to the wagon, settled Travis into the tangle of quilts. The younger boy curled up at once, a thumb in his mouth, his breathing deep and regular.

"Maybe he'll think it was a dream," King murmured, half as a prayer. Dee still clung to his arm. King sat on the tailgate of the wagon. With his free hand, he rubbed Dee's hair. "Tell me about it, son. What's all right?"

The boy swallowed a couple of times. "It wasn't the preacher I was scared of," he said. "It was—"

"What?"

Dee tried to speak, shook his head. He drew a deep breath. "It was my dead daddy from my dreams," he said all at once.

King tried to frame a question, but it wouldn't come. Instead, he settled his arm around Dee's thin shoulders and waited while the boy cried.

"Every night I dream I see him lying there blowed to pieces," Dee whispered finally. He started to sob again but gulped it back. His words came faster. "Then he rises up and asks me to find the ones that killed him and kill them for him."

"It's all right."

"No! Because then I run off screaming like a damned kid and leave him there instead of helping him. That's what I thought when—when—" He made a quick blind gesture toward the creek. "I thought it was him come to get me!"

"But you didn't run," King said.

"I couldn't!"

"That's all right." King put his hand on Dee's shoulder. "I know. I can't run either."

Dee shrugged away from the touch. He looked back at

King, his face filled with suspicion. "Huh! What would *you* want to run from?"

"My dreams."

"What dreams?"

"We've been waking up from our dreams in the same house. In my dreams, I'm nine years old, like you. It's Christmas. There are pretty Christmas things at one end of the parlor."

Dee turned a little more toward him. "That don't sound bad," he said.

"And two coffins laid across chairs at the other end."

"Coffins?"

"I walk toward them. I can't help walking on toward them."

"But you don't want to."

"That's right. I can't see in them yet but I have to keep going until I can look."

"What do you see?"

"My mother and daddy."

As if answering a question, Dee nodded. "What do they do?" he asked. "Do they rise up out of the coffins?"

"No. I wake up. Shaking all over, like it was cold."

"And you can't go back to sleep."

"That's right. You and I are in the same shape."

The boy leaned back, looked into King's eyes. "Do—?" He stopped, knuckled the drying tears from his eyes. "Do you always dream like that?"

"Off and on. Since I was nine."

"Doesn't it ever go away?"

"It never has. But you learn to live around it."

Dee frowned a little, still looking at King. Far down the railroad tracks, an engine's whistle rose and fell in a low keening moan. A mockingbird woke in the tree above the wagon, hopped to a low branch to stare at King and the boy with bright beady eyes, and gave a raucous call in imitation of the whistle. The whistle moaned again, nearer, and the rails began to thrum with the beat of the approaching train. Dee slid down from the tailboard and stood on the dry grass, facing toward the railroad bridge and the creek.

"You got to get him out, don't you?" he asked.

King stood up, too, let his hand fall on Dee's shoulder. This time, the boy let it stay. "Yeah. I'd better," King said. "Can I help?"

"Yeah. I want you to stay here, in the wagon." King saw the disappointment in Dee's face and knelt to look into his eyes. "I'm not pushing you out, Dee. I need you to keep watch here, to warn me if anybody comes. Mostly, I want you to watch over Travis so he doesn't wake up scared—the way we do. Understand?"

The train roared onto the trestle with a slam and clatter of wheels on iron joints. The wooden pilings groaned and trembled under the weight of the locomotive, but Dee didn't turn to look. He studied King's face for the time it took the freight to pass, then nodded with assurance.

"You bet," he said.

The body came up much more easily when King didn't have a boy under each wing. In the early light, King could see that Melton's collar was hooked on an old trotline that somebody had left running across the creek. The boys' throwline had gotten tangled in the same way. King pulled hard enough to bring the body back to the surface of the water, then tied off the line to hold it there. He went back to the wagon to get his rope and to release the hobbles on the brown horse.

"Better wake up Travis," he told Dee. "See if you can make some space in the bed of the wagon. We'll all ride up on the seat."

On his third try he lassoed the dead man around the arms and shoulders. The horse shied and trembled, but it had no trouble dragging the body free of the fish hooks and up onto the bank. King had his tarpaulin ready. He wrapped the body as quickly as possible, then he got the whole mess into the back of the wagon. As the boys helped him gather the rest of the gear, he shook his head, thinking of the story he would have to tell their mother.

* * *

"It's not his fault," Dee insisted.

"You be quiet, young man," Rachel snapped. She faced King, her eyes blazing. "Of all the—"

"It's not his fault," Dee said again. "It was Travis and me caught the damn fish!"

Scandalized, Rachel turned on him. "C. D. Hollis, Junior! You get in that house right now. Travis, you too, and not another word out of either one of you. We'll talk about this later."

The two boys withdrew to the porch, still rebellious. Rachel took a step toward them and they scampered inside. King saw them, noses pressed against the screen door, still watching. He grinned. Rachel caught him at it.

"It isn't funny! I should have known better than to send them off with you to look after them. You don't have a lick more sense than they do, and here they are defending you—" She stopped suddenly, listening to what she'd just said. "They are, aren't they? Defending you, I mean. Jeff, what happened out there?"

"We went fishing," King said. "We talked some. That's all." He closed his eyes for a moment. It had been a long day already, though it wasn't yet noon. It looked to be a longer one before he was finished. "And we found Wallace Melton."

She looked at him, concern gradually replacing the anger in her eyes. "Was it—awful—for the boys?" she asked.

"Pretty awful. Scared them—us—half to death. I'm sorry. The captain said—"

"I know."

She glanced toward the wagon. The brown horse stood patiently in the traces, except when a gust of wind brought the scent of the thing in the wagon bed. Then it would toss its head, big eyes showing white at the edges. Water dripped from the wagon's tailgate to spatter on the muddy ground. Rachel looked away.

"Poor man," she said again. "Jeff, do you have to go?"

"Yes. I need to get the body to town and get word to Slater. There's a lot to do."

"But you haven't even had breakfast. Do you want me to fix you something?"

He shook his head, grinning without much humor. "Somehow that doesn't much appeal to me. I'll eat something later. Tomorrow, maybe."

"Some coffee then?"

"Only if I can take it with me. I don't want to go inside until—" He stopped. It was hard to explain how he felt, how he didn't want to bring the feel of death into the house he'd shared with Rachel and the boys. "I'd better go," he finished lamely.

She seemed to understand. "All right. Will you come back and tell me what happens?"

"Yes. As soon as I can."

"Good." She took a quick step toward him, reached to kiss him, and moved quickly away. "I'll be waiting."

"Wait with that shotgun handy," he reminded her as he clambered up to the wagon seat. "We still don't know it's Spivey they've caught."

King had barely crossed the bridge at the edge of town and started up the hill toward the square when one of Myles Brewster's policemen waved him down.

"Chief wants to see you right away," the man said. He wrinkled his nose. "What the hell you got in that wagon?"

"Nothing good."

King drove to the jail and left the wagon out front, asking Newt to send for the undertaker and Doc Simmons. Myles Brewster came outside to meet him, extending a hand.

"Jeff, good to see you." The police chief's face was flushed, his voice strong, his grip forceful. "Two messages for you. The state doesn't think anything of spending telegraph money. First one says the body they found isn't Melton's at all."

"You don't say."

"Some younger individual, big, brown hair. Stabbed, though, like Melton was supposed to be." He held out a yellow slip. "Better read the second one yourself."

The message was from Trueblood. King smiled at the thought of Slater forcing Trueblood to send the expensive telegram. He wondered whether Trueblood had yet sent one to the governor of Wyoming.

"Prisoner definitely Spivey," King read. "Awaiting extradition papers. Will contact when business finished. Thomas Trueblood, Investigator." He looked at Brewster. "Why hell."

The muscles of Myles Brewster's face tightened into what might almost have been a smile. He got over it quickly, though, and said, "Well, that's got that out of the way." He frowned suddenly. "Shadow of death! What do you have in that wagon?"

"Some unfinished business," King told him. "The undertaker will be here pretty quick. And I need to send a telegram to Captain Slater."

King sent wires to Waco and Austin, hoping to reach Captain John Slater in one city or the other. He sent a second message to Tom Trueblood in care of the Waco chief of police to let him know he'd found another body. Then he walked over to Halstrom's Funeral Emporium, which doubled as the coroner's office. Myles Brewster was waiting in the dreary front parlor.

"It'll be a while," Brewster said. "Tomorrow, probably; can't ever get much done on a Sunday. Halstrom's on call over to Red Oak and Doc doesn't want to start without him."

"All right."

"Death is waiting for every one of us. Melton yesterday, me today, you tomorrow."

"Maybe the day after."

"Still, murder puts death out of its time, doesn't it?"

"Yeah." King stood up. "I think I'll go back up to the house, maybe get something to eat. Could you have somebody fetch me when they're ready?"

"Sure as fate."

As King reached for the door, it opened and Randy Foster came through. "I want to know what you've done with Rachel and those boys," he said without other greeting.

The tone of his voice and the loudness of it caused Brewster to raise his head. King took a step back and tried to smile.

"They're safe. No need for you to worry about it."

But Foster had the topic between his teeth like a big dog with a shank bone, and he wasn't going to let it go. "I worry about it when any man carries my fiancée off." He motioned Brewster forward. "Glad you're here, Chief. I call it kidnapping. I want to file charges," he said.

Brewster raised his eyebrows politely but said nothing. King stopped smiling. "To begin with, she's not your fiancée. And I haven't kidnapped her."

"The hell she's not. And the hell you haven't." He took a threatening step toward King. "Your friends saved you from a beating the other night, but if I find out you've compromised Rachel—"

"Now, listen—"

"I think that's enough." Though he moved as if the effort cost him great pain, Brewster was suddenly between them. "Shadow of death, men, life's too short for such foolishness."

"It's not foolishness. I want to press charges."

"Jeff, stand back! Mr. Foster, you have my word as an officer that Mrs. Hollis is safe." Brewster turned, moving the two of them apart by force. "Now, if you want to talk about charges, come to my office in the morning. Meanwhile, we need to have some respect for the dead."

Foster hesitated, then backed off. But from the doorway, he turned and leveled a forefinger at King. "Ranger or not, you haven't heard the last of this," he snapped.

Fifteen minutes later King caught the horsecar up College to his home. He built a fire downstairs to take the general chill out of the house. Then he made a pot of coffee and sat down to do some figuring.

If Randy Foster thought he was engaged to Rachel, there must be some fire under that smoke. Maybe Rachel really wanted Foster. It was the kind of thought King knew he ought to put out of his mind, but he also knew that some thoughts were harder to evict than others. He poured more coffee and turned to the job in hand.

Spivey was out of the way until he came to trial. King meant to see that trial was in Texas, where maybe they would decide to hang him, crazy or not. He had a body apparently of a man Spivey had murdered. If the local law didn't get along with the identification pretty quick, King would pull jurisdictional rank on them and bring in a man from Dallas. Or take the body to Dallas on the train. There was a limit to his patience, and they were all of them stretching pretty hard trying to find it.

Someone twisted the bell crank at the front door. King loosened his Colt as he went, thinking it might be Randy Foster. Foster carried a pistol, and he'd been pretty angry. If he wanted to continue their discussion . . .

Instead, it was the telegram boy. "Hey," King told him, "come on in the house out of the cold."

"Thanks. Two telegrams for you. Sure seen a lot of this house since you come home. Any answer?"

"Let's go back in the kitchen and I'll see. Have a cup of coffee while you wait. I won't be telling your employer, and I don't want you freezing to death on my account."

The first one he opened was from Austin: "Arriving first train Monday. Slater." There was no need to answer.

The other was from the chief of police in Waco. "Regarding your wire. Trueblood not here. Sought as witness. Have him contact me soonest. Asa Talley."

"Funny," King said. "No, no answer. Here, take this for your trouble. And thanks."

When the young man was gone, King went outside to the shed to see that Pistol had feed and water. He stayed out for a little while, rubbing the roan's sleek neck and talking quietly to him. He hadn't thought how it would be in the house with Rachel and the boys gone. He'd spent a lot of nights on his own, along cold trails far from lights and noise and people. He'd never been lonely. Now, in his own house in the middle of his hometown, he understood what the word meant.

Back inside, he put another pot of water on to heat and searched through the bookshelves in the parlor for something he hadn't read. In the silent house with the deadly shadows of night outside, he found he was in no hurry to go to sleep.

Captain John Slater missed the first train to arrive Monday morning, but he was there well before noon. He didn't want coffee or breakfast or conversation. He wanted to see the body. "Right now," he said. "Before it gets an hour older."

King took him to Halstrom's preparation room. Halstrom and Doctor Simmons were at work and did not wish to be interrupted, but the Rangers went in as if they'd been invited. Bobby Halstrom was twenty-four, a member of the new generation of scientific embalmers. Bent over the corpse, he wore the long white coat of a surgeon. Simmons was in shirtsleeves.

"Damn it all to hell," Slater said without enthusiasm.

King said, "What's the matter?"

"That's Wallace Melton."

"I believe you're right," Halstrom said. "But I wish you'd wait outside until we're finished."

King was ready to wait outside. "Tell us why you think it's Melton, and we'll wait."

"Clothes fit him. Clothes have name Wallace Melton embroidered in them. Industrious wife."

"We'll wait."

Slater paced the parlor floor. "No need to wait. I recognize him. It's my place to tell Lina."

"Are you sure it's him?"

"I wish I had the least doubt. Damned ice water kept him fresh as the last time I saw him. I want you to stay here and watch, though, in case your doctor of death can give us any proof who killed Wally. I'm going to catch the next train and get on up to Dallas."

"John, let's have something to eat before you get started again. Some coffee, at the least."

"All right." They went outside, started walking. "I'd forgot my job anyway. Best you tell me how you came to find him."

Over a cup of coffee and a sandwich at the restaurant nearest the depot, King explained exactly where and how he'd found Melton's body. Then he said, "What I need to know is about Spivey."

"Got him in jail. Thrown away the key on Trueblood's testimony. You and I'll go down and see him tomorrow."

"What do you make of it that the law in Waco now claims it doesn't know what happened to Tom at all."

Slater smiled. "Hell," he said, "I expect Trueblood's hiding out there somewhere by the jail with a rifle just praying that Spivey'll escape so he can get a clear shot at him!"

It was well into the afternoon of a dark and chilly day by the time King was through with trains and depots and ready for bodies and coroners. He returned to the preparation room with little enthusiasm.

"Well," he asked of Halstrom, "can you tell me how he died and who killed him?"

Halstrom smiled. "How he died, sure," he said. "Who killed him, all but the color of his eyes."

"Tell me his name and I'll look at the color of his eyes."

Halstrom threw up his nose and laughed in a quick, high bark. "That neither. But here, let me show you. It was a knife, but not a regular one."

"How do you mean?"

"Well, it's a big, round puncture. Like a shotgun at close range, right through the sternum. But a shotgun even right up close cuts a raggedy-edged hole. This one's smooth. Mighty odd shape of knife and mighty sharp." He paused for a minute, then said, "Now, Dr. Simmons thinks that was the cause of death. I'm not so sure. Some very severe damage—contusions, broken bones. And the sternum was shattered."

"Sternum?"

"Breastbone." He thumped King on the chest. "Right here. Like it was hit with a sledgehammer."

"If the knife was so sharp, why'd it shatter that bone instead of cutting through it?"

"That's what's funny about it. Something else broke the bone. A tremendous blow of some kind."

"Sledgehammer?"

"That's what it looks like." Halstrom laughed in a quick snort. "No. I've seen them where they'd been killed that way. Hard blow to the heart, broken bones in the chest. But I believe I heard this poor soul had been thrown off a train."

"Off a train and into a creek."

"Mighty lucky. For us, I mean. That frozen creek is the only reason we can still tell anything. Most likely the bones got broken when the body hit the bridge rail or the trestle or a stump in the water. Not much way we'd ever be sure about that."

It was more than King wanted to know, but he still had to ask another question or two. "You say it's possible for a man to do that with his fist?"

"Oh, yes. You bet."

"What about the knife? He used a real slender one and cut out a plug?"

Halstrom breathed in sharply, let the air out in a whine. "I hadn't thought of that. Like plugging a watermelon? No. I'd call it more like testing a bale of cotton."

"Cotton?"

"It puts me in mind of one of those coring knives a cotton buyer'll use. You know, like an auger to dig into a bale for checking the quality of the cotton."

"You mean with one stab? Blade shaped like a piece of pipe sharpened on the end?"

Halstrom nodded. "Sure."

"I've lived here in the cotton capital of the world all my life, and I never saw any knife like that."

"Why, hell, you know Randy Foster. He's got one. You've probably seen it right there on top of his desk. If you want to know what I'm talking about, go look at his."

"I'll do better than that. I'll go bring it to you. I want to see if it fits that hole."

"Now, I don't see any cause for—"

"You wait right here. I'll give you the cause."

King walked hard all the way to the square and across the north side of it until he came to the building where Foster had his office. The cloudy sky had already grown dark, but a light shone from the window of Foster's office. King was in too much of a hurry to wonder why the cotton buyer had stayed so late.

The street door wasn't latched. King slammed it open and left it standing back. He went up the steep wooden stairs two a time and swung left at the top. Foster's office door was ajar. King wasn't thinking about manners when he flung the door back and strode into the room.

That the door made no noise when he flung it back would have registered on King if he had not seen Randall Foster first. Foster was lying on his back near the middle of a round braided rug. The rug had served as a big wick for most of the cotton buyer's blood. In the middle of his chest stood the ivory handle of the coring knife Halstrom had mentioned.

King was just turning to see why the door had not rung against the wall when someone as strong as a bear clubbed him across the back of the neck and drove him to his knees. The second blow felled him flat in Foster's puddled blood.

He put his palms against the wet carpet and shoved himself to his feet. The room had gone dark. Somewhere a heavy man was running down a creaking set of stairs. No matter what Trueblood's wire had said, King knew he was in the same building with Edwin Spivey, that he had to make something of this one chance.

He staggered to the door, left red handprints where he clung for a moment to the facing, and then started down the stairs. A big form blocked off the moonlight near the bottom of the stairs. King got a wooden hand on his pistol, pulled it clear, and fired straight down the stairwell at the broad shoulders. But King was dazed and his target was moving as fast as a fleeing bear. King missed a step, slipped, fell against the wall, and slid down. His bullet shattered the glass in the street door.

Immediately the bear twisted in the darkness, angled an

arm upward, and sent two bullets into the shadow that would have been King's chest if he hadn't fallen.

Then his target was out the doorway and gone. Gone. King looked across the street and left toward the square before he turned right and ran toward the near alley. He stopped at the brick corner, listened for footsteps, bent at the waist to make a shorter target, and swung into the alley. He listened until he could have heard a mouse twitch. But no one shot at him, no one made a sound. Then a man was running toward him, waving a lantern and shouting. It was Curly Kincaid.

"He went down that way," King yelled. "He must have."

Behind him Kincaid came to a stop, holding the lantern high. "Jeff?"

"Yeah. Look, he went—"

"Jeff, put down that gun," Kincaid said, "and then turn around here to me."

"Curly, I'm not going to throw my good gun down on the bricks. Listen, somebody's just killed Randy Foster."

"You hurt, Jeff?"

"No." King turned. "What do you—"

He stopped. Kincaid's free hand held a pistol, its muzzle pointing at King's belt.

"No? Then you'd better put your gun down. And if that's not your own blood all over you, I hope you can prove you've been killing hogs."

From the Journals of Edwin Spivey

I WAS IN THE BARN, SADDLING UP TO TAKE MY WAY BACK TO Montana, when Milford Bransdon came down on the run. He stood a long while in the doorway blowing steam like a locomotive engine. When he got back enough breath, he cursed me. Still I was all forbearance.

But he kept on. He said things that one partner ought not say to the other. You will have a hard time accepting this, gentle reader, but I swear to you it is true. Poor Milford was so misguided that he actually accused me of being cruel to my own family.

"Cruel to *them?*" says I. I came over and faced him there where he leaned against the doorpost. "And how about me? I've been off by myself these two years waiting for this holiday. Look how they've all treated me. And you not the least by the way you've sided with them against me."

That got to him. He cooled some and asked me to loosen the girt and stay after all and that they would, too. He would talk to them, he said, and try to make peace. It touched him too close to be in between us all, he told me.

"It hurts me here!" he said. And he put his left hand up to

200

his heart the way a play actor does on the stage, and tears showed at the corners of his eyes.

It was the crying, I now believe, that settled it all out for me. It's always made me angry, crying has, and I saw he was doing it to spite me. At last I saw everything clearly. I drew back my fist and hit him in the heart with such speed that he never had time to move his hand nor get his back away from that doorpost.

I've always been strong in body as well as in mind. The force of that blow came near to breaking my hand. It did break all Milford's fingers, and it cracked that big bone down the front of his chest. Instead of making a fight of it, he drew up like a spider in a fire and sagged back against the post and died. It was only then my vision cleared enough for me to notice he held his pistol in his other hand.

It was a shame, losing a partner like that. But he'd turned on me, no question, and it had to be done. So that whole holiday season that had begun so well ended as pretty much a loss. But I did learn a valuable lesson. Even in adversity, a man can always learn something that will help him later. The valuable lesson I learned is that a man is easier killed through his heart than through his head. Ponder on that, gentle reader, and you'll see it is true.

Chapter 16

JEFF KING SAT IN MYLES BREWSTER'S OFFICE CONSIDERING HIS situation. On the surface of it he looked guilty as sin. He would have arrested himself on less evidence than Brewster had.

King couldn't deny having words with Foster twice in the last week, before witnesses. Once they had come to blows. Foster had threatened him, and his own words to Bobby Halstrom, the embalmer, could be construed—*were* being construed—as a threat against Foster. He and Foster were angling for the same woman, giving each of them a perfect motive.

"It looks grim as death," Myles Brewster had told him. "Everybody in the whole damn town knows you had blood in your eye when you saw-mentioned-thought about Randy Foster."

If that wasn't enough, King thought, he had blood on his boots, blood on the knees of his pants, blood on his hands and chin, blood all down the front of his coat. Blood even on his badge. Foster's blood.

He had just finished telling Bobby Halstrom he was going to go bring him Foster's fancy cotton knife whether Foster got in his way or not. Within ten minutes Halstrom was part of a crowd standing over Foster's body, looking at the knife King had gone to find. The more King thought about it, the more he knew he couldn't have set it up to look worse for himself if he'd tried. *Hell,* he thought, *I wouldn't believe the man who said I didn't do it.*

King wished he had Trueblood there to watch over Rachel and the boys. The three of them were out at the farm, completely unaware that Spivey was loose. Not that Spivey had any way of finding them, but King was sorry he'd ever let himself be taken in for questioning. Now there was no one except Myles he could trust to guard his family.

Of course, Rachel might be heartbroken over Foster's death. She might blame King. He had just begun to think along those cheerful lines when he heard Bobby Halstrom's voice in the hall.

"There's some swelling," he was telling somebody. "Impossible to be positive, but the cotton knife seems to fit about as well in Wallace Melton's wound as it does in Foster's."

King wasn't surprised at that news, but right then he didn't much care about proving who had killed Melton. He only cared about keeping Rachel safe.

Myles Brewster came back into his office as if he had been wandering aimlessly and entered the door by accident. "Jeff?" he said.

King looked up at him without comment.

Brewster held out a lifeless hand palm up in King's direction. In it lay a foot-long steel cylinder, plated with nickel, beveled and sharpened viciously at the end. It was fitted with an ivory handle.

"You ever see this knife?"

"No."

"Didn't you say a while ago you saw it sticking out of Randall Foster's chest?"

"All I saw was a handle. It looked like that."

"Hadn't you never seen it before that?"

"No."

"Not in his office?"

"Never been in his office before that."

"Well." Brewster crossed to his desk. He opened a drawer, put the knife inside, and closed and locked it. "Death's a mystery, Jeff. Murder seldom is."

"Myles, whoever told you—"

"I need you to help me believe what I want to believe. I want to believe you didn't—in the heat of anger—murder Randy Foster." Brewster sat down, looking more than ever like a post oak snag somebody had left in the office by mistake. "I need you to tell me why you laid down and rolled around in Foster's blood, if you came upon the scene all after the fact."

"He hit me, knocked me down in it."

"*Who* hit you?"

"Whoever killed Foster. Edwin Spivey, I'd think, though I don't know how in hell Spivey got away from Asa Talley in Waco. Whoever he was, I didn't see him. Listen, Myles—"

"Not when you shot at him?"

"He was in the dark a good distance from me by then. Listen—"

"And how many times did you shoot at him?"

King willed himself to patience. He'd done this sort of thing before, from Brewster's side of the desk. The quicker he got it over with, the quicker he could talk to Myles about Rachel.

"I shot once, as you very damn well know since you've been studying my pistol this past hour. I'd bet you found the bullet hole in the wall behind the door where I told you to look."

"I did," Brewster said. "But Kincaid and Halstrom both say they heard three shots."

"Right. One of mine. Two of his. You've heard all this."

"Just as you said, indeed. I'll even add it to your side of the story that the other two bullet holes are in the wall at the top of the stairs."

"Well then?"

"Jeff, those holes are right in the middle of the wall, not three inches apart."

King had thought about that himself. "If I'd been standing, they would have gone right through my gizzard. I'd never call him a poor shot," he said.

"Nobody's ever called you one either; all those bullet holes look like your shooting to anybody that's ever seen you shoot." Brewster stopped talking. For a minute, he pulled at his lower lip, and then he shook his head sadly. "Shadow of death, Jeff. Much as I hate even to think so, it sure makes a good case to say that you stopped at the bottom of the stairs and fired those shots back up at the top to make it sound like there was a second gun."

"But why—?"

"To make it look like there was another man there," Brewster interrupted impatiently. "Else it's hard to figure how those bullets would have missed you had you been where you say you were—high up on those narrow stairs."

"I'm tired, Myles. I'll lay it out for you once more. I slipped and fell on the stairs. If I hadn't, I'd've killed that butcher cold, and we wouldn't be wondering about it now. He whirled and shot at me before the last of the glass hit the floor from my shot. Your own witnesses admit they didn't grow any beard between the shots. You want to say I stood at the bottom and shot the door and then fired up the stairs. But there was only one shot fired out of my gun, Myles. You've seen that."

Brewster shook his head as if he were trying to teach a child not to lie. "It was a minute or so before Curly got to the scene with light. He says you had your back to him. Says you refused to put it down when he asked you. Says you could have been reloading two chambers to make it look like you only fired one shot."

"Hell."

"I asked you to help me believe what I want to believe. You'd better get to helping me."

"You figure I ate the hulls?"

Brewster hadn't thought about the empty cartridges.

"Go find the hulls if you think I reloaded. They wouldn't be any farther away than I could throw them."

Brewster hadn't thought about that either. "It's awful dark for that kind of work, Jeff."

"Just be sure if you find any that they're the same load I was using. Maybe you ought to dig those bullets out of the walls to be sure they're all three alike."

"Death's door!"

"It's past suppertime, Myles. I'm hungry and tired and I want a bath and some clothes that don't look like I've been in a slaughterhouse. Most of all, I'm worried about Rachel. If Spivey's really running loose—"

"If."

"—then she and the boys are in mortal danger. I need to get back out there. We can settle the rest of this tomorrow."

Brewster tugged at his lip again. "Well, now. As to Rachel, you and I's the only two in all the world who know where she is. If there's a ghost of a problem, I'll send Newt out come morning." He frowned. "As to settling the rest—"

"You don't think you're going to hold me?"

"Jeff, you've done right well helping me believe what I want to believe."

"Good."

"There's just that one other thing."

"What other thing?"

"There's a third witness."

"Witness?" King looked up. "Witness to what?"

"To the number of people that came and went through that street-level door. Says he'd just moved into his hotel room and wasn't watching out the window and didn't see who went *up*. Didn't look out till he heard shots. Two shots, he thinks. Anyway, he looked down there right away."

King grinned. It felt good. "Why, hell, Myles. Why didn't you say that to start with?" He jumped up, motioning to Brewster. "That settles it. He can tell us which way Spivey went. Don't just sit there like a totem pole—let's get after him!"

Brewster hadn't moved. "Not so fast," he said. "Death

comes soon enough. Thing is, Jeff, he says that only one man came *out*. And it sounds like that one man was you."

"What lying son of a bitch told you that?"

"One you know." Brewster reached down to a desk drawer and took out his pistol. "Name's Thomas Trueblood. I think you'd better come along this way."

"Why, hey, now, hold on, Jeff," Trueblood said. "I told old Myles here different the minute I realized what he was getting at."

He stood next to the police chief, the two of them staring through tall iron bars at Jeff King. King sat silently on his bunk. In the adjoining cell, a small man lay snoring loudly.

"Somebody could surely have got out the door before I got my curtain open to look," Trueblood said.

Brewster shifted like a tree pulling up its roots. "Your first statement said your curtains were open to start with," he said.

"Did I say that? Well, hey, *now* I don't remember."

"You ought to know right well what you said. It hasn't been a half hour since you said it."

Trueblood snorted. "I didn't know we were talking about Jeff King as the person to be suspected in this thing," he growled. "If I had, I'd've seen things a power differently."

Brewster thought about it. "You didn't recognize King when he came out the door?"

"Why no."

"Seems like you would have."

Trueblood set his jaw. "Can't testify to it."

"Angel of Death! You'd risk perjury!"

King said, "Myles, let me talk to Tom for a couple of minutes. Alone."

"Why?"

"So I can talk him into telling you straight what it was he saw. I don't want him lying for me."

Brewster frowned and pulled at his lip. "It's irregular," he said.

"Myles."

"Well, don't take long. Death won't wait." Brewster

plodded back into the hall, closing the iron door behind him.

Trueblood said, "I feel like a dad-damned fool for talking to the police. Durned if I knew you were the joker in this deck!"

"We'll sort that out later." King stood up and walked over to the bars, looking at Trueblood. "Tom, what went wrong in Waco?"

"Why, hey, I can't say. Everything was just fine there when I left. But about what I saw—"

"Then what are you doing here? Your telegram said you were heading back to Wyoming."

"Well, now," Trueblood said. He frowned at King. "Truth is, I was on my way when I got word Spivey had slipped the leash again." He wagged his head. "I tell you, you were right as could be. It won't do to put him in jail. Only thing is to kill him outright."

"Got word?"

"Anyway, my very first thought was about Rachel and her two lambs. I couldn't close an eye for fear that wolf was on their track again."

King put his hands on the bars. "Got word?" he said again. "How'd you hear about it, Tom?"

"And he's here," Trueblood went on. "He must be. It had to be him killed Foster, just the same as them two colts. I heard you had a clear shot at him."

"I had a clear shot at Foster's killer," King said slowly. "Just as he ran out the downstairs door. I don't see how you could have missed seeing him, Tom."

"Truth is, it took me longer to locate the shots than I let on. Had I seen Edwin Spivey come out that door, he'd be dead this minute!"

King shook the bars. "If that's the truth, call Myles back in here and tell him so. Then you and I'll go take care of Rachel and the boys."

"Chief Brewster! Why, hey, Jeff, I should have thought of that sooner. Where will we find them little lambs? I already stopped by the house."

"They're—" King stopped. "They're safe. Call him again."

Trueblood went to the cell block door and knocked. The little man in the other cell opened his eyes but did not sit up. He kept his quiet attention on Trueblood. When the door opened, Trueblood spoke softly, then stepped through.

"Tom?" King called. "Tom! Myles! Myles Brewster!"

Warner Wilson sat up on his cot. "It's him," he said.

"What?" King half turned. "Myles, damn it!"

Myles Brewster came back into the block. "All right, Jeff, all right. All that noise can't wake the dead." He shook his head. "I wish you'd spoken to me first. I don't think it's a good idea."

"What?"

"I told you, I'd send Newt out in the morning. You might've trusted me. But if you want Trueblood out there instead—"

"What? Myles, what are you talking about? You didn't tell him where Rachel was?"

Brewster looked puzzled. "Well, he said you had. He asked me the way out to the farm. Said he knew it was out south of town and you'd told him—"

"Lord God," King breathed. With sickening clarity, he remembered pointing the location out to Trueblood. He shook the bars frantically. "Myles, stop him! Get me out! He's Spivey, Myles. And he's going out after Rachel."

Brewster stared at him. "Shadow of death!" he said. "You've gone crazy, too."

"Myles!"

"It's true." Warner Wilson was on his feet now as well. "He's the one I saw that night. He's Long Spike, upon my sacred honor."

King turned on him. "Why in hell's name didn't you say something sooner?" he demanded. "We could sure have used that information the day I arrested you."

"But I didn't know." Wilson spread his hands helplessly. "Surely you could see it tonight. He was—well, he was a different man. Tonight, he was Long Spike."

"Then—" Brewster's pale face flushed. "Hades! I'll get the keys!"

He ran for the door, disappeared through it. His steps rang in the hallway, then stopped with a grunt of surprise and a sudden stumbling shuffle and something like a snarl.

"Myles?"

Brewster came through the door, slowly, his feet dragging. "Jeff." He held his hands pressed tightly to his chest. "I—"

Blood began to seep through his fingers. He made another step, fell to his knees, tried again to speak. Then his hands slipped away. Blood fountained from the great hole in his chest and splashed on the hard stone. As though his stiffness had left his body with the life, he slumped bonelessly forward until he sprawled on the floor, one twitching hand almost touching the barred door of King's cell.

"It happens that way sometimes."

The strange voice jerked King's attention back to the doorway. Tom Trueblood stood there, a Trueblood that King had never seen before. Now the change Warner Wilson had sensed was obvious. His eyes looked wider and deeper; his relaxed smile had become a tense and crafty grin. The lines of his face, the hunched set of his shoulders, the loose swing of his arms all said he was a different man. His hand held a long blood-soaked cotton knife. Warner Wilson moaned and drew back against the back wall of his cell.

"Spivey," King said.

"It happens that way sometimes. Man had a deathgrip on life." He raised his wide eyes to King. "That's right, Tex. Ed Spivey." Looking down at the knife in his hand, he grinned and tossed it on the floor at King's feet. "You be sure to explain you didn't do it, now."

King started to grab for the knife then held up, his hand an inch from it. He looked up into the muzzle of Spivey's pistol. King straightened very slowly. After a moment, the other man laughed and holstered the gun.

"I'd made a pledge not to kill you, Tex," he said. "Told Trueblood I wouldn't, back when he was pretending to be me. But if you had given me a reason, why, it would be different." He shrugged. "Well, I have to be going now. They're waiting."

Keep him talking, King screamed at himself. Maybe somebody would come. Maybe.

"Tell me the one thing first," King said. "Even if I could understand why you killed those ponies, I'd always wonder about this other. Why'd you kill Randall Foster?"

From the Journals of Edwin Spivey

"WHY'D YOU KILL RANDY FOSTER?"

Why, I killed Milford Bransdon for the same reason as last time. For the clear and simple reason that Sallie May was paying him attention. Not that I ever believed a word of the scandal that was talked about them. Sallie May was true-blue; I know she was. But I couldn't allow him to come between me and my family.

"What family?"

Why, my family, of course. The selfsame family you yourself have been trying to separate from me.

"Me?"

Especially you, Tex. But you know all that. You who have been wandering around telling people that you will make a good father for my boys.

"*Your* boys? What do you mean, *your* boys? No, wait. Hey!"

Chapter 17

Warner Wilson said, "I didn't know that a God-fearing man could curse so fervently."

Jeff King directed a yet worse invective toward the little hobo in the next cell. He threw himself against the door of the cell in blind anger. The heavy steel bars quivered, clattering against the door frame like a tray of dropped silverware, but the only damage was to King's shoulder.

"Hey!" King yelled. "Newt! Kincaid!" He slammed into the bars again. "Somebody! Damn it, somebody hear me!"

"Ranger, you'll do yourself some injury," Warner Wilson said. "There's really no need—"

"No need, hell! I've got to get out of here!"

"Supper was finished an hour ago," Wilson said with infuriating calm. "Everything's locked down. The jailer won't be back until morning. No one can hear you, not even the other prisoners, who couldn't help even if they did hear you. But—"

King snaked an arm through the bars between cells and grabbed Wilson by the lapels. "Listen, that rotten bastard's gone to kill innocent women and children. I've got to get out!"

"No violence, please." The little man hung inert in King's grip. "You will be best served if you release me and compose yourself. You've been most kind in your treatment of me. In return, I believe I can alleviate your problem."

King blinked, trying to make sense of the words. His head hurt, and blind panic was clawing at him like a treed bobcat. But hadn't Wilson once said that if he didn't like the jail, he wouldn't stay?

"You mean you can get me out?" King asked.

"Precisely. So I believe."

King let him go. "Do it then. Please."

Wilson pulled himself erect, straightened his coat, then went over to the cell door and studied the lock with minute care.

"Yes," he murmured. "Very secure. The good people here spared no expense."

"Warner—"

He fumbled for a minute with the lapel of his coat. When he looked up at King, he held a long, thin metal rod in his hand. "I would most assuredly like to see that," Wilson said aloud.

King gripped the bars with both hands. "Hurry!"

Wilson bent over the lock, reaching through the bars to get at its other side with an arm that seemed as long and supple as a monkey's. "So I must both ask and answer, must I? 'What is it you'd like to see, Mr. Wilson?' you might ask. 'Why, an innocent woman,' I should reply. That's what I've never seen—an innocent woman." He withdrew the rod from the lock, peered critically at its end. "You wouldn't happen to have a pair of pliers about your person?"

"Warner, in the name of heaven—"

"I'm hurrying," Wilson said. He clamped the tip of the wire between his front teeth and bent it. "The lack of tools is a perpetual problem. It's so difficult to carry all that one needs."

He twiddled with the lock again, staring blindly past King while his fingers moved ever so slightly. In the tense stillness, King heard a sharp, metallic click. With a satisfied smile, Wilson swung open the door of his cell.

"Warner! You did it!"

"Certainly." Wilson stepped carefully around the mess of clotting blood around Brewster's body. He bent over the lock to King's cell. "Where might I find her, this innocent woman? I would gladly journey any distance just to view such a phenomenon of—"

The lock clicked open. King hit the door on the run, sweeping Wilson out of the way as the cowcatcher of a locomotive sweeps the track.

"—nature."

King grabbed Myles Brewster's pistol and rushed through the cell block door. He turned right, boots skidding on the tiles of the hallway, and clattered down the stairs. At the bottom, he stopped short.

Curly Kincaid was just coming into the building at the other end of the main hall. He caught sight of King and grinned automatically in recognition. Then he remembered and the grin froze on his face. He drew his gun.

"Halt!"

But King was already bounding back up the stairway. Kincaid broke into a run.

"Jeff, stand still. God Almighty, Jeff, I've got to stop you."

King dodged into Brewster's office, shooting home the bolt behind him. He stopped inside, looked frantically around the room for any chance of escape. There was only one way out. He hesitated. He could wait for Kincaid, give himself up, explain what happened with Wilson to back up his story. But there was too much danger in that. Kincaid might not believe either of them. At the very least, it would mean delay, a delay that might be fatal for Rachel.

"Jeff!"

Curly Kincaid pounded on the door. King tensed himself, ran straight across the room, and dived headlong through the window. He hurtled into the big oak outside the office and fell crashing through the branches like a cannonball. Broken limbs snatched and slashed at him until at last he managed to grab hold of one with his strong wooden arm.

The shock of his stop almost yanked the arm from its socket, but he hung on, swung until his feet were under him, then dropped ten feet to the flower bed below.

Above and behind him, he heard the office door smash under the impact of Kincaid's shoulder. King wasted no time wondering if he'd broken any bones or how badly he might have been cut by the glass or branches. He ran.

His first thought was for the house and the shed and Pistol waiting in his stall there. Once mounted on the roan, King would take his chances on any kind of race, even with the lead Trueblood-Spivey had. Putting a little distance between himself and pursuit, King turned north.

He kept to shadows and alleys, coming up finally behind the shed. He reached the back gate, pausing to listen intently for anyone who might be nearby. Then he worked the latch and slipped through. In a second, he was inside the shed and fumbling for matches to light the lantern there. The sudden flare of light showed the stall door standing wide. The horse was gone.

"That son of a bitch," King whispered in despair. Spivey! It had to be. Edwin Spivey, mounted on King's horse, was on his way to kill King's family—and probably laughing about it with every step.

Concealment forgotten, King ran outside and headed for town again. He had to have a horse, a wagon, anything. He had to get on his way. His breath rasped heavily in his throat and the cuts and bruises from his escape were beginning to hurt, but he had no idea of stopping. Then, as he passed a corner, he heard someone shout.

"There he is!"

King turned sharply, came to the square, and ran straight through the rubble that had been the courthouse.

"Where'd he go?"

"Not this way. Cut over to Rogers. Cover the bridge."

That was Kincaid. He hadn't believed Warner Wilson then—or hadn't talked to him. Headed into a trap, King turned sharply south, ran down the alley between Jackson and College. Something loomed in front of him. Before he could stop, he fell sprawling over the low fence of the railyard.

"What was that?"

"Down this way. Come on!"

King scrambled up and picked his way more slowly through the tangle of rail sidings. He ducked between two boxcars as someone with a lantern came his way. Coming out on the other side, he almost ran into the green teakettle that pulled the local freight. Mason Irons was just climbing into the cab.

"Let's back her down and pick up our string, Cletus. Time to get on toward Dallas."

"What's all that commotion, Mr. Irons?"

"Law after somebody. None of our damn business."

King didn't hesitate. He caught Irons with one foot still on the ground, shoved his pistol into the engineer's back, and jerked his other hand toward the cab.

Irons's face went ugly. He lifted his fist. "You—" he said.

King said, "No time. Get up there."

"Don't have nothing up there. I ain't run as much as a damn bottle of whiskey since the last time you—"

"Climb or die."

Irons peered back at King's face for a moment, then went up the steps to the warm iron floor of his locomotive. King dogged him step for step.

"I don't care what you're carrying. Build up some steam. We're going south to the Bethel siding."

Irons laughed heavily. "There's other damn trains rolling the rails," he said. "Not even you can do anything about that. Whyn't you take a damn handcar?" He laughed again.

King saw a shadowy movement, swung the pistol toward a tall, massive shape in the shadows of the cab. "Cletus," he said. "Don't make me."

Cletus lowered the coal shovel and took a step back, staring at the gun. King jerked the barrel toward the firebox door

"Build up that steam."

"No. I won't do it unless Mr. Irons says so."

Mason Irons said, "Hell, no. There's a northbound express on that line. It'll be here under an hour."

"Then we'd better hurry." Someone shouted from down at the far end of the depot platform. King ducked lower behind the iron walls of the cab. "I don't have a whole lot to lose. Build up the steam."

"What about the express?"

"Beat it to the siding."

"Beat it to the siding! You're crazy. You *want* to die?"

"Doesn't matter. There'll several people die if I don't get to that siding in time."

"Well, I don't aim to be one of them."

"Me either."

The noises began to move closer. King estimated there were at least five men looking for him. They'd spread out now and were methodically searching the yard. He had at most five minutes before they closed on him.

"Mason," he said. He cocked the pistol and put it to Irons's head. "Mason, I've never driven a locomotive. But I swear to God Almighty that unless you get us moving, I'm going to start learning."

Cletus sucked in his breath sharply. Irons licked his lips.

"You mean it," he said.

"I do."

The engineer looked into his eyes a second longer. "Cletus," he said, "shovel."

"What if the express is early?"

"We can pray about it on the way. Shovel."

Cletus slammed open the firebox door. A lurid orange glow filled the cab, throwing King's blood-soaked clothing into sharp focus.

"Sweet Lord," Cletus breathed and dug into the bank of coal in the tender. Irons swallowed audibly but said, "Listen. Can you stand maybe a hundred people on your conscience? That's how many could die if we get out there on the tracks in the way of that express."

King thought about it. "How fast will that express be running?"

"Sixty. Hell, clear night, no stops, schedule to meet. Might be pushing seventy."

"How much can you get out of this one?"

Irons pressed his lips together. "She's not as spry as she used to be. Forty, maybe forty-five, running without a load." His voice turned pleading. "Think about it now. You'd be better off taking the fastest horse in town and riding him flat out. Little use as I've got for you, I'll help you do that if you won't kill all those people."

"I'm half an hour behind a man that's already taken the best horse in town. I'd appreciate your offer more if I'd figured you to be so sensitive."

Irons laughed without humor. "Sensitive? Hell, King, you must not never've seen a train wreck." But he began opening the throttle. "Cletus'll have to open that switch behind us. And we'll be running backward all the way."

King nodded.

"Cletus," Irons said.

The fireman dropped his shovel and went to the lowest point of the steps. The teakettle backed toward the switch at the main tracks. A commotion of voices rose from the depot as the grimy old engine swung past it. On the other side of the locomotive, Curly Kincaid was bouncing down the mule lift track on horseback, waving his hat and shouting. King didn't try to make out what the people were saying on either side.

Then Cletus was off the engine and running. King saw him bend to the railroad padlock on the switch. He didn't want to think what would happen if the fireman didn't get it open in time. Then Cletus threw the big iron lever over. The tender hit the switch and swerved smoothly through it. Irons slammed the throttle open.

More and more voices were shouting as the locomotive rolled out onto the main line, but they were falling farther behind with every chuff of the great vibrating steam engine. Cletus sprinted alongside, hooked a hand into the handrail, and swung up onto the steps. Three or four bullets spanged off the ironwork as he vaulted into the cab. Others were running, lacking the big stoker's speed, dropping away to be lost in the dark. Then the train was over the creek and away from town and rolling smoothly through the empty night.

Mason Irons said, "You're a damned fool, Cletus. You were out of it."

Cletus spoke between panting breaths. "I figure—your onliest chance—is to get to that—siding powerful fast. You going to need me. To shovel. And if we make it, you sure going to need me to throw that other switch!"

King hadn't thought about the siding switch. Not only would Cletus have to get it thrown to shunt their little locomotive out of the way of the crowded passenger train, but he would then have to get it open again in time to let the express through. Otherwise the switch would derail it. To Cletus he said, "I'm grateful to you for being a damned fool."

King stretched to stare around the coal car. It was true he'd never seen a train wreck. What little he could see of the dark tracks made him think of the yawning gates of hell. He turned his attention back to his unwilling companions, thinking that after something like a midpoint, they wouldn't need watching any longer. Once it was too late to stop and return to Waxahachie, they would be as anxious as he to reach that siding.

Irons was leaning out to stare south along the track, his face set hard as a granite tombstone. Cletus slammed coal into the firebox with a powerful, desperate rhythm. It came to King that he'd been wrong. The railroad men had reached that point of no return the minute they hit the main rails. Both of them were working like sinners in the jaws of the devil. The stoker's half-naked body glistened with rivers of sweat and the flames grew like a barn on fire.

Icy wind howled around the top and sides of the tender. The regular blink of the firebox's monstrous orange eye blasted the cab with heat. In between, the moments of darkness were bitterly cold. King sweated, and he saw the shine of sweat on the engineer's face in the intermittent bursts of flame. Irons pulled the cord and let the whistle go in a brave blast.

"You figure that'd slow them down any?"

Irons stared at King in the moment of light. "The angel Gabriel blowing his trumpet couldn't save *us* now," he said. "But our headlight's pointing the wrong way. Kind of like to warn any poor bastard that might be on the track between us and the express."

King didn't even want to think how fast they were going. "How far's the siding?"

Irons laughed with a sound like railroad spikes falling on a tin roof. "Hell of a time to wonder that," he said. He gave the whistle another long blast. "Put your gun away. We'll be there inside three minutes if we get there at all."

A minute went by as slowly as money falling down a well. King looked at Irons with his question. The boiler blaze reflected in the engineer's wide eyes.

"If I don't get on the brake right quick now, we'll overrun the siding," he said.

"Then get on it!" King said.

He put his pistol in his coat pocket and peered with blinded eyes out into the wailing night. Irons threw out the throttle and sat down on the brake. The big churning drive wheels locked down with a rending squall of metal, slamming King back almost into the empty void between the engine and tender. He grabbed for support, caught a handrail, and clung to it while his feet kicked over the moving darkness. Irons caught Cletus by the arm and stopped him from shoveling.

"You done it, Cletus!" he yelled over the racket. "By God, ain't another stoker on the line could've got us here! Get ready to hit that switch!"

The big fireman staggered back a step, reached out for his balance, missed, and fell in a puddle of sweat. His eyes were wide, fixed, staring, in total exhaustion.

Irons said, "God help us now."

"Stay on that brake!" King said. "I'll throw the switch."

King had seen the switch a hundred times. He asked about it anyway. Cletus half lay on the catwalk, his great chest working in convulsive gasps. Irons looked at King with the kind of confidence mice invest in snakes.

"God help us. There she is!"

"Finish your praying after you tell me when to jump," King said. He saw the reflection of a headlight in Irons's eyes. He swung round, looked into the eye of the San Antonio express, and felt his heart balking at the task.

"Now," Irons yelled.

King flung himself out into the darkness, hit on the sharp rocks of the right of way, and rolled all knees and elbows and ears through a dozen bruising yards. He ended in a tumble. He was pretty sure his neck was broken as well as his legs and probably both arms. It didn't matter. He stumbled to his feet and ran. The teakettle's brakes were wearing its great wheels flat on one side and grinding the rails away in a storm of sparks as King caught up with it and ran past it toward the switch.

The express might have been a mile away, coming on like the last trump of doom. The chances were its engineer had not yet seen the other engine sliding toward it. Then Irons let off the brakes. He was coming on as fast as he could roll. If King got the switch thrown, Irons might almost clear the express. If he didn't, it wouldn't matter.

King tore his attention away from the trains. He found the switch, bent over the heavy padlock. There was no time for a key, even if he'd had one. He grabbed for the pistol, found it was already in his hand, and fired three times into the body of the lock. Then he wrenched the freed shackle out, flung the lock aside, and threw all his weight against the iron lever. He'd no sooner leaned through to a stop than tender and locomotive whined past him on the left, the rims of its wheels half black, half red from the braking, the exhaust scalding him with steam.

Behind him the highballing express was screaming. Its whistle was constant, its brakes now on fire, its headlight grinding down on King like the eye of the devil roaring out of hell. He leaned on the bar until that one blink in time when the teakettle's wheels released the switch, when the eye of the express was so close that he could feel its heat, when the weight of the world fell on him and the lever at the fulcrum of that open switch.

He put all he had left into the bar, felt the switch rails begin to slide grudgingly, and forced them on home straight and true in perfect line with the main line. Immediately the great white-hot thunder of the express swept past him and burned him on the other side with steam and sparks. High in its cab a white-faced engineer screamed open-mouthed at King and the lucky teakettle. Whatever he said was lost forever in the bellow of his machinery and the horrible sliding squeal of his brakes.

Lighted cars went by like a half-dozen cannon balls shot at once from the same barrel. Passengers were flailing in turmoil, looking out the windows, cursing the engineer for spilling their coffee. Quicker than King could count they were gone into the darkness of the night, red lanterns of the last car shrinking into pinpoints.

King saw that the teakettle had stopped before it came to the end of its siding, that it stood chuffing softly, probably trying to catch its breath. He turned, leapt onto the ties between the warm rails, and plunged down the west side of the embankment. Halfway along, he lost his footing, fell tumbling down the steep right of way, righted himself, and set off at a steady pace toward the farm and Rachel and the boys. And Edwin Spivey.

From the Journals of Edwin Spivey

CERTAINLY THEY ARE *MY* BOYS. BACK BEFORE YOU INTERLOPERS and ghosts, I was their father and I knew it and they knew it and Sallie May knew it.

"Knew what?"

Why, that Jeff is in jail.

"Jail! Why?"

Hadn't we just been talking about that? About how he'd killed Mil—Randy Foster? Didn't you understand me?

"Well, I don't, I don't believe it at all. Do you mean to tell me you've been sitting there all this time writing in your diary and just now thought to tell me Jeff's in jail!"

I hadn't thought to tell you at all, but now you've entered my writing, haven't you? Writing is thinking. But you don't know that. You neither write nor think. All you do is—

"Oh! Couldn't you have told me about it before you started *thinking?*"

I'm afraid that I was a witness.

"That doesn't mean Jeff did it."

Surely. I explained that very thing to Myles Brewster. But then Jeff admitted it to me himself that he did it.

"Why would he have lied to you that way?"

You who are sometimes Sallie May and sometimes Miss Rachel and no longer at all any kind of ghost but the woman I want and mean to have and always had said more. And I said more.

But *why?* is the kind of question a person asks when he wants to be contentious. It has been my rule never to answer a why question unless I feel contentious. At that moment in her house, I did not feel contentious. I was merely trying to *think* in peace! What I do *NOT* like is to be disturbed when I am trying to *think!*

Chapter 18

Jeff King ran along the ridge in the moonlight for fifty yards before he dropped off into a brushy draw. In the semidarkness he tripped over a tangle of barbed wire and fell flat into the muddy trickle of water than ran along the bottom. The rest of his half-mile run was littered with rocks, broken fence posts, and old wagon wheels. It was too dark to be certain, but he was pretty sure he stumbled over every piece of refuse available. Some remote part of his mind noted that it was time to clean out the draw—maybe burn it off—the first warm day he could, and King laughed harshly at the thought.

The draw shallowed out into the middle of a field not two hundred yards from the house. King went down on one knee to catch his breath, to watch for light or movement at the barn or at the house. All he saw was lamplight shining so softly in the back bedroom windows that the lamp must have been in the kitchen or the living room.

There was no way he could tell whether Edwin Spivey was there ahead of him or not. What he could be sure of was Spivey's dangerous lunacy. Or maybe Spivey as Tom

226

Trueblood had told him the real truth: *"Mean. Just plain goddamned mean."*

Had that been Trueblood or Spivey talking? King wasn't sure he would ever get the two of them straight in his mind. Even now, it was hard for him to accept that they were the same man. But it wasn't the time for reflection. It was time for killing.

Keeping as low as he could, Jeff King moved toward the house. He came to a line of scattered, untrimmed hedges his father had planted to hide what he had considered flaws in the field. He knelt behind the biggest one he could reach and fixed his attention on the house. Nothing moved. No one made any noise. But someone was in the house, or there wouldn't be lamps lit.

From his present vantage, he couldn't even see the peak of the barn roof. He watched the back windows of the house until his eyes ached. Nothing moved. He could not afford to wait any longer.

He ran across the dirt of the flower beds and rolled under the low railing onto the porch, hoping the boards wouldn't creak. He should have removed his boots, he thought, but it was too late now. Coming to his feet, he crept as softly as possible to the parlor window and listened. Through the thin wall King could hear voices, one a woman's and the other clearly a man's. They were in the kitchen.

Staying next to the wall and bending beneath the windows, King went around the house. He paused at the northwest corner. On the inside of the wall, the man and woman were probably not six feet from him. Their voices were clear.

"Well, I don't, I don't believe it at all," Rachel was saying. "Do you mean to tell me you've been sitting there all this time writing in your diary and just now thought to tell me Jeff's in jail!"

The man King was accustomed to calling Thomas Trueblood said, "Why, hey, a fellow's got to do his writing when he can. Writing is thinking."

"Oh!" she cried. "Couldn't you have told me about it before you started *thinking?*"

"I can't hardly believe it either, but I saw him myself when he come running out of Foster's door."

"That doesn't mean Jeff did it."

"That's what I told Myles Brewster. But then Jeff, he admitted to me himself that he'd done it."

"No! I don't believe that! I know he didn't do it! He wouldn't. Why would he have lied to you that way?"

"I've been asking myself that very question, right along beside of why he wanted me to come out here and bundle you up and bring you back to town."

"Back to town? You mean tonight?"

"Why, hey. I'm not sure how we'd do it otherwise. It is kind of late, though, and you say them boys is already asleep. I guess we'd be safe waiting here until the morning."

King heard the change in quiet voice and his skin prickled. Rachel might have heard it, too, because there was a silence before she said, "I don't know."

"I wouldn't want us to rush into anything after waiting all this time."

"All what time?"

"Since the day we met."

"Mr. Trueblood, I don't understand you."

"I sure wish you wouldn't say that. You've always understood me from the very first. You're the only one in the world that ever did."

King waited through a short pause in their words. He took Brewster's revolver out of his pocket. He'd used three at the railroad switch, he remembered. He fumbled with the cylinder catch on the unfamiliar weapon, got the cylinder open, and counted with his thumb. Five. Two left—if Myles hadn't left an empty in there.

He closed the Smith and Wesson's cylinder with a tiny click and leaned to listen to the two inside. He would have given a great deal to be able to see them, to know how they were situated in the room. Time was passing, and he couldn't afford to wait much longer. He knew how quickly Spivey could switch from kindliness to murder.

In a different voice Rachel said, "I'm sorry, Mr. Trueblood."

And he was quick as any other lunatic to spot the change. "And I'm really tired of having you call me that," he said. "I want it to be like it was when we met."

"How was—"

"Before they put me in prison."

"—it then?"

"Back before we had the boys."

"We?"

"Back to that first time I seen you."

"Me?"

"With your arms up to the elbows in washwater, scrubbing the winter out those sets of long underwear." Now there was no question about the difference in Spivey's voice. "Through all the nightmares and ghosts, I haven't ever forgotten the way you looked up at me then—like I was some knight out of Sir Walter Scott, come to rescue you from that life. That's the moment I want to get back to."

"How would we get back to that?" Rachel asked carefully.

"We'd start with meeting all over again. With calling each other by our Christian names."

"Have another cup of coffee then, Tom. I want to check on the boys."

"No! That's done with. Tom's dead for good and all this time! We're going back to the way it was before all the ghosts. You hear me, Sallie May?"

"I hear you. But it's been so long. What did I call you that very first day?"

"Ed. You called me that because it was what I gave you rather than my whole name."

"Are you really that Ed . . . Spivey?"

Spivey chuckled. "Thank you, Sallie May! After all these years of you being no more than a ghost!"

"Yes, Ed. I'm glad it's over. We're together again. Just let me check on our boys, and then we can talk."

"All right—no, wait! That's wrong. It's too early; the boys aren't here yet." A sharp click came through the wall, the sound of a cocking pistol. "Wait, don't go."

King thought of the shotgun leaning inside the door of Rachel's bedroom. He knew then what she had in mind. He also knew what Edwin Spivey could do with a gun, knew how quickly Spivey could whirl and shoot, knew how carefully he could put two or three bullets inside a breath and a jar lid.

King would have to be certain that Rachel didn't put herself in that harm's way. He moved, scuttling along the porch around the corner toward the kitchen door.

"But, Ed, I wanted to surprise you. I was going to change into the clothes I was wearing that day we met. Can't I? Then we can—start over."

"Then you do remember how it was," Spivey said. "Of course. And I'll step down to the barn in the meanwhile and get my things to stay the night—just like that first time."

Rachel said, "Hurry back, Ed."

King got back around the corner right before the kitchen door opened. Edwin Spivey stepped out into the bitter wind. King took two long strides and jammed the muzzle of Myles Brewster's gun into the middle of Spivey's back.

"You freeze right there, you son of a bitch," he whispered. "Just so much as twitch and I'll blow your backbone in two. That's right! Don't even quiver."

"Tex? Tex Hollis, is that you?"

King got hold of Spivey's gun, jerked it out of the holster, and dropped it into his coat pocket. Then he dug out his handcuffs.

"Put your hands back behind you where I can reach them."

"Tex?" Spivey laughed. The sound made King's scalp tingle. "You're the only one that ever got around me, Tex. The only one I never killed. Don't break my head, Tex."

"Give me your hands."

"I wouldn't give them to anyone else. But you're too late. I'm back past you now, back to where I belong with Sallie May. You can't get between us."

King fastened the handcuffs. "I didn't intend to take you in."

Spivey laughed again. "You can't take me in. You'll be gone in a minute, just like Trueblood, just like the other ghosts." He stood like a broad post still facing the barn, apparently with no thought of turning. His voice was full of joy. "I'm back now, back past the all of you."

King breathed, drew the words in as he said, "I could kill you right here. Easiest thing in the world. It's when I remember what you've done that I want to be sure you spend the rest of your time drying up to dust behind a set of bars."

"Now, Tex, you of all people ought to know that no set of bars can hold me. I'm free now. I've got it all back. Don't you remember?"

"*I* remember," Rachel said. She stepped down from the porch with the double-barreled shotgun held at her waist. Spivey still did not turn. "That you, Sallie May?"

"He's the one Holley told me about," she said to King. "A long time ago. I'd forgotten until tonight. He's the crazy one."

"Not me. No." Spivey was still staring at the distant barn. "You're the damned ghosts! No."

"Mama," Travis called from the door. "Why are you out in the cold without a coat?"

"Go inside, son."

Beside him in the doorway, Dee wiped at his eyes with a flannel sleeve. "What're they doing here?" he demanded. In his other hand he held a shiny new air rifle.

Spivey said, "It's all right, Davey; I'm coming. I'll be back to you here in a minute. Don't be afraid of these ghosts, boy. Don't let them get between us."

Rachel ignored it all. "He's the one," she said. "He's the one they were looking for when he suddenly came back to see his family. His wife turned him in."

"No," Spivey said, his voice gone quiet.

"The posse was waiting, Holley and the others. But when they called out to him to surrender, he shot her—shot his own wife and boys!"

"No!" Spivey cried. His voice echoed into the night like the cry of a cold, lonely wolf with his muzzle toward the moon.

"And after they captured him and had him chained like a wild wolf, he saw what he'd done and he broke the chains and would have killed them all if Holley hadn't got behind him!"

"Noooooooo!" Spivey howled and slung himself away from King's grip. He groaned, his body trembling all up and down from foot to head, his muscles tensing and bunching like coiled snakes under his shirt. The handcuff chain broke at one of the links, and Spivey whirled around as quickly as a mad dog chasing its tail. The broken chain slashed across King's upflung arm, which was instantly numb and useless. His pistol went flying into the night. King bent double, nearly touching the ground while he gripped his wooden wrist in agony.

Rachel had started lifting the shotgun toward Spivey when he tore it from her, got an arm around her waist, and dragged her against his chest hard enough to take her breath. Still screaming his howling denial, he held her dazed while he got control of the gun with his free hand. King was straightening up. Spivey pivoted half around on his heel, bringing the shotgun down toward King's level.

C. D. Hollis, Jr., did the very thing he had been cautioned never to do. Worse, he did it on purpose with malice. He knew even as he pulled the trigger of his new air rifle that he would never get to shoot it again. But he did not hesitate.

The lead BB shot struck Edwin Spivey in the corner of his left eye. Spivey roared like a wounded bear, his roar lost in the boom of the shotgun. A bright orange sheet of flame lanced two feet above King's head and an arm's reach behind him. Spivey slung aside the woman and the useless shotgun at the same time. Clamping his left hand over his eye, snarling and whimpering, he lurched off toward the barn in a shambling, slew-footed run.

Half deafened from the shotgun's blast, King bent over Rachel and shouted, "Are you hurt?"

"I'm sorry!" Dee cried.

"Mama," Travis whimpered. He dropped at Rachel's side.

Rachel said, "Jeff, I want you to kill him."

"What?"

"Kill him." She gripped King's coat with frantic strength. "He has to be killed!"

King read her lips. "You boys look to your mother!" he said much too loudly. To Rachel he said, "Go inside and reload this shotgun and lock the door. Don't open it for anybody but me. If you don't hear my voice, fire both barrels right through the door."

He waited for her dazed nod, saw her and the boys on their way toward the house. Then, still stunned from the roar and concussion of the shotgun, he turned toward the barn. Spivey was disappearing through the wide front doors. King flexed his right hand into some kind of life and trotted after him.

At the doorway, King took Spivey's gun in his hand and listened. From some unseen spot within the barn came a deep growl from a large animal waiting in pain, waiting without fear, waiting without thought of right or wrong, waiting without any *doubt* of its ability to overawe any enemy, waiting in particular for Jefferson Davis King and wanting him to know it.

King growled out loud in reply, flung the doors open to throw a wide street of moonlight onto the barn floor, and went quickly inside. Then he shifted to one side to listen while his eyes got used to the darkness. The injured animal screamed, a kind of sound King had never heard before, and leapt on him without any hesitation or any concern for the gun.

King fired as his back hit the barn wall. The orange streak of flame told King his shot had missed Spivey. The sharp pain down both legs and arms told him that his spine had hit one of the strong tall studs close to the door. The heavy weight on his chest told him that Spivey had him in a bear hug and had thrown him to the ground.

King lifted his right hand and swung the heavy pistol into Spivey's head just behind his ear. The instant pain along the heel of his palm told him he had lost the gun when he fell. Spivey's vicious new snarl told him he hadn't swung hard enough.

He stretched against the steel bands that restrained him, felt the grip give a little. King squirmed, drove his head forward, felt it slam into Spivey's twisted face. The animal howled and pulled a paw completely loose. King knew what that meant. He threw his left arm up to protect his head, but instead the heavy closed paw struck King in the middle of his chest and all but crushed his heart against his spine.

The pain was paralyzing. Only later would King have time to understand how such a blow must have killed Wallace Melton. He pushed up with his arms, legs, head. He desperately needed to breathe. Spivey hit him in the ribs, on the jaw, across his unprotected temple; then he reached for his coat pocket.

King thought of the wound in Melton's chest, of the knife in Foster's heart. With his good left fist, King shot a short punch that caught Spivey on the jaw and rocked him sideways. King pushed hard enough to unseat Spivey, rolled free, came to his knees.

Edwin Spivey was getting the coring knife out of his pocket when King put all the weight and strength he had left behind his wooden fist and drove it into the middle of Spivey's chest. The knife fell. King lost his balance, stumbling forward as Spivey's ribs collapsed and gave way.

Spivey's one good eye showed round and white in the dimness. His mouth opened in a great soundless cry and he stumbled back against the wall, and his face taking on an expression of amazement. King plunged forward and drove his fist at Spivey again in the same place.

This time there was no give, no chance to move away. It was like punching into the wall itself, and King heard a crackling that he took for breaking boards. Black as paint in the moonlight, blood suddenly frothed through the rips in Spivey's shirt, rips made by the jagged ends of broken ribs. King had his bloody hand lifted for another blow when he realized that no more blows were needed.

Jeff King stayed in the barn a little longer than necessary. On his slow, staggering way to the house, he dragged along Edwin Spivey's possessions, stowed in King's own saddlebags. King remembered that he had left Rachel Hollis waiting like a cocked gun with a string on its trigger. He started calling her name before he reached the porch. She drew aside the curtain to stare out at him through a kitchen window. Then she threw open the door and came out to welcome him back to the world of the living.

"Jeff. The blood."

"Not mine," King said. "Not much of it."

Heedless of blood and all then, Rachel flung herself at King. Framed in the door behind her, one boy brandished a small .32 pistol that hadn't worked for twenty years that King knew of, and a suddenly much older boy held an air rifle more carefully than he'd held it before.

Much as he wanted to, King did not sweep Rachel Hollis into a close embrace. Instead, he held her with a strong encircling arm that shouldn't offend the boys but should make his intentions clear to her.

Dee said, "I didn't forget what you told me, and I didn't mean no disrespect, but I know you're going to take back my gun anyway."

"No," King said. "What you did was to exercise your judgment like a man has to do. I think you did right. You had it in mind to protect your mother and your brother. I trust you with your rifle, son."

"Where did you get all that blood on you?" Travis asked. "Are you going to die?"

King shook his head. "Not anytime soon," he said.

"Then are you going to be our new daddy?"

King said, "Your mother and I will be talking about it."

Rachel Hollis said, "Travis, you can't get a new daddy like you get a new pair of boots. You boys get back in the house by the fire before you freeze to death. And you, Dee, you should say, 'I don't mean *any* disrespect.'"

When the boys had shut the door, she lifted her face toward King. "Spivey?"

"Dead."

She shuddered. "It was so—" She put down her face and trembled under his hands like a frightened deer for a moment, but when she raised her head, her eyes were dry.

"We'll be talking about it, all right," she told him. "Where *did* you get all that blood on you? Come on in the kitchen where I can see to get you cleaned up. When we talk about marriage, we'll talk about your job. You'll still say that somebody has to do what you've just done. And I'll say you ought to let somebody else do it."

Jeff King stood with his arm around the very strong-willed woman whose energies were certain to play their part in shaping the rest of his life, one way or another.

"You may be right," he conceded as they went inside. "But I'm the one that was here." In his mind it was clear that nobody else was quite as good at his job as he was. "But I want you to see another side of my job, maybe to have a hand in it yourself."

King dumped the saddlebags on the table then sank down on one of the chairs. The furious energy that had carried him through the fight was waning, leaving him weak and sick. He tried without success to find a part of him that didn't hurt. Rachel bent and started cleaning his face with a wet cloth, washing away the blood and looking for its sources.

"What side's that?" she said without much warmth.

King pointed a bloody finger at the saddlebags. "Open those if you will. The right one."

She put down her cloth and began to unstrap the bag. Inside she found another volume of the killer's journal, which she hastily put aside. Underneath was a gallon of small white envelopes in a jumble. She looked at one.

"Oh my dear God," she said. "These were for those orphans at the Methodist Home." She looked up at King, who nodded to her.

"You and I and those boys will take the train to Waco tomorrow and deliver those orphans' Christmas together. That suit you?"

For a moment Rachel Hollis said nothing. Then she looked at him and nodded. The promise in her eyes was what he'd been waiting half a lifetime to see again. She reached out and took his hand, bowing her head over it. Then, finally, she began to cry.

Authors' Note

The city of Waxahachie, Texas, thirty-odd miles south of Dallas, is entirely real. In 1895 the town and the surrounding countryside looked pretty much as we describe them in our story. The town square hasn't changed a lot since then, although the unpromising pile of rubble King saw in its center grew into one of the most admired of old Texas courthouses. Today, Waxahachie retains a lively interest in its past. Its well-documented history and the many homes and commercial buildings carefully preserved from a century ago make it an irresistible place for the roving writer to do research. We appreciate the help of the people there in preparing this book, and hope they will forgive whatever errors we've committed in appropriating their geography and some of their local history. As always, the characters in the story and the events surrounding them are completely fictional.

About the Authors

Successful Writing Team Puts Up with Hassles for End Result

by Georgia Todd Temple

Midland Reporter Telegram

"'He has to die! There's no two ways about it!'

"The words rose in the still air of the judge's chambers to resonate in the iron-framed skylight . . .'"

Thus begins *Manhunt*, Midlanders Wayne Barton's and Stan Williams's third co-authored novel.

"We thought it was a good way to start a book—the old nail-them-in-the-first-line approach," Barton said.

The book was released in November 1992 by Pocket Books, yet Barton traces the inspiration for it to a brochure he was browsing through some years ago.

"I saw a Fort Stockton tourist brochure which mentioned the fact that at one time several of the town's leading citizens had drawn lots to see who would murder the county sheriff," recalled Barton, an engineer with Atlantic Richfield Company.

"I collected some more material on that and intended at the time to do a magazine article on it and took a trip down to Fort Stockton to see what more I could find out.

"And I found out enough to see that I could not write it as nonfiction because there was not enough background material available. But I decided it would make a heck of a novel, and after a couple of false starts, Stan and I finally turned it into one."

The two writers remember first being introduced at a meeting at the University of Texas of the Permian Basin. They did not see each other again until years later when they found themselves serving on the same jury.

"We realized that we had seen each other at some writing function and we were both writers," said Williams, who has spent the past 20 years teaching English at Odessa College.

"For several years, we talked about his writing and my writing. Wayne had had maybe 50 stories published. He then had two Western novels published."

At the time Barton asked Williams to co-author a novel, his agent had cut a deal with Pocket Books for four novels from Barton. The first two were reprints of his previous novels: *Ride Down the Wind* and *Return to Phantom Hill*. The others were written by the two-man team, who first wrote two stories together before tackling a novel.

"We really get together and talk over what we intend to do, and then I do a rough draft—just a chapter at a time," Williams said of the process of co-authoring books.

"And he then does a second draft staying about a chapter behind me so that I will know what changes he's making that will affect my rough draft.

"We really don't sit down and write together. We sit down and talk about it together, but we write separately."

Having two minds work together has its advantages.

"We each bring something a little different to the book—a different approach and a different way of looking at things," said Barton, who with his wife, Margie, has two children—Charles, 25, who manages a theater in San Angelo, and Kristin, 21, a senior at Texas Tech.

"It's pretty good discipline for a writer because one of you is always around to keep the other one on track. Also, I feel that we get better stories than either of us has done individually.

"Stan is responsible for a lot of the depth that goes into the characters and a lot of the narrative density that goes in the plot, and I have a lot to do with—for want of a better word—the directness for getting from point to point in the plot and the sense of place in the story."

The problem of limited time also is addressed when a writer has a partner.

"If you have limited time to devote to this, it's much more effective to have more than one person work on the project," said Barton, who has received the Spur Award and the Medicine Pipe Bearer's Award from the Western Writers of America.

Of course, working as a team also has its downside.

"The greatest dilemma is the tendency sometimes to fall over your own ego," Barton said. "I will undoubtedly come along and cut out some of Stan's most treasured passages, and sometimes when I see what he's doing ahead, the character of the situation is working out a little differently than I think it should.

"You have to be prepared to compromise and make concessions and see what the other person is doing, but the results have been more than worth the hassle."

"I imagine sometimes I feel the way he does," said Williams, who has been married for 30 years to Jill Williams, chairman of the English Department at Lee High School. The couple have two grown children—Midlander Wendy Tomlinson and Stan (not junior), who is working on his master's at New York University.

"There's this or that I would have done a little differently if I had been doing it by myself," Williams said. "But when I was doing things differently by myself, no one would publish them. So, I'm really quite pleased about the whole process of getting to work on some that are published."

Although both enjoy writing, Williams said he had previously "never really gotten quite the sense of fulfillment from it I had hoped for.

"The last time I went back to school, I decided what I wanted was to be a writer and so I studied creative writing. That was what I intended to teach, then there weren't any jobs in teaching creative writing. I was more interested in doing the writing anyway.

"And so I have been intent upon writing fiction for 20 some odd years now. I never had gotten very much of it published until the opportunity to work with Wayne came along."

The way they address the discipline of writing is different, Williams said.

"I work in spurts and fits and starts," he said. "Wayne probably works a little every day."

The most important aspect of working as a member of a team, Barton said, "is to have a very clear understanding of what each person's role is."

For those considering a larger effort than two writers working together, Barton said he recommends talking "to a lawyer and getting a contract drawn up. I can see how this would be very complicated for more than two people."

Working as a team has worked successfully for Barton and Williams, who are currently working off a six-book contract with Pocket Books for co-authored stories.

"Very few professional writers make their living entirely by writing," Barton said. "My intention has always been to get paid for doing this, but there's a lot of truth in writing for the love of it."